Lost Writings

Lost Writings

TWO NOVELS BY MINA LOY

Edited and with an Introduction and Afterword by Karla Kelsey

Yale UNIVERSITY PRESS | NEW HAVEN & LONDON

Published with assistance from the foundation established in memory of Calvin Chapin of the Class of 1788, Yale College.

Yale University Press books may be purchased in quantity for educational, business, or promotional use. For information, please e-mail sales.press@yale.edu (U.S. office) or sales@yaleup.co.uk (U.K. office).

Set in Source Serif and Source Sans Pro Regular types by Newgen North America.
Printed in the United States of America.

Library of Congress Control Number: 2023944733
ISBN 978-0-300-27612-1 (hardcover)
ISBN 978-0-300-26942-0 (paperback)

A catalogue record for this book is available from the British Library.

10 9 8 7 6 5 4 3 2 1

Contents

Introduction

An iconoclastic figure of European and North American modern-ism, Mina Loy wrote poetry, novels, manifestos, plays, stories, and uncategorizable prose. She was also an accomplished visual artist and designer. Best known for her poetry and for her involvement with the artistic communities of futurist Florence, Dadaist New York, and surrealist Paris, her poetic sequence "Songs to Joannes" (1915–1917) thrilled and scandalized readers with its daring free verse and erotic content. Her highly original verse epic "Anglo-Mongrels and the Rose" (1923–1925) engages with her childhood to address the impact that gender, ethnicity, and class have on self-identity and artistic pur-suits. Loy was exuberantly creative beyond these works and through-out her long life, even though much of her artistic production did not have a public audience until after her death.

Among this output is what she referred to as her "Book," a suite of autobiographical novels that draw on her childhood, student days, and artistic literary life. *The Child and the Parent* and *Islands in the Air* are part of this project of fugitive prose, and were both written when Loy was assumed to have fallen silent after her celebrated poems of the late teens and early twenties. Enigmatic and philosophical, *The Child and the Parent* begins with infancy and early childhood before branching off into a lyrical meditation on the repression of women. *Islands in the Air* reshapes passages from *The Child and the Parent* into the story of Loy's alter ego, Linda, following her into her teenage years as she strives to become an artist and independent woman.

Unpublished prior to *Lost Writings,* Loy's manuscripts for these books have nevertheless played a leading role in her legacy.[1] Significantly, Carolyn Burke's groundbreaking 1996 biography *Becoming Modern: The Life of Mina Loy* derives many details of Loy's younger years from the novels. According to Burke, Loy never learned that her mother, Julia, the daughter of a cabinetmaker, was seven months pregnant with her when she married Loy's father, Sigmund Lowy, a Jewish tailor who had immigrated to London from Budapest in his early twenties. Although the pair were temperamentally mismatched, Sigmund was soon making clothes for the upper class, which afforded Julia a coveted ascent in social standing. When Mina Gertrude Lowy was born in London on December 27, 1882, the couple were living in a boarding house, but they quickly moved to more spacious quarters. Dora, the first of her two younger sisters, was born in 1884 (the second, Hilda, was born in 1890), and by the time Mina was ten the family had acquired their own semidetached brick house in prosperous West Hampstead.

The Lowys were part of London's recently affluent newer middle class, anxious about slipping backward, eager to strive forward. We can imagine Julia consulting Mrs. Beeton's popular *Book of Household Management,* not having learned from her country mother how to command servants or manage a budget. She would not have found a Jewish Central European head of the household, a tailor no less, in such a book, and Julia's increasing social ambition, fed by her anti-Semitism, led to a punishing relationship. However, while Julia was controlling and severe, Sigmund was a Sunday painter, loved beautiful objects, and believed Mina might achieve the most important thing in her future: a good match.

When Mina completed secondary school at fifteen, Sigmund convinced Julia to allow her to enroll in the nearby St. John's Wood Art School. Although there was no question of her becoming an artist or learning skills with which to make a living, their daughter might join other respectable young ladies in cultivating refinements that would make them more attractive to the marriage market. Mina was disappointed by the school's conformity but nevertheless excelled and was praised for her visionary drawings. As tensions at home increased, Sigmund arranged for her to study for a year at the Society of Female Artists' School associated with the Munich Academy of Fine Arts, where she was one of the star students. The birthplace of Jugendstil, the German counterpart to art nouveau, Munich at the turn into the twentieth century was second only to Paris in its reputation for the arts. These are the years covered in *The Child and the Parent* and *Islands in the Air*.

As the stay in Munich of Loy's alter ego Linda draws to a close, *Islands in the Air* ends, and Linda boards the train alone, a young artist bound for destinations unknown. But although Linda's story might be over, Loy's had only just begun. She moved to Paris, lived and studied art in Montparnasse, and, in 1903 at the age of twenty-one, married the artist Stephen Haweis. Loy was four months pregnant on her wedding day, and her daughter, Oda, died of meningitis just after her first birthday. During this period Loy began to show her artwork, most notably in the *Salon d'Automne,* an annual exhibition famed for helping to launch impressionism, fauvism, and, later, cubism. (It was for her first *Salon d'Automne* exhibition that she adopted the spelling "Loy" in 1904.) In Left Bank galleries and cafés she was noticed for her hats, which she trimmed herself, while her flowing dress designs set the trend for an uncorseted silhouette several years before Paul Poiret brought the look into general fashion. When she and Haweis briefly separated, she became pregnant by her lover, but Haweis persuaded her to move with him to Florence, which was then popular among Anglo-American writers and artists.

In Florence, Loy's daughter Joella was born in 1907 and her son Giles in 1909. At the American heiress Mabel Dodge's lively Villa Curonia salon she embraced modernism and began enduring friendships with Carl Van Vechten, Gertrude Stein, and Isadora Duncan. Loy read psychoanalysis, sexology, philosophy, and across spiritual traditions, including Christian Science, which she practiced throughout her life. When her marriage disintegrated and Haweis abandoned the family in 1913, she rented his studio to the young American artist Frances Simpson Stevens, and together they dove into futurism. The two women were the only representatives of their countries to show work in the 1914 *First Free Futurist International Exhibition* in Rome. Loy became romantically involved with the writer and philosopher Giovanni Papini, as well as with his rival, the founder of futurism, Filippo Tommaso Marinetti. Although her encounter with the movement was brief, she channeled the resulting energy into her latest form of creativity: writing. Loy's literary debut, a manifesto titled "Aphorisms on Futurism" (1914) published in Alfred Stieglitz's *Camera Work,* leveraged futurist techniques toward the liberation of creative consciousness; it was quickly followed by the publication of poems in avant-garde magazines.

Upon Italy's declaration of war in 1915, Loy volunteered as a nurse in a surgical hospital while laying plans to relocate to New York City. Joella and Giles would remain in Florence with their trusted nurse; the antiques Haweis had left behind would be sold for her passage. When Loy arrived in 1916 she was welcomed into the center of New York Dada: the nightly gatherings at the apartment of modern art collectors Louise and Walter Conrad Arensberg. Profiled in the *New York Evening Sun* as the quintessential "Modern Woman," Loy started a modestly successful lampshade business, acted in experimental theater, and contributed prose to *The Blind Man,* edited by Henri-Pierre Roché, Beatrice Wood, and Marcel Duchamp, a lifelong friend. She continued to publish poems and exhibited a painting in the notorious 1917 *First Annual Exhibition* of the Society of Independent Artists, which opened just four days after the United States declared war on Germany. At the exhibition Loy met Arthur Cravan, born Fabian Avenarius Lloyd, a Swiss poet, artist, and boxer legendary for his provocative, anarchistic performances. By the time Cravan left the country to evade the draft that summer he had become Loy's greatest love. Her divorce finalized and the financial strain slightly alleviated by the small annual allowance she began to receive upon her father's death, she joined Cravan in Mexico City in December. They married soon afterward, in January 1918.

During their year in Mexico, Loy and Cravan were barely able to support themselves, coming close to starvation. When Loy became pregnant, they decided to leave for Buenos Aires, she on a hospital ship and Cravan, who did not have official papers, on a small fishing boat. He took the boat out to test repairs and was never heard from again. Compounding this loss, the mystery of his disappearance was never solved. After waiting several months in Buenos Aires, Loy sailed for London in spring 1919, and her daughter Fabienne (called Fabi) was born in Surrey, where Loy's mother now lived. The next four years were a period of great itinerancy as she moved from London to Geneva to Florence to New York, back to Florence, and then to Berlin, before landing in Paris in 1923. Despite the continual uprooting, during this period Loy published drawings, political and commercial pamphlets, and several of her notable short poems. These include "Brancusi's Golden Bird" (1922), which appeared alongside a photograph of the sculpture in the issue of *The Dial* that introduced American audiences to T. S. Eliot's *The Waste Land.*

The Left Bank that Loy returned to in 1923 was the capital of the modernist avant-garde, the place where artists and writers important to her such as Duchamp, Stein, Man Ray, and Djuna Barnes gathered. *Lunar Baedecker* (1923, so spelled), the first of the two books of poetry Loy saw in print during her lifetime, was published by Robert McAlmon on his Paris-based press Contact Editions alongside volumes by Bryher (Annie Winifred Ellerman), William Carlos Williams, Ernest Hemingway, and Marsden Hartley. It went out of print almost immediately, in part because U.S. customs officials confiscated literature thought to violate obscenity laws. The first installment of her groundbreaking verse epic, "Anglo-Mongrels and the Rose," was published in *The Little Review*'s important 1923 "Exiles' Number," edited by Ezra Pound, and she exhibited a painting in that year's *Salon d'Automne*. Amid this creative homecoming, however, Loy received the shattering news that fourteen-year-old Giles, whom Haweis had taken from Florence to live in Bermuda without her consent, had died unexpectedly of cancer.

In addition to her grief, Loy faced the financial pressure of supporting herself, Joella, and Fabi, and turned to decorative art for a solution. *Jaded Blossoms,* a series of paper collages in antique flea-market frames, earned enough money for them to move to a larger apartment in 1925. In 1926 she opened a lamp and lampshade shop at 52 rue du Colisée, partially financed by the art patron Peggy Guggenheim, and managed it with the help of Joella. The shop was a success, but Loy became overwhelmed as the business grew, especially after Joella married and relocated to New York City. Loy sold the shop in 1930, planning to devote her attention to writing and painting. She published very little between 1925 and 1930, but it is likely that in this period she wrote the novel "Goy Israels," probably her first use of events from her childhood in long-form prose.

From 1931 to 1936 Loy earned a small salary as the sole "Paris *représentante*" for her son-in-law Julien Levy's New York City gallery, which was instrumental in introducing surrealism to the United States and an important venue for modern documentary photography. A significant conduit for the art that traversed the Atlantic, Loy represented artists such as Giorgio de Chirico, René Magritte, Richard Oelze, and Salvador Dalí and encouraged Levy to show Luis Buñuel's transgressive film *L'Age d'Or.* In 1933 she exhibited a suite of her own paintings at the Levy gallery, and while she published only two new poems she developed *The Child and the Parent* during the early thirties. In addition, another novel, *Insel* (1991), draws on her relationship with Oelze and was likely begun around this time. Posthumously published, it is Loy's only novel to be released before the present volume.

In the face of Hitler's rising threat and well aware of her Jewish heritage, in 1935 Loy sent sixteen-year-old Fabi to live in New York with the Levys and followed in 1936, selling her apartment at a loss and saying good-bye to Europe for the last time. Loy was fifty-four years old, and this difficult shift from Paris expatriate to Depression-era refugee was compounded by the decrease of her inheritance to forty dollars a month. In an attempt to supplement her income she devised a series of inventions ranging from children's toys to a posture-correcting corset and a reflective, multi-layer plastic material she christened "Chatoyant." Most of these designs were never realized. After initially staying with the Levys, over the next seventeen years she first roomed with Fabi and then in a series of communal houses off the Bowery, where she lived in near poverty until moving in 1953 to be near her daughters and grandchildren, who had relocated to Aspen, Colorado, in the mid-1940s.

Even without this context of struggle Loy's robust creative output throughout her New York years would be astonishing. She wrote dozens of poems documenting the down-and-out figures of Lower Manhattan, whom she befriended. She continued work on *Insel*, wrote *Islands in the Air*, and produced reams of shorter prose, such as a review of her friend Joseph Cornell's 1949 Egan Gallery *Aviary* show, as well as an extensive philosophical meditation, "History of Religion and Eros," and a long poem on Isadora Duncan. Nearly all this work was posthumously published or remains in manuscript form. Loy also continued as a visual artist. Dressed in the wine-red robes she favored during her Bowery years she scoured the streets of Lower Manhattan for tin cans, egg crates, mop heads, and other trash, which she assembled into depictions of her neighbors, calling her constructions *refusées*.

When Loy moved to Aspen in 1953, the town had one paved road and less than a thousand residents. Now in her seventies she wrote little, but she continued to make her constructions and undoubtedly cut a sensational figure in her costume-like velvet dresses and antique brooches, walking through her neighborhood in the American West, gathering trash she would transform into art. In 1958 Jonathan Williams's Jargon Press published her second book, the slender *Lunar Baedeker & Time-Tables,* which brought select earlier poems back into print alongside a few of her newer poems. In 1959 her refusées were shown in New York, and she was awarded a Copley Foundation Award for outstanding achievement in art. Loy died on September 25, 1966, and was buried on a hill in Aspen. Her grave is marked by three stacked marble discs, modernist in style and enigmatic, like the moon.[2]

Islands in the Air opens with a woman's arrival home to her apartment, astonished at its disarray. Although she tidied it that morning before leaving, a carelessly flung pair of shoes now directs the woman's gaze toward objects scattered across the floor: tissues with their "lipstick corollas" blossom among "Faded piles of ivory paper. . . . Half one volume had gone to the mice." The woman narrating this opening scene—we later learn her name is Linda—recognizes these "Ghosts of manuscripts written at odd whiles" as part of the "Book" she had once "felt impelled to write." Compelled to resume her project, she will expand these pages into the novel that unfolds, offering "A life for a life. My experience to yours for comparison."

Loy titled this chapter "Hurry" and called it an "Experimental Introduction" in a note scrawled on the back of one of her manuscript pages, instructing that it should be set in a different typeface from the rest of the novel. Its invitation to consider life as an unfinished book anticipates Loy's focus on self-fashioning as well as her refusal to confine herself to a single narrative. It also hints at the intimate connection between the novels in this volume: *The Child and the Parent* is the very manuscript strewn across Linda's floor. As the "Experimental Introduction" indicates, the opening chapters of *Islands in the Air* take Part One of *The Child and the Parent* as their foundation, reworking it into Linda's story.[3]

From the outset *The Child and the Parent* is provocative, and it is easy to see why Loy returned to this material. The book begins with an experience common to all but forgotten: the free state of infant consciousness, not yet formed into an identity. Born of the continuous spiritual stuff of the cosmos, the infant does not initially distinguish between itself and the physical world. Clocks, horsehair sofas, carpets, dominoes, buttonhooks, numbers, and the entrails of women squished by corset busks communicate without language. As the passage from infancy to childhood strips this oneness away, social values take its place, shaming and molding the child with expectations guaranteed to lead her to define herself by her male suitors' desires. "What would you like us to be?" the ladies who live in an aviary ask the men who woo them with the "sugar of fictitious values" in chapter 7. In chapter 4 the narrator notes, "Not realizing that my very survival depended on submitting to that psychic pressure that church and state and even the police force would see to it that I should, and that failing their protection, the economic system would throw me out of life itself if I tried to escape, I decided to ignore it." Of course, as Loy's narrator well knows, she cannot ignore it, and the novel examines the internalization of these structures along with the creative spirit necessary to strive against them.

Throughout *The Child and the Parent* Loy uses details from her life to reveal social values that both ensnare and surpass the individual. For instance, Part Two introduces insect-like newlyweds as they embark on their honeymoon. Called Bridegroom and Bride or, alternately, Simon and Ada, these characters are presented as the narrator's parents-to-be and are placed in Brighton Beach, the quintessential honeymoon spot of the British Victorian era. As they clumsily navigate their first sexual encounters, Loy depicts not two individuals but a larger cultural order that ignores the female libido, with grave consequences to the psyche.

A work of feminist lyric philosophy, *The Child and the Parent* is breathtaking, unique. Infused with the energy she describes, Loy's language in this novel is both abstract and sensuous. Sentences swell to paragraph length, then shift to the succinctness of cut glass. Her tone ranges from scathing, irreverent irony to crystalline lyricism, while her imagery is alternatingly beautiful and grotesque. Long before 1960s feminism directed attention to the political in the personal, *The Child and the Parent* draws out the ways in which the most intimate issues of domestic life and female sexual pleasure are structural and systemic.

Islands in the Air pursues a related journey toward freedom through Linda's feminist plot, though its language is less abstract and its narrative more conventionally structured. The components of Linda's childhood and adolescence mirror Loy's early years, but more important than how *Islands in the Air* maps onto her biography is the novel's investigation of what it is to be in the world and how to forge a creative life in an environment that might, in the words of Linda's mother, "crush 'it.' " As Linda matures, even the objects that surround her threaten to constrict her—corset busks, machine-made furniture, the "brick box" of her parents' house, its iron staircase described as "the backbone" of "a nervous system entirely deranged."

In response, Loy crafts a narrator who is both passionately sentimental and coolly ironic; both wickedly satirical and endearingly sincere. Linda is allowed to hate her mother, violating a powerful taboo, and often infuses her narration with sardonic humor, which she has no problem turning on herself. While Linda's experience is specific and personal, Loy exposes toxic gender dynamics that extend beyond her. Many readers will blush with recognition when Linda is shamed by her mother for developing a figure. Who will be surprised to learn that a visiting male art critic "practically licked his chops" over her drawing of a beautiful woman? Yet Loy's narrator discovers what many women never do: telling her own story in her own way is a crucial act of resistance.

Neither of these texts and none of Loy's larger Book were published in her lifetime, despite efforts by Loy and her daughter Joella in the fifties and early sixties to interest James Laughlin, the publisher of New Directions. He was sent *Insel*, which he returned in 1953 with a note saying the press had too great a backlog to publish it. In the 1960s he was sent a larger version of Loy's Book under the title "Islands in the Air." This manuscript probably combined *Insel* (German for "island") and several of the other novels, including some version of the two texts in this volume. He called the larger manuscript "touched with genius" but not publishable in its current state: containing multiple manuscripts the book was too big and needed editing, which he did not have time to do. Laughlin forwarded the manuscript to an editor at Simon and Schuster, who thought it too long for a commercial press.[4] While correspondence indicates that these manuscripts were returned, they seem, like other copies mentioned in Loy's letters, to have been lost. However, four of the eight archival boxes of the Mina Loy Papers housed in the Yale Collection of American Literature at the Beinecke Rare Book and Manuscript Library preserve drafts of six of her seven known novels. After *Insel*, *The Child and the Parent* and *Islands in the Air* are the most complete and survive as developed typescripts annotated with Loy's hand corrections.[5] The present volume is based on these manuscripts, and readers interested in Loy's fascinating drafts can find the whole of her papers digitized and free to access through the Beinecke website.

The Child and the Parent and Islands in the Air have waited for decades. They provided the foundations for Loy's biography and have inspired an array of scholarly responses. All that has been missing is the publication of the manuscripts themselves. Reasons why they have remained unpublished until this time are both speculative and revealing. Loy's critique of heterosexual values was tremendously bold for the time in which the books were written. Perhaps the novels have had to wait for so long because Loy's legacy is based on her poetry, and even this reputation has been tenuously gained. And while she held genius in the highest regard, she had little interest in reputation and status. Indeed, her poetry might be entirely unavailable today if not for Roger Conover, who edited the first comprehensive collection, *The Last Lunar Baedeker,* in 1982 and the subsequent edition, *The Lost Lunar Baedeker,* in 1996. He has similarly seen to Loy's legacy as a visual artist, initiating her first retrospective, which took place in 2023 at the Bowdoin College Museum of Art. Furthermore, while Loy's value as a poet has been secured, only relatively recently has the audience for her prose begun to grow alongside an understanding that her creative output constitutes a lifelong, multi-genre body of work. Edited by Elizabeth Arnold and initially published in 1991, *Insel* was out of print until rereleased in 2014 with additional content and an introduction by Sarah Hayden. In 2011 came the publication of a collection of almost entirely previously unpublished short prose, *Stories and Essays of Mina Loy,* edited by Sara Crangle. In 2013 Sandeep Parmar published *Reading Mina Loy's Autobiographies: Myth of the Modern Woman,* a scholarly volume that eloquently makes the case for the value of Loy's novels. This recent editorial and scholarly work, done by women, has taken place in a larger context of interest in innovative prose and in projects that recover marginalized writers from their dismissal.

If the entire range of Loy's output has not been as available as it should be, each period seems to find its own Mina Loy or to find in

Mina Loy the writer and artist it urgently requires. Writing and rewriting elements of her experience, Loy not only broke new literary ground but also enlarged the very definition of a life. Essential to this redefinition is her insistence on being the author of her own story, even when such a pursuit is necessarily a project that must remain "tenuous stuff . . . not all of a piece." Our time needs the vision Loy expresses in these novels of a never-finished self that insists on being free.

The Child and the Parent

PART ONE

The Child

1

The Bird Alights

When I try to recall the dim beginning of my human life, before the world as I know it took shape in my mind—that sheer existence when matter scarcely perceptible and the ether not entirely invisible together formed a cosmic vapor that dispersed so soon and for later years left a blank introduction to memory—I find that beginning keeps a certain distinctness as an infantile sensation of having come under a spell.

Such an undecided condition can only be figuratively conveyed, yet there would seem to be no symbol for that dual dawn of flesh and aspiration—a new-born consciousness—unless its whole significance lies hidden in the stucco dove which, since an alate Ghost signaled the girded loin to rise from baptism, is splayed on holy ceilings.

Seen from beneath, the soles of its claws are like naked stars stamped on its useless underparts—the immobile unsullied abdomen of the Third Person who is claimed as her sole property by the church. But, as a bird, it is entangled in so much half-forgotten legend that it reminds one more readily of that theoretical soul said to encumber even the unredeemed, for, if Life after all should prove to be a divine emanation, we partake of the Ghost from the time we come into being, and the dove presents an image of our animation. For, as we look up at its everlasting descent in a puff of gold to serve for the breath of God—breath which is at once the conveyance and animus of the conveyed—we wonder whether this secret that has hovered over the centuries, if seen from above, would be revealed as the spirit of man suspended in intelligential ether.

Call it Holy Ghost or consciousness, or what we will, a bird in flight is not unlike the roving passage of the intellect between the known and the unknown. I have always felt an unaccountable pang of recognition on coming upon this dove in whom the whole hush of the altar is concentrated above our heads as it showers down from the arches its ethereal influence.

So it is, with the aid of this primitive symbol, that I have tried to retrieve from oblivion whatever awareness a bird-like spirit of life enjoys when, through the jugglery of birth, it is first confined to three dimensions.

But the very faint remembrance we might have of how it came to incorporate with us is so overlaid with the things we have learned, which do not necessarily coincide with our experience, that we should have to get rid of nearly all we take for granted to regain our first reaction to phenomena—a fleeting impression of having recently been drawn out of the world around us—of being both liberated and trapped in a sudden ambulant individuality.

When the Infinite performs its impossible stunt of omniprevalently remaining, while infinitesimally disappearing through some seedling point within itself to emerge as a human soul, the feathered metaphor is brought to earth. But a winged perception, newly come to the concrete, shows little concern for the body allied to it and no choice of location, for, although it has been snared in our atomic mesh, it persists as an untethered sensibility, that—like the breath from which it emanates and whose omniprevalence it briefly continues to share—must first, in order to identify itself, drift through the identity of all things. During the initiation to its environment it flies the circles of our consciousness and, conceiving no distinction between the "thing known" and the "knowing of it," will become, in turn, everything it encounters, the while remaining at large. And the last object to be located by it is the center from which it diffuses; the body of its pending individuality. Being so far unbounded, this sensibility, loose as the air, magically exceeds its surroundings or shrinks to minute concentrations, as consciousness, unfettered on its introductory flight, establishes that intimacy between subjective and objective on which the intellect must later rely.

Therefore, an infant feels no surprise on becoming a clock, when its attention is touched by a striking hour, or a crystal reflected in its own iris. But the only proof I can offer myself that I actually passed through a stage of being "everywhere at once" is a memory of having been thus diffused that survived my discovery of something I since have known as space intercepting my relation to all other contents of the nursery.

Even when this dove or this infant consciousness that encircles and darts and alights on its bird-like survey no longer actually amalgamates with chance phenomena, the blossoming-into-view of the object of sense—which for us is a process so discreet that they always seem to be here to meet us or hang waiting round the corner of our eye—will ram its gaze so suddenly that a flower will "go off" like a firework.

The give and take of consciousness has something of the mediumistic in the facility with which the parties to the contract "appear." This predecessor of myself, however, being a bit of cosmic consciousness in process of isolation within a dimensional fence, can only be made out if we pay attention, for it looks like nothing but a clot of flesh in a plain room; a state of affairs that is still unconditional to a bird unfamiliar with capture.

Even if, after months of such spurious liberty, common to its kind, of looming with the light of day or dwindling to the flicker of a toenail, the bird of consciousness more often, but still by chance, decides to settle upon this circumscribed creature that it is going to inhabit—a baby kicking its legs out of curve to oppose the girding of the loin—neither the tangible pressure of the nurse's hand can make the baby lie still nor the intangible urge of Nature's design keep the bird within bounds. The enticement to belong to itself only succeeds when the bird, being dumb, at last discovers the advantage of association. The flesh has a voice.

So the bird alights. Now we can catch its ecstatic throb in the cooing throat, recover the flap of its wings in a fountain of arms conducting the fanfare of self-expression, and behold the child—an aerial infinity from which a body of grace depends as a plumb to hold it to the level of phenomena.

2

The Beginning of the World

As though I were a monad, a universal giant who should retain during infancy something of the serene continuity of the cosmos, for my life preparedness the world had no beginning, for both take part in the eternal Presence that is familiar to itself.

The state of pure apparition in which this world is at first revealed is not of newness, but of being reknown in a novel relativity of something to which the child has hitherto been inherent become separate, and as this change is not altogether interruptive, the world retains sufficient continuity to make it seem indestructible and in so far perfect. For, whether it is of any significance or not, the first concept that the mind can form is of perfection, and the first thing we demand of perfection is absolute duration; and the second, that it be unconditional.

This concept of Perfection only lasts until fact, in founding our suspicions, transforms the perfect to the impossible. It was an almost increate world, where hearing and seeing interchange and stationary bodies give chase to words that materialize. On entering it, I paraded my glorious insuspicion of the world of fact, making advances in a fairy air to communicative furniture which joined with me in a veritable dance of consciousness in which we can no more take part than we can hob-nob with a micro-organism, in its universe of concentrated distance, which is also out of scale to our dimension.

I had the art of animating ideas in a universe at once inside and outside the real world. For the things I saw appeared to no one else—or at most to suggest immediate transformation of experience, as horse-hair sofas turning into ships. My improvement on three-dimensional conveniences was, almost invariably, their conversion into engines of escape.

Perhaps in that transcendental factory the child proceeds from in which the word is made flesh, there is no inertia? Its superior mobility suggests that radio-active onrush that comes to a standstill in our reality. To what indignity of occult shrinkage has its spirit been submitted to account for the incalculable contrast between its perilous stagger and its air of dominion—the defiance of remoteness and the tiny stretch of its arm. An infant is always *attaining* something it cannot touch.

* * * * *

Fitful moments when the bird of consciousness alighted crystalized on the emptiness of the cosmic haze in clear vignettes that will never fade.

When I was twenty-three months old I had my first concrete impression of phenomena . . . not so very concrete.

The wife of our family doctor had taken me home with her to keep me "out of the way" while my younger sister was born. I was not aware of this visit at all except of Dr. Monks, who had one of those bulbous purple faces that have practically disappeared with the caricaturists who exploited them (however, he had not as yet materialized as far as I was concerned), carrying me down the staircase to a carriage waiting in the drive.

There may have been some sort of laboratory giving on to one of the landings, for we passed a row of glass bottles filled with colored liquids standing behind a fanlight over a door. The afternoon sun was shining through the bottles, through the fanlight, firing the drastic reds and yellows in a double transparency that was so bright it caused a blazing explosion in me. I was riddled with splinters of delight. Quickened by that fundamental excitement whose elements are worship and covetousness, which, being the primary responses to the admirable, very likely composes the whole human ideal, my arms, like antennae, were waving towards the glittering bottles, and, through a sort of vibrational extension, came into as good as bodily contact with them. As if I were capable of a plastic protrusion beyond my anatomical frontiers, in spite of the fact that the doctor who held me so firmly was headed downstairs, he having no idea that out of his small charge an impalpable bird, trailing a certain degree of my atomic energy along with it, had flown onto a sunlit shelf above us. At the same time, I could distinctly feel that something not far away from me was being held in a clamp, but even while my body struggled, as it seemed, independently, I was not yet enough of a piece with it to find out that this "something" was attached to my own elasticity until after future experiences. Although a vague unease in the vicinity of the clamp forbidding any further extension on my part, as the doctor descended another step, constrained to follow in the wake of my body, once having been drawn off the bottles, my consciousness had no time to attribute its forced displacement to the haul of his arms, for when his descent did divert its course, it anticipated his intention—my airy consciousness was out in the glow of the garden, while he must carry its load downstairs.

Or perhaps what really occurred was an immediate transportation of a bed of those pantomimic flowers called "red-hot pokers" to the middle of the stair carpet—these first impressions being of such lightning nature.

I cannot explain why the actual scene—a strong man carrying a small child downstairs towards a door opened on to a garden, the waiting carriage or the knowledge that I was being taken home—did not exist for me at the time. It seems as if it may have taken shape subsequently, as if stored in an embryonic state to mature in the practical compartment of memory which only opened up for me later on when I accepted rational standards.

As a background to my first encounter with color, they attended me only so far as in a dream a particular person accompanies us, although on awakening we should be hard pressed to understand *why* we had presumed he was there, as the dream contained nothing to indicate his presence except our *conviction* that he was with us.

Perhaps at that early stage the realities were cognized vaguely as having the final unimportance which transcendental things take on for the adult. It is possible that the infant's realities consist in very clear impressions made on a natal mind-stuff that is about to fall into desuetude, while the earthly realities are making very faint impressions on a more utilitarian mind-stuff that, as it gains in substantiality, shows them up more and more clearly. For, as the facts stand, all I was alive to at the time were the flaming bottles and red-hot pokers, and my only reference to the visit and its cause is a remark made casually in my presence twelve years later. At all events, in infancy, the tremendous, the obsessive "reality" lies in the magnetic property of attractiveness to incorporate the chosen object with the choosing child, while accessory circumstances print pictures, even maps, that are not, as it were, taken off the press until later on. Also, the intentions of the people taking part in an event were registered but not *received* at the time.

* * * * *

We can define everything about the child except the quality of its experience, for we can hardly imagine the mysterious ability of this stranger to our order to float around itself, any more than we can realize how often, when we stress a word in our educative way, it takes it for granted that we are expressly giving the signal for embodiment.

It was not very long after I had first been bashed into consciousness by the doctor's glittering glass—and transparency has always been a revelation to me—that my mother was playing a march on a piano with a long black tail.

"Listen," said my nurse who, together with the player, had only the tenuous dream proximity, "that's the soldier's music."

Instantly before my eyes a file of soldiers sprang from the carpet. All shining and alive they jogged across the drawing-room floor with a full-blown military swagger, notwithstanding that they grew like rooted plants only from the waist up out of a soft golden-yellow pile lying in the light from the "French" windows through which they vanished.

After they had gone, the room and all it contained resumed the monotony of practical conditions I have always found so unconvincing.

It is curious if the real and unreal are interchangeable in a mind, for which such materializations are a matter of course, that the child should so very rarely mention them to an elder. Does it know instinctively that for us words are not in the habit of materializing to disturb our conviction that nativity suffices to bring our offspring into the same world with ourselves; or else, why should it make reservations in view of adult standards, as if it could not get into touch with them?

These magical embodiments that do actually take place within the adults' range are more simple than they would seem were we aware of them. They are the result of the child having received such intense first impressions that it is able to externalize memory.

I have often groped back in that hazy mist of infancy for an explanation as to why that vision had no legs, whereas real people were only, when at all, tangible up to their waists. I dimly recapture an impression of being so held that only the upper half of a passing regiment was visible to me beyond a low garden wall.

Experiences like these seemed casual; having myself only lately been embodied they naturally caused me to neglect the practical knowledge handed on to me, as it was quite useless in working the senseless miracles I took as a matter of course. On the other hand, I was nonplussed as by an abnormity, when, shortly after, I asked for the march to be played again and the living soldiery failed to appear.

* * * * *

If man, when undecided as to his relation to phenomena, at the mercy of mystery, fumbles, the child brings absolute assurance to its maddening enterprises of destruction. When I approached the bibelot, the candle, or anything else I was about to spoil, I came upon it with the virtuosity of a past master—but in the name of Hermes of what art? The child seems to have the preconception of what it wills to create, which, at a later age, comes only to genius.

Of what transformation of form or matter is the child prescient? What supernal object is it so sure of making out of almost anything? This inverted creator who can never let well alone as if nothing to it seems well enough.

All its anticipations appear to miscarry in breakage and mess. Yet nowhere shall we find a more rocketing surprise or deeper discouragement than that of a little child who, when struck with an unexpected impotence, also begins to fumble—like ourselves.

Evidently it is not informed of the laws governing matter, but as we watch it we could almost swear it has been accustomed to a different order. It always seems to be seeking something that must have disappeared.

We may suppose it to be very much of a monkey; that all this is symptomatic of the riddance of atavism such as is said to enable the newly-born to hang by one hand from a bough. But what *is* this monkey bent on destroying the mechanisms proper to its own future as if it does not find them perhaps sufficiently convincing? The mystic tenacity with which it guards its seemingly idiotic treasures suggests that all religious wars and wrangles may originate in this infantile conviction of possessing the best magic.

To one who cannot find the way we point out the direction, so this stranger is put through a harrowing discipline to eliminate the peculiar principle of its useless activity; an interference necessitated by some sadistic evolutional experiment to which child and preceptor are submitted alike. Its final reclamation from an ante-factual awareness coincides with the extinction of that indefinable luminosity distinguishing it from the adult.

Until the crisis in which it exchanges its universe for ours, the child is not only alive but alight.

Intact in its qualities; responding only to beauty, joyous without rhyme for its joy, heroic unneedful of arms for its heroism; its April dolors only real as rehearsals of a future it tries to postpone, the child is prompted by a clearer reasoning than ours to avoid the perils and disgraces we hold out to it, and to linger in an unseen region it inhabits that is staked beyond fear.

The meditation of the philosopher is little more than the assumption of a responsibility the mother shirks in forbidding ridiculous questions to parry the insane logic of the child mind. Perhaps if it is ever proven that there is a distinction to be drawn between faith and insanity it will be by the light of this child consciousness that makes no beginning of being born—

When I got into the real world, I was frightened in the dark of dangers threatening the rear, and this may be in memory of primeval ancestors or because the first remonstrance in the nursery sprang on me from behind. It is also possible that I felt hampered in my facilities for self-protection by my *blind back* that had slammed like a shutter on a lost dimension.

3
An Intimation of Death

As I was already half living in the same place as my elders, they needed to come to an understanding with me. But on what basis? For, in parrying the insane logic of my infant mind, the why that lets chaos into their cosmos, they found themselves in the predicament, rather than composing their world for the questioner, of disintegrating it for themselves.

The meditation of the philosopher is little more than the assumption of a responsibility the mother shirks in forbidding ridiculous questions.

The child, still under the influence of some indefinable cosmic memory, stands inquiring on our threshold in infant innocence of *what* is to be expected *under these conditions* like adolescent eagerness to learn *what resources this* life has to offer—as if a fundamental certitude in the human mind that such conditions and resources would have had to be selected by some transcendental arbiter from among an infinity of possible ones must underlie the curiosity as to *which* have been selected for *here,* suggesting that a questioning consciousness is rather a visitor to than an inseparable component of this world. When we consider what it is that tangles our long argument with the child on the threshold of life, we discover the thread of death to be tangled in our every explanation.

Death to their experience was inevitable, while I was unable to accept it. This absence of presence appeared impossible, to deny existence itself until our failure to justify the necessity for it. In face of the child's conviction that it could do without it, we are brought to the point of wondering whether all death's terror and enormity may depend merely on its being an event taking place beyond range of our apprehension, except for its beginning that thus seems like an ending; in exact opposition to the cosmic continuity the child is so loath to let go.

Perhaps if it is ever proven that there is a distinction to be drawn between Faith and credulity, it will be by the light of this unbroken child-consciousness that makes no beginning of being born.

For is there not something less than conviction in the pang of paradox that wrings us when we discover that we can only present our world to our child as rational when gauged by death, which robs it of all rational value?

As the most reliable milestones directing the intellect are painful realities that lead to decease, it may not be only a coincidence that my particular consciousness after making its fitful survey should choose a slight pain in the leg from the tweak of a buttonhook as a signal for entering the sphere of actuality.

I can see myself now as a small girl whose nurse has lifted her onto the marble slab of a hall table to keep tidy for her walk: a speck at the bottom of a well of light lined with the unfurled fan of the staircase rising towards a sky-light in the roof.

As a patient under an anaesthetic feels agony drawn out of the body like an elastic that finally gives way, inversely, I became aware that a discomfort taking place at some distance, yet more distinct than was the doctor's grip, was drawing nearer; until in a last operation of my curiously detached attachment I located it in a slim black object lying in front of me like an overthrown post, in an uncustomary sharpness of perspective.

The mind, in an effort to define the nature of anything it faces for the first time, grasps at comparison. I thought of the legs of furniture that pillared so much of my adventure. But this, in spite of seeming rigid, was secluded from the insensate stuff of its surroundings by an aura of viability and a certain tenderness in which I was alarmed to find myself beginning to take part.

I tried to recede, but the space that had hitherto intervened between myself and such things as I did not *require* failed to expand. Bound in a new relation of inseparableness, I could not get away. The pinch of pain, unhindered, darted from the protruding solid to my brain; and the world congealed in a clap of inertia.

The tempo of my consciousness, the hilarious riot of vibrant infancy slowed down, the scene dimmed, as when the weather changes. Distinctly as if a film of radiance and velocity should transform before my eyes to arrested motion and monochrome; for after the violently superlative values I had been used to, I was unable to at once make distinctions among a milder coloration, so at first the actual world presented its lethargic performance in photographic greys.

A woman, of the color of shadows and strangely slow, was pressed against and bending over me in an intimate partnership of my concrete plight.

"Can't you keep still," she asked, lifting with a long exertion the buttonhook in her grey hand, "while I do up your gaiters?"

There must be something ominous about a hue refractory to light that led our ancestors to choose it for the pall of death (often an infant in arms will scream with terror at widow's weeds). The sight of the matte black sheath of my gaiter with its row of boot-buttons, stirring an inherited reaction of the eternal subconscious, was my first alert of mortality; although it is incredible, unless the condition for entering the adult's world is the acceptance of finitude; Death was staring me in the face.

And the heaviness of the flesh incurs its psychic counterpart, an apprehensive sullenness when by some sly, slow, fourth-dimensional stunt one finds oneself trapped in a brick box, caught by the leg.

"Now, Goy, don't sit there sulking, it's time - - - ."

The marked propensity, in children, to hop like broken birds - - - - - - .

4

Arrival on the Scene of an Accident

I see myself again in another brief flash, looking like an untrained ballet-dancer in my short embroidery. I was hopping about among the furniture of the day-nursery of which I cannot make head or tail. To me it is nothing but a lot of wreckage piled on the site of a Perfection that has fractured to time and space; for, as there is no knowing why incipient life, when first it turned towards the light, should have headed for this particular form of civilization and as, with an organism that responds to only a limited gamut of vibrations, it is hard to find our bearings, it looked pretty much as though an accident had happened in the dark.

Indeed, it had left everything in this commonplace room so entirely out of focus that I couldn't discern whether I was a hopping child or really an old crippled instinct poking about in the shadows for something to save.

A sense of disaster penetrated to that core of consciousness which would seem to be sensible of a matter intermediate to the palpable and the impalpable, so similar to the physical is its impact with the thing concealed that the subconscious is more present than the person. For repression will muster such rebellions as to pack the atmosphere until there is no room for the spirit.

I was blockaded by doubles of women sitting their patient sit; and the effort to reconcile their actuality with the pretenses they projected was one of the deep preoccupations that prevented me from communicating with the adult.

For my brain, so highly sensitized in being new, humanity was broken in half. I was just on a level with the souls of their entrails. My mother was only a corset-busk that gave an ominous creak as if nursing resentment for some unimaginable affront, under festoons of silk. Her subordinates were legs that hid behind panels of cloth. Sometimes Papa came in and smiled at me. He was straddle-legged in two tubes whose summits were magical sources—trouser-pockets. He would stand and rattle the coins in those pockets, while I could almost see great houses and colored raiment and every provision pour out of them.

Although people in the concrete did not extend for me beyond the waist, and this was because the things near my head conveyed solidity as their vibrations went straight through my brain, I could look up into their faces; so I could see my father's smile, but, being above me, it seemed almost visionary.

Out of the women's mouths floated words and words, some of them were addressed to me, but although I had more or less settled down in my body I could not quite place it, so, not knowing exactly whereabouts I *was,* I would miscalculate their direction and often failed to reply; and on that uncontacted visionary plain I would hear a rumble about a child too young to understand, while their subliminal selves were making appalling confessions to me, for the women of the eighties were filled with a different stuffing to the upholstery they resembled. So, in spite of my seeming inattention, I was paying that over-taut attention of feeling depressed. For the psychic pressure that hemmed me in was the blind emergence of their crushed life.

Not realizing that my very survival depended on submitting to that psychic pressure that church and state and even the police force would see to it that I should, and that failing their protection, the economic system would throw me out of life itself if I tried to escape, I decided to ignore it. Only when I turned my back on it all, I was brought face to face with the elastic Ogre, Time. And this huge duration which was unfamiliar to me drew itself out to its infinite length until I was terrified to imagine it. It wound itself about me.

"Feel me," drawled Time, "How endless I am, Feel how I am all bare, with nothing *on* for you to distinguish me by. Count me," jeered Time.

Hoping to save myself in space, I turned to the room again and tried to cling to form; but design on a scene of devastation is so unruly that I could find nothing to sustain my equilibrium. I tried to balance mass, to rearrange pattern, and keep them in place, but everything fell back into the same wrong shape again as soon as I moved my mind.

A sanity may depend on a sense of proportion and enough of my infant vision had lasted for the blatant purity of an inconceivable aesthetic to serve as criterion for anything I should ever see.

But in the ACCIDENT even symmetry has been seriously injured; for if one of the aspects of form is a contour of utility, it remains a fluidic carving of the atmosphere which, flowing as it pleases, can also be *pushed* contrary to the tenor of our nerves.

The mystery of Nature's beauty is only more baffling, in being sublime, than are the senseless hazards that mold the object of daily use to the taste of a majority who waive the moral restriction of aesthetic choice.

And yet, selection may be deteriorative if the secret of a lost proportion inheres to structural types that had no precedent, to a sort of "the way it comes out first time" being forever right. For, after a waning classicism, the offices of Wall Street arise in a virgin conformation as lovely in its necessity as the cliffs of homing gulls.

Thus Beauty may result from a divine insouciance, and ugliness be deliberate; but as we are already beginning to gurgle with delight in curiosity shops over the very furnishings that assaulted me in my childhood—as it were in revenge for the hocus-pocus to which I had so lately put them; Beauty may in some cases be a compensation to the discarded. Still a room that has been composed in a quarrel between display and thrift cannot hold out the arms of its walls to us and gather us in as it should. Yet I would sit staring at it moodily for hours as if I were sure that the tawny indefiniteness, like the very excrement of color, spread upon so many homes at the time, must be the matrix of an imagined jewel.

The convinced are always confirmed, so at last, while fiddling with the high wire guard around the fireplace, I pricked my finger, the lucent embers in the grate glowed through the liquid drop, and I came into possession of a living ruby.

The origin of symbols is not fortuitous, Destiny having also its subconscious whose seeming accidents are omens of its ends, the modern story may follow the ancient myth and there may be really something redemptive about a magical blood.

* * * * *

The bird had settled. I was jammed in the conditional; yet it took me some time to narrow down to myself, or pick myself out from among other people. The muscular responses to past illumination still persisted, every now and again lively arms would fly up to embrace a blaze that had hardly had time to extinguish to a ceiling. They would wave so wildly in the air in spite of the admonishings of a lethargic audience, by whom, could they behold it, the revolutions of the planets would be blamed as fidgets.

This happened to me once when I had been playing with some heavy dominoes, and one of them lay forgotten in my unclasping, outflung hand.

There ensued a train of events.

The words that used to sail away to unknown destinations descended, stinging me with a vocal shrapnel of "wicked temper" and "smashed window!" But all I could make out was that when my arms assumed a vertical position, other, horizontal, arms shot out from all sides to surround me with pointers like craning geese and converged towards a large placard of light I had not noticed before.

Sound increases. The mystery of all things visible becomes audible to culminate collision in a supreme Voice rising from the steel-bound abdomen, in exact antithesis to the promise of self-expression that lured the bird to earth.

If life is a promise made to be broken, such is the Voice that shouts down fulfillment, being a very echo of the Accident in which all trends or ideas, rushing from opposite sources within the same confines, crash into one another and splinter to bits.

And I was bound to listen, for although unintelligible to me, it reached the child intuition that has no need of language.

Like an ungovernable wind, it rushed its way through me crying, "You—you who have no conception of evil—I will show you evil—Look! doesn't it frighten you to death? And where do you think I found it? Right inside you. You never knew it was there? You'd rather throw it away? Nonsense! How could God chastise you if you have nothing to chastise?"

It was a strange accident, in which the intellect colliding with the Absolute split apart into Good and Evil; and I could just catch a hint of what caused it to occur when the Voice summed up, "Original Sin"—and puffed my future equilibrium to the devil.

The final achievement of consciousness, meditation, is perhaps misconstrued, when, owing to a general concession that a certain degree of subjugation of the body is required to bring it about, it is demeaned to a form of punishment for very young children. For there is also that other essential preliminary, concentration, and when I had been told not to move while everyone else went down to tea, I just sat pushing my fingers through the holes in the cane seat of my chair.

But as one half of our mind seldom knows what the other half is doing, I was at the same time tremendously engrossed with the rectangular clarity set in the air, that had been so surprisingly mixed-up with a series of excitements for which, try as I would, I could not find myself responsible. It was the "being there" of its "not being there" that intrigued me. Only one thing had become quite plain to my child consciousness. The soiled light of these strange new days did not come in by itself, for an implausible wound in invisibility whose zone is fine as a spider's line revealed a clearer distance.

"Never mind," says Mary Maude Munn, whose eyes, that are like violets too bashful to fade, steal into the nursery with their maiden lady to look at the hole in the window—"It was an accident."

5
The Will

The last thing of which I can accuse myself is lack of courage fighting against infinite odds in the determination to make sense of myself. Still, I could not have endured in the almost sub-physical helplessness of the child among the specters of the subconscious that crowd into its company when, like Adam from Eden, Lucifer from heaven, it is "cast out."

For, being by nature an evolutional phonograph record, the child reincarnates not only the biological stages, but also among the litter of ideas peculiar to its race those sparks emitted from the depth of being to illustrate reactions, of which the first were the physiological myths of Rise and Fall that, inspired by the unconscious effort of breathing, align the sacred and profane concepts with paranoiac alternation in the human past.

The time allowed me for such a large recapitulation was so restricted, that I must often enact remote and recent stages simultaneously; so that spurts of primeval magic in my mischief would coincide with a distinct intellectual acumen, a fallen angel become a savage. I had to pick myself up and pull myself together. The insupportable monochrome comparison with my bird-like liberty had got to go.

Nature took care of all that. She stoked the sun to an intensity compensating for the sublime, and I emerged into clarity once more—.

* * * * *

I was as high as the hedge-grass. An horizon of immediate sky descended to my estate of insects and undergrowth on the edge of an open country road, and the residuum of its azure splashed one blue flower against immensity. Isolated in this grounded perspective in which the tops of my parents vanished in leaning over a fence, above the knee I saw nothing of the hills and plains that were spread out before them.

I urged my body through the lower bars of the fence to get into the field and gather this innocence. Its beauty was reassuring after the mirage of the ruby blood. But even a flower held in the hand is not possessed, there is something more about it than itself; the aesthetic suggestion: to make beauty one's own through some dimly conceived and incalculable transformation—

Flooded with sudden determination, the physiological vehicle is wiped out; for a moment consciousness overflows and there is nothing *here* but infinity and where my body had been standing was left only a nucleus of *power*. As consciousness came upon my body, I came upon my will. Redeemed by self-sufficiency.

When I narrowed down to myself again, something of this power that had absorbed me remained within me; it is the power that hovers over our eyes and through our eyes reciprocates the light. The light that makes the inside and the outside One. And I said to myself, "I can know all things, achieve all things. All is in me; ready to emerge at a sign, a hint, with little cooperation, on some reflection." What certitude of the whole future before one. There were no barriers to that solar golden future; the light had washed it up at my feet.

The relief of readjustment, of perfect equipoise, when I grasped my heritage of dominion over all things, elated me, that the regenerative intervention of the will stirs up a great bravado, as if, having been held in thrall by specters and providentially released, it should prefer to pretend that it has overcome them.

So perhaps, because it is the nature of individuality to look upon the rest of the world in the light of an audience, I got the idea that "an impression is to be made." I tried to astound everyone with my unexpected potency and as often happens with the ambitious, I bluffed a little. I would climb a tree and from my foliate pedestal play monument to the sky, or in the dark ascend that indoor tree, the staircase. It is easy enough to be brave before you know what to be afraid of, and my elders praised me; but they were being deceived, for I knew nothing of valor, I had only that intuitional trick of keeping the body of jeopardy in custody of the spirit. It seemed so easy.

In ancient times Sorceresses were accompanied by their familiar. Likewise, the Will-to-Achieve may be seconded by an impulsive genie who can, if he cares, direct all the currents of hazard to further its course, and who advertises his presence by the showing of signs.

It seemed for a time as if I had come under his tutelage, for like the aboriginal who, on issuing from his hut, encounters omens, I picked up a diamond and other precious things when I went out for a walk.

"Gracious, Miss," said my nurse, "you've got good luck."

So this is luck, I reflected, now that sofas no longer turn into ships, Nothingness itself will crop up in values that remain. And I reveled in the promise of my luck. I was convinced that not only should there be no hindrances, but that all the hidden forces of Fate would actually cooperate with me.

And, being an optimistic throwback, I knew perfectly well what to do about luck, for I had just been taught how to count up to ten. So watch me escape from the Victorian era, in spite of the strain entailed in reaching the handle of the door, driven by some inner necessity to shut myself up in an unpeopled room to enclose myself with "what has always been" alone with the air that is "knowing" what I really am.

Once alone, I would turn round and round until objective reality dissolved and stop when I found myself attracted in a direction. It was imperative that I should bow low in this direction while certain numbers I had learned made a great to-do in my head. Numbers that are forces for my protection, at once very remote and very present. Numbers that must not only be muttered, but also spoken to. The awe they inspired was overpowering and only offset by the security they bestowed. They must, moreover, be bowed out to the measure of their own count. And by some strange chance they were numbers immemorially holy.

However, my indeterminate impressions of the solids and shadows that formed my home could hardly incite willpower, they having in the period of magical play been drained of all conjurative properties except a lingering tendency to disappear and allow the gradual outreaching of the imagination to superpose an inchoate facade of the future, built to the indiminishable perspective of curiosity on my actual surroundings, even as the natal inspiration had once masked all phenomena.

For if the will is a force, it is so much the complement of curiosity that the call of the unknown most efficaciously stirs it to action and the unyielding limits of the home afford the most urgent pressure in ejecting it into a larger world.

So while I was as yet nothing but a bud of animation, so exactly like a toy from its miniature face to the lace on its drawers, in falling after a rubber ball I decided to conquer the world.

It did not matter at all that the words "world" and "conquest" were absolutely unknown to me, for concepts are embedded in the human mind long before they become communicable. Just as degrees of impetus are defined by mathematical processes, I intuited my impulses and their oppositions quantitatively if not in kind.

According to the etiquette of mythology, the will must encounter a dragon, but at that toy-like stage the parental, or counter-will is still lurking, for unconsciously it awaits the convenience of seizing its opponent on common territory. So the formless premonitions of a conquestorial future continued to hang about me undisturbed, like the lace that ambitious arachnids spin out of reach; for desire puts its own construction on emptiness. Yet nothing pertaining to my phantasmal conjectures materialized until one day I happed on a little door. But there are many thresholds that may be crossed for entrance into non-existent sanctuaries.

It was a door that lay on a low table, prostrate for lack of any palpable jamb to support it. I opened it and found that this entrance gave on to another door; this one so flimsy that it fluttered back to disclose what seemed to me an infinite succession of white, four-cornered flaps. They were covered with linear conundrums.

This was the first phenomenon that had come within my range that had nothing about it of the "déjà vu" of infantile continuity. For these signs of signs that record the centuries of intellectual intrication have no cosmic prototype, but mark a certain independence of man that did have a beginning.

As the result of many inquiries I gathered at last that such doors as these open onto the contents of time; that behind them is stored the composite brain of humanity preserved in microscope slides; the final answer to the whole question. And all that was needed for access was to decipher the unfamiliar markings.

I became such a pest invading other people's occupations, pointing to a mysterious page, that I was given a fat book of rhymed alphabets. Enormously I concluded that I held the doors of the universe ajar with my hands. By the time I was four years old, I knew how to read and my life as a scholar came to an end at that age. But I could not guess when I came to "Z is for Zantippe, who was a great scold" that again the methodical accidents of destiny's subconscious had, through my first scrap of knowledge, predicted the overthrow of my will.

Now that the child has begun to show off a little, she is nothing but an actor on our own stage, but had we, while she was yet something either nebulous or absolute, been able to get into touch with the child microcosm, we might have found in this seedling of all evolution not only the reflorescence of the past, but also a germination of the ultimate blossom of consciousness, and that, in the cyclic manner of secret things whose end is in the beginning, it starts its unfoldment in a flashing synopsis of the eventual illumination of man: as if will were the urge upon us of Evolution, to arrive, through a patient voyage of elucidation, at the point of departure. Only this time by light of our own reason.

6

The Link with the Parent

When the human animal, on reproducing himself, was faced with the living riddle of the future, he suspected that he had inadvertently animated something destined to surpass him while its initial weakness raised the hope it could be held in check.

For if this riddle is aloof to a degree that indicates an assurance of being self-solvable, it finds it very hard to assume an erect posture.

The parent being himself a cheated child with only one miracle left him to perform—the creation of his own duplicate—immediately preferred to regard it exclusively in this latter trainable aspect. It was not his fault if the point at which the spirited aspirations of his youth became obscured by the domestication of the flesh was the very point at which the provident genius of Evolution, to avert an imminent lethargy, chose for generating fresh impetus; but it was voluntarily that the parent subjected the incentive renewed in his offspring to his efficiency as prototype, in a kind of fixation he seemed to hanker after as proof of his own significance.

No authority less than the divine can be maintained without a threat, and even God is presented as a bully in exoteric religions. The problem of Evil arose when the parent, desirous of power, invoked the first Bogey as aidance in a world whose sheer conditions are perfection and accident.

If savages outrage our respect for initiative in the prolonged convention of their ceremonial masks, they at the same time convince us that primordial Papa knew the secret of keeping the children's wits "in the home." It is obvious, in the phantasmic grimaces of these headdresses, that the magic they picturize is the initial wish of the forefather to frighten humanity out of its wits. He did not say, "I am frightening *you*." He said, "*You* are frightened by a malevolent spirit."

The parent's caprice is often the child's destiny. The first patriarch has not yet loosened his grip on the race. The lasting ideas of brains that die are refleshed through the generations. Our very emotions reflect the sequent ideas of the past. Tracing intellection to its simple origin, we find the first stir of the will in the face of the obstacle. Affirmation and opposition. Creation and destruction; God and the Devil. God and the Devil have undergone many transformations as opponents, often the one has been substituted for the other—a God indulging in ugly vengeance; a Devil monopolizing delight—to fuse in a single inhibition. They originated in "yes" and "no."

The pendulum of the intellect, as we exercise it, will never swing to any to-and-fro other than of positive and negative. The Eastern mystic uniting the pairs of opposites induced an indefinable Nirvana. The utter Christian comes to think entirely in affirmatives, and to him his heaven is revealed.

"Yes" is the word of salvation, "no," at the last, is murder.

Evolution, the cosmic will, is up against the parent, for if infancy exhibits atavistic tendencies, parenthood, reverting to Nature in procreation, revives an instinct for ceremonial masks.

The Victorian parent having scrapped the mask, terror becomes more insidious; for where there is nothing visible to inspire it, the child is free to imagine its source; and while in the Old Testament woman was disregarded, she has since been instated. In the home, being considered a fitting ally for the patriarch, she has become so influential as almost to have usurped his authority. The sense of this power that is new to her has made her even more insistent upon its exercise than he, in whom a long familiarity may have bred a certain contempt; so the fear of God and the flame of Hell are laid in her lap, to be learned at Mother's knee.

And she the more earnestly defends a creed that damns incredulity the less she finds it credible, as if hoping that in convincing her offspring she may convince herself, in the same way, that religious institutions maintain their permanence by passing the buck.

But to understand why, as if to follow the role of a divinity one should rehearse it, she feels impelled to appear so august to her children that heaven and hell must be invoked to enforce her motherhood, or why she becomes magnified in the nursery to exactly the inverse of the inconsiderable proportions she attained in the world where she was only in evidence as a picture, let us measure the conventional frame in which she was set, or rather, let us look into the cage that confined the women of the eighties.

PART TWO

The Parent

7

Ladies in an Aviary

They are so lovely and they cannot get out. Their breasts are pouting as they trail their lacy bustles among the azaleas. Dispelling the shadows of their lashes in a starry veneration, they lift that flat look of the naive to the visitor, a man with a loaf of sugar.

It is so sweet this sugar, the sugar of fictitious values.

"What would you like us to be?" they inquire in a flutter of modest aspiration; while the solitaires on their fingers shift up and down the wires that close them in.

"Angels," their visitor replies, holding the sugar higher; and a flock of satin draperies settle on poufs, as if on clouds, waiting, with wings sedately folded, for a diamond star to rise in a massive fringe.

"Here is Love," cries the great strong man, " 'tis woman's whole existence." This loaf of sugar more glistening than the gas that burns in groups of frosted globes with a light as forgotten to us as the hourglass figures it throws into relief.

There is a tremor of ribbon, a hasty sweep of feathers as inquisitive ladies, running to eat out of his hand, agitate these tassels of the soul in their impatience to be satisfied; and it is very wistfully that they recompose their ruffles on retiring from the scene to gnaw a pocket-handkerchief or fall into a faint.

An even sweeter offering to the captives is "the sanctity of marriage," and although it seems to evaporate as they taste of it, they do not demur, for marriage is something the neighbors suppose, while the married, shut in with their sanctity, hunt for "marriage" all over the home. The wires of the aviary resonate with a buzz of slender sighs.

Why are these ladies kept in captivity with their bodies almost severed in the middle—they appear to be tame?

It is the fashion.

Their plumage is not their own. For when God hung the jewel of the body upon breath, the sun made much of it; but "morality" hid it from sight. And this prey, which unintentionally, in covering, morality protected from her own scourge, impelled by its inextinguishable beauty to weave from its very veil countless revelations of a hidden allure, defeats eclipse with utter compensation; so that at last there is nothing to choose between Venus and Queen Elizabeth.

* * * * *

How incredible it would seem to this Belle of the Season, whose whitened arms describe the handles of an amphora against the shadowy plush of a wine-red curtain to hang a pearl in her ear, that she has thus been decorating herself eternally, to camouflage the vehicle of a primary inertia to which all creation has recourse for replenishment, the female principle in nature. Or, that her lifting gesture should be loaded with invisible chains, securing her at once to something within herself, and to something beyond conjecture.

In the face of her slumbrous conservatism Man flees in pursuit of an ultimate conquest, the drill of the intellect bores deeper into the unknown. The centuries conform to their several destinies: woman is still hanging a pearl in her ear.

Fashion alone, in varying her adornment, saves this being, who, unable to invent herself, is available to be fitted to any shape Society considers plausible, from sinking into complete inanition; and it is impious to mock at her frivolities as whims beyond reason, while our intellect is powerless to apprehend the intentions of a creator whose

"Species" may also have been designed as models for antedeluvian spring.

* * * * *

In the perspective that diminishes a period of time to a grimace of fashion, Society of the eighties appeared to live in a gilded cage. The female pets could never escape, but the men enjoyed a certain amount of liberty. A transcendental observer might be able to explain why their morals and their feathers followed an identical curve, their early steam-engines and their intellects had each that particular degree of velocity: why their sermons were bombastic as their bric-a-brac, their pampas grass as fussy as their emotions, their stomachs the shape of their souls: why the back of a prayerbook had the very accent that was being threshed out in their musical *operettes;* whether these formations on their idiosyncrasies make shapes that assume a significance from his point of vantage and fall into place as part of some unguessed structure.

The structure we can see is quite amusing, being over-carved, over-draped, and over-stuffed, for the cage is lined with the fussy surplus of Man's conquests of Nature; those minor inventions he multiplies to celebrate the passivity of one, who, so much of an angel and rather like a cow, is after all the sole suavity of his civilization; until woman, showered with accessories whose folly accentuates their charm, comes to look as if reclining among plumes that she herself had shed.

There may seem to be a visionary confusion about this showing of both child and woman so much in the likeness of birds, but woman has to some extent the same volant consciousness, the same dilatoriness of the ego to settle upon itself as we found in the budding intelligence, and it is undeniable that these ladies also spend their time in watching for words to materialize, in a flesh-trap more nearly than the condition of man recalling the snare for the dove.

Fixed in the center of the aviary is a fancy tree; giving inmates the illusion that they are at large, and an observer the impression of its being doubly familiar, for with maidens perched on each branch with plumage outspread as they sit at easels or embroidery frames, it has a somewhat genealogical aspect; while we distinctly perceive a serpent coiled about its stem. A serpent of whom we cannot see the end, so interminably does it encircle wisdom and almost make one with the tree, that the part of it left disengaged seems to be afloat as independent evil upon the air, while the lightning of its hiss streaks back and forth as if on guard above a trap-door that lies within the shadows of the lowest boughs and is like enough to a tomb for a fall that is not exactly death.

For these birds, who need not be anxious as to any scarcity of feathers, are liable to an ailment known as impurity; a sort of spiritual molting that deprives them of their wings. The one who contracts it is incurable; and who would dare to risk contagion?

So down goes the untended invalid who becomes aware of her infection through whispers and withdrawing of skirts, down through the social oubliette, often in an equal innocence with many of her wholesome sisters of the sensational climax considered as inoculatory to the disease, for the passions supposed to animate her have perhaps not been hers at first hand. Yet all the same she drifts out of view on a current that, in the aviary, is known as "the streets."

For it is not always so easy to conform to fashion, the soul itself is dressed in troublesome cloths; it feels too warm, its bustle has shifted so that it will not be able to sit beside the still waters; it wears enormous panniers of avidity that prevent it from entering in at the straight and narrow gate; here, cold, it is sewn into its bodice, or venal, keeps its purse in its drawers, and here is a soul that has dropped its powder-puff into the bottomless pit.

* * * * *

The apple on the tree of knowledge is so often invisible fruit—we wonder with what they nourish their gossip on a subject that is tabu, as they sip their tea; the subtle tattle they contrive despite the tabu being tacit consent that "this subject" retains a traditional coherency only if left untouched. For the romance of the pre-nuptial sugar has melted, leaving nought but the onus of domestic farming: among the hidden preoccupations imposed on them, those crucial questions of planting, irrigation, and the regulation of crops, they have reaped no harvest of promised ecstasy; they are like earth become excruciatingly conscious of the tilling.

Thus they can only valuate their licit love, not according to any intrinsic satisfaction they find in it, but by imagining something really too awful which may be disparagingly compared to it; and this is not difficult, prepared as they are by the scission in the human mind resulting from the sacro-profane combine that makes the magic spring of life at once our most superb inspiration and a *cloaque d'immondice* which lingers, even now, as the basis of an ethic whose insidious influence forces both *révolté* and conformer to an absolute illogic of thought and action.

Being, for the sake of their self-esteem, in honor bound to identify a love elegiacally exalted with the grave discomforts of the matrimonial bed, they suspect the shameful secret that lured their sister through the trap-door of ostracism must be Pleasure; an acquaintance, perhaps, with the solution of their internal enigma into which the segregations of society forbid them to inquire; or if it were not so, could there exist so base a creature as to vilify herself from choice in a sordid procedure without that act of God that constrains them to put up with it?

Logically it would seem to be this latter guise they conclude is the more plausible, for else would they not in their vast irritation break through the ostracism and implore her confidences? Then is she not a legitimate object of their opprobrium? Or have they no opinion one way or the other in their dread of a rationality their masters condemn?

Ah, one can hear which way Eros' wings are wafted when they fish from the dregs of the subconscious their befuddled disgusts and chuck them from their married immunity all over "her."

The transubstantiation of the communion altar is not unique. What happens at five o'clock to the mysterious wafer, the fruit of the tree; symbolized in the aviary by all these petty cakes and sandwiches laid on occasional tables? Looking from our long distance we can see them gather together from all over England and aggregate to a sole volume.

Sequestered on the omniprevalent tea-tray, trussed with shadowy conjectures, prone in the coma of the evoked lies the nebulous body of the fallen woman. Mute, unrebellious, she lies where she has dropped among the glitter of cups and spoons under the lamp that dyes her with the brand of its scarlet lace; so near and yet—"I feel as though a gulf were fixed between us," peep the birds of the aviary, but nevertheless they nibble at her, they gobble her up; and having thus trammeled her in their crops, piquantly they speak of her as "loose." But how make sense of a mystery? For in those days, with their remarkable distances, a veritable gap in consciousness lay between the scraper* and the pavement; the only measurable areas being of the home. The streets were the unknown; the track on which the erotic revelation paced. Pleasure elusive is become furtive, only to be picked up at the street corner, where decent women dare not venture lest they be mistaken for—.

The people of that era were conscious of nothing but somebody else's assumption of the contents of consciousness of a hypothetical somebody-else; the unlocatable arbiter of their morality. For they were unaware that their moral standard, whose non-existence they did not suspect, was not a moral standard.

Thus the Myth takes on the direction of impractical life; at every doorway lurks a downfall for virgins who go wandering; in every suburban fireplace shines an embered edition of "Marble Halls" and the girl who "dreamt that" she "dwelt in" them, while submitting to the insane monotony of staring into the coals, is shown by Prince Charming over the ideal edifice which will in real life turn out to be another bird-cage or—a brick box.

We have been watching the habits of these ladies so attentively that we hardly noticed an eerie gloom creep in upon them; the foliage of the tree as it fades away looks queerly like faces in the Albert Hall

---

*An iron gadget outside front doors for scraping the mud off one's shoes before entering the house. [The footnotes throughout are Loy's own.—Ed.]

upturned to a waddling Patti whose endless trill lifts "Home Sweet Home" above all human hearing, until darkness that has gathered imperceptibly, like the cover thrown over a bird-cage, blots them out. Nothing is left in the boundless shadow but the nacreous figure of the woman with the ear-ring, and even she is becoming blurred.

A sudden tremor stirs her arms to motion, to graceless gesticulation in a downpour of infinitesimal particles that fill the air; her arms are flung out before her to avert the assailment, or fall in consonance with her bowed back; to mow, in spasms, at something inimical that has surged about her feet.

For the earth not only reclaims her offspring, but seemingly outraged at being inhabited, with the aid of the winds and the friction of her swarms, pulverizes her superficies and all waste products of life, in an effort to choke and inter mankind by covering herself with a supplementary crust.

So hour by hour this other aspect of womanhood; the eternal cleanser scours a track for the daily emergence, only to find that the obstruction she cleared away on the eve has collected again at dawn; as the spectral filth overhanging drudgery trails a dusty veil over everything she has sweetened, so that even her pretty children are unrecognizable.

Still, for one moment she comes to rest in something of her former semblance, but the languid curves for adjusting a jewel have changed to awkward angles, the *poudre-de-riz* to a fearful rawness; the circles of her rings have given place to the smarting fissures of toil.

The amphoral pose is transformed: she is stuffing her fingers in her ears to muffle the cry of hunger from multiplying mouths.

Shriller it grows to a fineness of pitch that matches the hiss of the snake, and as if some disturbing reminder had brought her up short, the hand that suspended an Orient clutches hold of a wooden spoon, to rotate with hectic monotony in the midst of a column of steam.

This cruel metamorphosis was not anticipated by man, who loved to pop sugar into a leisured mouth and smooth his lean steel face on down when relaxing from his struggle with the elements; it is not at his desire that she is driven from her couch of roses to receive him on a burst mattress; yet the circumstances arising from the domination of Nature have originated an unnatural force that would seem harder to control than a natural one; the economic factor which drags him down from the very citadels of his achievement and yokes the doll it was so urgent for him to coddle with his senses to the same irksome harness as himself.

So within the extremes of the bird-cage and the storm of dust, the nervous system of half a universe is consumed with desires that, being unformed, are seldom consummated; but it is only recently that we have come to realize how disproportionate the woman's role in the sugar-drama has been, having always interpreted her unselfconscious acquiescence for a general and serene lubricity. We can only suppose that this martyr to Nature's enervating propensity for keeping secrets to herself and throwing dust in our eyes is endowed with a complex organism for the long incubation of some intrinsic quality she needs for the future.

With the lapse of time, difference to itself becomes indifferent. The monuments of the past resemble a little millet spilt on the bottom of a bird-cage; the cultures of all societies are composed of such *débris* as might litter the floors of an evacuated printing house, or the miscellaneous pages for wrapping groceries in the poorer quarters; the essence of history lies in a few scraps left of a letter torn up so that nobody should read it.

A scrap of paper looks very like a rag—and lying in the rusted pan at the bottom of the cage is a limp tatter; the bustle has fallen, leaving those flanks to which is allotted such poor armour, again heavy with child; stirred by a feeble draught it folds and unfolds its soiled frill, an exhausted phantom bowing upon itself, spreads in the blown agony of a wing that would rise again, and subsides at last even as old ladies of the aviary died in paralysis, like a lace butterfly for their caps, stuck in a pincushion.

8

The Hewn Tree

To discover the hidden influences that affected my childhood, I
have had to seek further and further back until, coming to the prenatal, I must inevitably imagine events that took place before I was born.

For this I have to use a little hearsay, a few confidences, some personal observation, and above all, evoke that voiceless converse I held
in my infancy with the souls of entrails.

To do so is simple. I need only lift a "feeling" out of the past to find
that this long-buried impression is still so distinct I can re-experience
it in the present, and submit it to mental analysis, just as a poet repro-
duces an impression with an *exact* word.

So in some strange way I give to a past generation a more lucid existence than they had at the time; they who were so little conscious of
themselves they went into eternity undefined.

- - - - - the bustle has fallen. It serves as a clue to the whereabouts
of one, at any rate, of those women of the eighties, for we find it abandoned under a gas-jet turned so low that its last light pricks the fields
of darkness with only a blue crocus.

Tossed over the back of a bed-room chair by a prospective mother,
it lies among cambric underclothes whose unexpected angles form
a dim model of shaken cliffs; an abandoned fortress from which Innocence, like the soul on leaving the body, sets out upon an endless
journey when it puts off its chemise.

- - - - - - The Tree of the knowledge of good and evil has fallen, chopped down, sawn off, pieced together, converted into its present equivalent: a bed.

Between its linen sheets, two tender bodies, the one impetuous, the other reluctant, are folded in a capricious space that "shutting open" softens upon or recedes from them as they draw their breath; a situation which would hamper the artificial forms they have shed as much as the everyday world would abrade nakedness. For however thin a veil may be, it has the actual density of the tissue of conventions that separates the body from the brain. Draperies being tentacles into which the nerves project a secondary corporality whose rhythm complies with corrective contours, the man who tripped on a lady's train experienced some of the remorse he would feel on wounding the wearer.

And these bodies in the bed, who still held their own in a familiar pantomime as long as they retained the idea-laden chemise or shirt that formed their liaison with their environment, stripped of their sheath have lost their space and time, and all their customs. The incentives that clung to their clothing have disappeared. They are so entirely isolated from all vested values that no re-adaptation is possible, except to the innermost retreat of a primeval selfhood, of which little remains but a blinded atavism.

So Bridegroom, who is the impetuous one, to meet an emergency in which instant forgetfulness of three decades of moral discipline is imperative, finding darkness the better part of shame or seeking that utter darkness in which the spark of his instinct smolders, has turned down the gas. Or else across the curtained air the well-stitched corpses of their civilities might mock the untrained ghosts of flesh that, having forsaken them, relapse to a state of obtuseness like that of the newly born.

He has brought Bride to Brighton on a honeymoon in pursuit of a pleasure that marriage, in legitimizing, or so the implications of their upbringing persuaded them, has guaranteed.

But in the hollowed-out Tree of knowledge its ancient lore seems so awkward to learn, as if the long residence in a woven modesty had made the human body somewhat clumsy of attainment. They who lie as the Tree has fallen are finding its wisdom no less banned than it was in the days of Eve, and the solution of its secret is almost entirely lost in protracted temptation; for whenever they asked to be informed as to *what* consummation tempts the flesh, the Censor at once intervened.

Whatever the final utility of the body may prove to be in future laps of evolution, Simon and Ada live in a cycle of time when the body, having incurred, but according to what justice we cannot know, the liability to reward and punishment, is a vehicle for pleasure and pain. Its vital instability tips between these two; yet so much more towards the latter that our great concern for that miraculous pulp has been its protection rather than its delight. For while pleasure confirms our most tenacious intuition, pain is the major opposition to our will, and being submitted to by all humanity alike, it arouses a certain sympathy that is never extended to the pleasure-seeker. The excitation around an accident having inspired the humane sciences, Society recognizes little responsibility for the individual before he feels unwell and is almost prohibitive to pleasure. Notwithstanding that, the greater the area of consciousness preserved for the culture of pleasure, the less will be available for the experience of pain.

Under the "raptureless regime" the Apostle appointed us to doff the flesh and invest ourselves of the spirit. The ecclesiast ostracized the flesh, the laity were persuaded they indulged the flesh, while Eros distributed the misleading literature.

Both Eros and the Apostle err. The fleshly discomforts for which the ascetic is notorious, of adolescent friars who vanquished Satan in his guise of urgence towards self-consolation, were as nothing in comparison to those of venerated mothers and light ladies; of male householders trapped with the "eternal feminine" when debarred from the climax of "love." In the matter of discomfort the ascetic was the slacker, for what is abstention when set against participation entailing effects such as pre-anaesthetic childbirth, or, for our really rollicking sisters and brothers, illicit abortion and the syphilitic debacle?

So the tentative progress of that nincompoop, The Flesh, devolved upon the layman who, taking all the sporting risks in suffering, has succeeded in pressing some sparse essences of Beauty from biological life.

The airplane and the dragonfly are not released from the same hand. Deity alone makes soft machines, the subtlety of whose material allows that articulate tuber, the living entity, to carry on the work of its Creator, in being conscious.

But in how far conscious? For the least phenomena with which we are involved could only be entirely embraced by a universal consciousness inasmuch as all relations are illimitable; while our small share in the universal consciousness seems to be in some way restricted by the dominant movement of life; forwardness. We are featured forwardly, we look, sound, toe and finger forwardly, and the time we take to make use of our senses moves forward with Life. As if we would flee from our blind back because life began as an impulse to issue from nothingness.

And this consciousness, so like an effluence in continual escape from the body to mix with the outside world, cannot revert and explore the territory from which it emanates that lies behind the frontiers of instinct; for the body, like the vastness surrounding it, is interpenetrated by intangible dimensions of concentrated distance to which our intellect has no access, except with the aid of the instruments of our sciences. For if one aspect of the fall of Man is the descent of his intellect into the microscopic universe—when an alternative, apparently beyond his choosing, was offered him to train his intuition on the diffused nearness of things enormous and divine— even so the body is not self-conscious, for by reason of the necessity for such instruments its data of itself are second-hand. The body is unknown to itself, as it is to its clothed impersonator.

A transcendental observer could look into this unexplored territory where our Being is sustained through the shaping of the indiscernible destinies of microscopic collaborators; could see in that flesh which, when accidentally exposed to us, is nothing but a butchered horror, an island in the air, whose routes bear the rush of infinitesimal races among the fronds of forestal nerves; would be able to hear the boom of the sensitive dynamo to which the currents of our life are confluent, receiving and expelling their pouring velocities through ivory aorta and arteries, to scatter in ruby spray on arrival at capillary terminals.

Whereas we, ourselves, are deaf to the whole roaring factory of our impulses where the ceaseless signaling of the cerebellum flashes commands from an unknown control; as deaf as though we were in no way connected with it. Only in such rare moments of inverted consciousness such as occur when we are coming out of a swoon can we listen to the action of our own heart.

Sidling up to his virgin, Bridegroom begins to fumble and she to shrink away, for not only are their bodies unreal to them but the intellects they anchor consist mostly in the hallucination that words will materialize without any assistance.

"I am now experiencing marriage," they say inwardly. But being conscious, as it were, by hearsay, they leave the word "marriage" to its own devices, in that intellectual incapacity to come to terms with instinct which causes so many of human-kind to succumb to symbolism.

Theirs is such a hazy hymen that it makes us wonder if the tradition of Love did not arise in the able passion of some pagan god, transcribed a long, long time ago in an Olympian ode, to dwindle down the ages.

Mistaking automatism for initiative, and the echoes that ring in their brains for the birth of ideas, Bridegroom and Bride are no more originative than records played on a gramophone.

Yet there is nothing for which they have more respect than their own personalities. But as personality is the stamp of ideas, and only exceptional minds are capable of conceiving them; while an idea, once it has been handed on by its originator remains as little more than a symbol, or even degenerates to a prejudice, this man and woman safeguard their private stock of symbolic prejudices with almost the brutish obstinacy with which felons hang on to ill-gotten gains.

Yet under all this there still lies the cripple instinct with its own diabolical obstinacy of the sub-conscious; for after all, Man is little else than a vehicle for forces whose inherence to himself he cannot explain. So that, when we listen to arguments in favor of the survival of personality, it is not so much the plausibleness of the Immortal we call into question, but the existence of any personality for survival.

So if we push past the signals of approach to the supposed personalities of Bridegroom and his bride; these eyes that are humid with an excitement they share with even the insect world, we find only the eternal modus of invasion and resurrection, and the eternal lying-in-wait of a cavernous passivity to be fulfilled of anything extraneous to itself.

Yet Bridegroom fumbles on, for the Presence of Nature has invited his instinct to take part for a moment in cosmic sentience, a moment in which the generations, with their countless hair, their enormously bamboozled souls and all the detail of their idiosyncrasies, are mustered in the invisible spermatozoa, and urges that instinct to combine with the intellect, that together they may learn to keep up with the instant and vast operations that are concluded in fractions of time; as when Life, conjoining with the Absolute, engenders the fresh organism in a blaze of sensibility whose sources of enlightenment we have not yet tapped. For it is sensation itself that has the lightning intelligence we shall have to share, if we are ever to gauge the entire extent of our consciousness or the larger import of our reactions.

A wooden bed in Hampstead Heath is less like a tree than is this slender stalk of grass that grows on the other side of the world, where, while Bridegroom's gas is low, the sun stands high in heaven, drawing the grass erect to his ray lest it be weighed down by the chain of coupling life that clings to it. Standing as if in a draught from the open door of the furnace of summer, the stalk is pendant with loves and the pairing of crowded insects takes place, under cover of their modest chitin, in a haze of heat so fine that it looks as if light had been caught in its own golden web.

United in a passion as inscrutable as the enduring eyes of the Boddhisatva, only once in as long as patience lasts the onlooker they are jerked in a single tick of convulsion as intense as the throb of this open noon.

The female does not let go of the stalk; the male continues to clasp her abdomen - - - - -

9

The Dissatisfied Bride

" - - - - - - my fingers meet about your tiny waist."

The Beaux of the eighties choose brides with slender waists; for fashion, which must some way spring from our subliminal efforts to catch the illusive pleasure by inventing new snares for it, seems at this period to have reached the conclusion that it were best secured by compressing a woman's internal organs within a circumference of seventeen inches, and that the ensuing congestion and prolapsus must be pleasure's proper element.

Ada has somewhat expanded on release from her corset, but the livid circlet in her flesh and a marked degree of flatulence persist.

East and West the knees of the bride are strained from the uneasy sacrum; her penetralia in such pose being so taut as to become insensible to the percussion of Eros.

The fine point or inextinguishable light in her brain, the lamp of instinct, is intensified to a lucent nucleus of animation that knows its desire. The desire to orchestrate the Life-fusion to an audience of body and soul. While her brain, a tabu-record on the human gramophone, plays on reverse, selections from love literature, - syringa - circlet - tulle - Hymen - amen. Virginity - ripening expectancy, passivity - Trust to male principle in the universe for axis - kiss - bliss.

"Ooooh - oh!"

"Don't cry, darling - - - it only hurts the first time."

Next morning at the breakfast table, an elated bridegroom smiles on a bride most unaccustomedly subdued, in a sort of creative patronage of one who, according to the morals in vogue, he could only make his own by deflowering her.

"Sweetheart—your eyes—all different, don't you know. Anyone may see you are a woman now—That sacred sovereignty, your womanhood."

"I feel so ashamed before the waiter."

Under the bride's *coutil* corset, the lacerated inconvenience melts to a clammy excitation, to a more localized temptation than was diffused during virginity.

* * * * *

The sun sets in the sea; an incandescent magnet drawing the senses down in his descent, leaves lavender the skies appeased.

On the windy pier, the bride's young flanks yearn to her groom. Although her incident of wedlock has been no more than the slightest of surgical operations, her emotions have been educated to tie the hymenal bonds into a mystic union with her mate. And this occult relationship, aided by the hypnotic influences of tradition, stimulates the latent tactile impulses of a satin-lined Venusberg.

The nucleus of animation, knowing its desire, expands the healing tissues of the bride like flower-petals opening to the light.

"Isn't the sunset lovely dear? It makes me feel so er—r—almost holy. There's something *in* me yearns to melt with the sun into the golden sea—it's *so* peaceful."

Since pubescence her dynamic life-currents, swift-currents, cross-currents have seethed, to rush confluent in an unimaginable concussion; and sink at last into some shoreless lake of sentient calm.

Driven by the sensuous grandure of the setting sun, the wedded pair fade in the dusk and return along the Esplanade to hide in their hotel for fresh embraces.

In bride-body, the dews of Eros descending, the passional storm gathers for the release of beatific lightning. The lightning does not strike. Her nerves, undelivered of the burden of their desideratum reverse from pleasure-seeking excitation to an excruciating cramp.

"Well, it will be all right next time; you have to get accustomed—you know, darling."

The bride awakens with an aching back.

For the nucleus of animation communicates its known desire, but not the means of satisfaction. So every night of honeymoon, the bride prepares young nerves and flesh for the banquet of the senses.

What yearning. What straining.

Ah, surely, now this unbearable aspiration of the body is about to be relieved, to be most beautifully allayed.

The rocket of the senses has been lit. The rocket splutters out in nervous irritation. No inward body-star illuminates the bride in tremulous revelation.

The bridegroom gasps. He sighs. Groans gradually in consummation.

The bride is numb with doubt. Of what lop-sided miracle has the bridegroom partaken?

Space is incommensurable to the separation of one knowing pleasure and one not knowing.

The bride and bridegroom are one flesh.

Above the breakfast table, an ill-sustained coquetry of the bride shifts in her eyes to allow for egress of gleams already envious.

What is it that the secretive implications of her upbringing promised her? That *he* has known through her? Why must she give and not receive? The body transmits its irritation to the brain. "Monopolist"- her mind screams - - "monopolist" - - -

"You know very well how I dislike that tie" -

"Ah, is that the reason you forgot to put two lumps of sugar in my tea?" -

Sugar—sugar—why should he have all the sugar?

The nucleus of animation persists in knowing its desire through endlessly concatenated generations of bodies, independent of an imperfect engineering of bodies, the experience of bodies; latent if unproven.

Under the fleshly shed of genius and dunderhead alike this nucleus, in protracted spring-tide, renews expectancy, even in the disappointed body of the bride. She shall again turn to her mate, and again.

"I hate men," pouts Ada, "They are so selfi - - -"

The Maître d'hôtel is bowing another honeymoon couple to a table. Their eyes are blurred, their faces slightly bloated—Ada's antagonism is drawn off her bridegroom on to the scent of the new enemy, a far more awful enemy—for this other woman—has *she?*—

"—er, I did not quite catch?" the husband inquires.

"I mean—they are so silly. How can you need sugar when you have me," asks the bride, become provocative again.

"Ah, now you smile as you used when I was courting you."

Dear God, am I not even as other women are? Why should all brides be happy while only I—? That one at the further table; has *she?* Ah, the mystery of the night for her, for *every* woman. To every woman how valuable my husband would be. Anyhow—if I can't have *it,* no other woman shall have *him.* I will not be deprived of everything.

"And you, dear, must never, never—do you hear?—stop courting me."

Ah, that other woman. Why should she have all the pleasure? It's too unjust.

Meanwhile at the further table—

"No, dear, I don't feel like walking this morning. I have such a wretched pain in my back."

The honeymoon, perfect month of a woman's life—never can come again—has drawn to an end.

The bride leans over her husband with unguarded face. He lies profound.

"Wretch—how to sleep so peacefully."

When he awakes he will kiss her. Those awful kisses that crawl down her spine and bid the body hope all over again.

"Dearest—*not* this morning, really, you've no idea—how tired—after all the packing. Yes, *of course* I love you. Of course I like it—only it's so *awfully* fatiguing."

"Look here, child, when we get back to town, you'll just please run along and see a doctor. Sir Digby Bing, the big woman specialist—set you right in a jiffy."

Sir Digby Bing—has dissected how many female corpses? How long was intern of the "Lying-In"? Has scrutinized how many films of female diseases under the microscope? Has observed woman in every stage of pregnancy—in every stage of decay; at puberty at the climacteric. Knows the womb inside out, upside down.

Unfortunately the Sphinx is solid.

And there is no consulting specialist for delight.

Dear Lady Bing herself is *very* delicate.

One guinea for the great strategist.

"No *nice* woman *ever* likes it."

And in that era when humanity went to the doctor, crying—"Teach me how to love"—Ada says—"Good afternoon," sniffing her lavender salts.

10

A Certain Percentage of Women—

Pleasure is a biological illumination in which the body perceives its origin in cosmic sentience. The child is a spark kindled in that sequestered flare, and one who belongs to the certain percentage of women who conceive unlit would have no tie with the child she bears, were it not that woman so often achieves a mystic maternity which fetches its inspiration from far beyond participation in the regenerative spasm.

Although the shock of unsatisfied intercourse is a form of murder that leaves her desire alive in the corpse of sensibility, in spirit she is the durable convalescent, who, forgetful of her wounding and distress will welcome her successor with a babble of delight. —She is so surprised by the immaculate bud that has formed in the troubling of her flesh that to celebrate it she can find nothing pure enough but white to wrap it in, and the swaddled babe is the living truce to the brawls of good and evil.

On crowded streets, in quiet parks, right under the throne or down an alley, this oasis of the flesh as it is before the "Accident" has made it lewd, draws little knots of people round it, to exclaim at its sudden purity: to poke a dimple or tickle the soles of this laughing flower, as if even sensation may be come by in innocence.

However, the flesh will sometimes come to such a pass that a mother carries in her arms a fearful thing, yet even she will claim the rights of motherhood to be reconciled to the outrageous and for her the holy church of Rome, the most subtle diplomat at the court of Nature, has set aloft an eternal nurseling, the prototype as God conceived it, to allow this swindled mother to make a mask out of the Infant Countenance that rules the catholic skies, to cover the features of her offspring while she is loving it; that she may look at it.

But woman is insatiable for fictitious values, her life is the steadfast adventure in make-belief; give her a stone and she will swear that it is bread, throw it at her head and she sinks into a swoon of sentiment from which nothing can arouse her.

Accomplishing the impossible, she will manage to be *constant* to a man who has broken off all relations with her. A frigid woman whom a transient mate has infected with syphilis; maltreated, cheated, and left with an illegitimate idiot on her hands will spend the last flickers of her sanity prattling of the sanctity of love.

Often her very appearance is a mirage, for subject to valuations as inaccessible as those of the aesthetic, a face has no love-lure if it does not picture some one or other of the nuances of sexual transport. The expression of the most popular beauty is a "still" of some evanescent reaction associated with the orgasm: her eyes are always turning up for the spasmodic oncome, so that men may plunge a preliminary gaze into this seeming promise that their senses have come upon something to share.

This would be natural enough if these chance fixations on handsome faces registered the sexual capacity of their possessors but often the more adorable girls are impassive to erotic stimuli, just as the gigolo who looks like a static of rapture is frequently subject to Ejaculatio Praecox.* The sensory scale of the erotic symphony must in some way accord with the unknown laws of proportion in beauty, as if perfection in art induces in the intellect a consummation comparable to that with which the harmonies of a human face crown some aesthetic craving in the genitals. So certainly is Nature urging Life to beget itself in loveliness.

*See Krafft-Ebing

And again we wonder in what personality consists when faces express familiarity with sensations their bodies may never have known. There is some consciousness in Instinct that knows what woman wants, while she, herself, so often fails to find out. And we may be mistaken in supposing that the intuition of rapture is the product of organs and hormones through which rapture is ultimately conveyed. It may be treasure which, even when irretrievable from the darkness it lies buried in, enriches that darkness nevertheless.

It must be something very like the child vision of latent miracles that sustains these sentimental women bearing the ardent load of their passional compromise as lightly as it were a sigh. And very like the infant residence on the rim of a supplementary dimension is their state of being in-love, in which the simplest reactions to being alive take on a richness of quality no actual values bestow, love being one of the three avenues of escape for the dynamic inquietude of our sensibility, which is never entirely consumed in our struggle for existence, but subsists as a surplus potency to foment our ideals and our dreams.

Three avenues of escape—love, intoxication, and religion—give on to a universe which, for losing some of its concretion, is compensatory in brightness.

So if the church holds out its cross, the brothel its blush and the bar its sign, over doors that for the people in the street serve as vents bored in the solid of a routine that stirs the drained human essence into such cruel alloy with the pavement; is it not in simulation of those avenues that open up in the human mind an escape from actuality?

And if behind these three doors the least light, that of the votary taper, is the most penetrating, even to the concavity of darkness, it shows us nothing; while at the zinc* altar is transubstantiation most likely to take place, and the stagger, not the genuflex, precedes our one disinterested embrace; we conclude that the functions of church and bar have become confused, or that intoxication, being an undesirable liberation, is one most surely attained through tangible means.

*Zinc—French bar

Yet all the same when the door of the church claps on one, who, aloof as if in certitude, ploughs the routine of the streets with his hermaphroditic trudge; how many from among the crowd, maddened by the whys and wherefores that crack the inadequate brain on the enigma of suffering, how many, in the belief that the priest has outknown bewilderment, have hurried after the black petticoat he assumed on being ordained to ease the intellect's despair out of a customary into an uncustomary dimension—(even as the teller of fairy tales eases the child mind into the actual world, and the myths of Eros reconcile women to life)—and catching up with this symbol of solution, as with a salvation, have stared into priestly eyes even less comprehending than their own.

Now should we pick woman out from among the crowds on the pavement, who are longing all alike for some opportunity to release the major rhythm of their eternal aspiration in spite of the minor rhythms to which more fleeting matters constrain them, we should find that when she gets an opportunity to enter the transformative state of love, she cannot wander in and out of the sphere of normal conditions as men do, or present, as it were, a surface to Love's contacts and associations, but she is bound to absorb the phantasmagoric values to be found there, until they become integral to her make-up.

And as it is only the charge of the male electricity that can hold this egoless amalgam together, when he withdraws his galvanic presence, woman ceases to glow.

He returns to the world he has his business with, while she remains ethereally attached to his magnetic center, as the child is materially attached to the umbilicus.

Even the woman who is known as cold, but who would be more accurately described as smoldering, is capable of an esoteric kind of union with her man. For sexual anaesthesia does not necessarily prevent her taking part in the mountaineering exploits of her partner's nerves. A sort of vaginal clairvoyance will enable her to follow in her emotions—(which his contact will whip almost to delirium)—the same graph as, in his senses, does he.

And the passing of the passional storm will leave her with all the shaken consequences of *something experienced*.

Thus so many impalpable tentacles have reached out of her to fasten upon him, that when he wanders away, he leaves her as nothing but a tangle of snapped nerve cables or wounded feelers dripping with a vital sap that she had drawn from him; and that, even when healed, will, while still at a loose end for a new attachment, dart about on the surface of her sentiments in the pattern of lunatic pentagrams that hydrometer beetles make on pools of water.

Such women, when closeted together, will carry on a conversation whose burden is hung upon a hiatus that stands for the ultimate fictitious value haunting the back of their minds while they, becoming entirely void, exhaust the atmosphere; as if a garden of flowers awaited a thunder-storm in which a male lightning should resuscitate them.

But what takes place when man enters this pre-gravid atmosphere? He will catch an eye in the full of its lusterless pretense and, finding it has gathered little light in rolling on the world, will polish it with his lubricity until it dazzles him in the very radiance he induces.

And when he prints on its dilating iris a glorified image of who looks out of it, she takes on an aspect of herself that he alone can evoke.

For woman requires to be praised into animation, being a toy that to be played with must first be colored up.

So as life was breathed into a sod of clay, as if her mind, like her body, must be impregnated by him, man puffs woman full of a vanity that can only be exploded by the one who arouses it.

This brings us to the interrogatory point where woman begins and where woman ends. For if it were possible that she alone throughout evolutional Time had had the inhabiting of the earth to accomplish for herself, she might, with no model to which to conform, have spread like melted wax, and by now be covering the greater portion of the globe with a fungoid layer of flesh-colored inertia.

In which event supposing that man, having been bred apart on another planet, should suddenly come to earth and tread in her, she would show as his perfect foot-print.

For Eve was created a little late. That lapse of time which corresponds to inception is Adam's own. —While her very beginning was of an initial secondariness that left her the whole gamut of development, except the creative impetus or starting point.

. The fecund chaos from which all creation arises, that is brought to order by the decisiveness of man, in her wells up against an aimless aspiration and ebbs in turmoils of frustration.

While man will convert time itself into achievement so that the centuries condense to flashes of his genius, the inconclusiveness of woman is of the very nature of duration in its aspect of mere *being*.

So, by reason of his taking Time by the forelock and of her being carried along on the Everlasting's back, she cannot coincide with his achievements. Just as the child is only half in our world, woman brings only a partial presence to the pursuits of man; including for that certain percentage of women—his concupiscence.

But if he suspects that even in the biological illumination she does not always see eye to eye with him, coming upon everything as she did on existence a little late; he, unable to cross over to the feminine side of sense and discover from there what impression the crowning act of his virility makes on his only audience, has chosen, rather than seek information, to persuade woman collectively to play the Sphynx.

She could not refuse this personification while unable to form her own conception of herself, and it suited her very well, as, the answer to her riddle being thus indefinitely postponed, it allowed for infinite conjecture.

Also, it so successfully confused the woman enlightened by Eros with the woman who is not that there is hardly any way of recognizing which is which; notwithstanding that the latter became indeed "the Sphynx" inasmuch as she never uttered a word to the effect that in the marriage bed as at the crack of doom, "the one shall be taken and the other left."

And perhaps because this secret is such as it would never occur to a rational humanity that she could *keep,* the man who was the least concerned with finding out concluded that women are Sphynxes without secrets.*

However, like Happiness that has no history, the satisfied make no publicity, while the unsatisfied, being mysteries to themselves, are very intriguing, so that it would appear to be this anomalous Sphynx, the one who conceals her empty secret beneath the vaguely teeming secretiveness demanded of her, who most, like elusive prey does the hunter, leads on the fantasy of man.

She it must have been who, lacking one knew not what, inspired the spectacular arts to spin endless designs for her completion.

For that which need never have been put out of mind—(were it not for the "Accident" shaking perception so awry that we cannot consider biological detail with the same unbiased finality as any other diagram)—the core of her attraction, being likewise hidden, has acquired a symbolic identity with the Sphynx's secret and like any other sheeny butterfly can be chased across the largeness of the social landscape with the light of a changing fantasy playing upon it at will.

Meanwhile, its ostracized reality has become so firmly embedded in the cache-sex as to form a solid moral basis so prohibitive to the senses that they seem almost to have forgotten where it is and to be satisfied with an ocular indulgence in the trunk lines leading up to it; now that the virgin leg is bred to be brittle and fleet as a Derby mare's to race excitement to the winning-post.

Where an audience of the eighties were kept contented with even one girl ripening her pink cotton tights, who had little else to do but carry "it" about with her; our multiple modern attention is drawn to a composite monster set on a revolving platform. Her constellatory flesh whose substance is a troupe of female acrobats; myriad-limbed, over-disciplined, falls into kaleidoscopic arabesques that dwindle and swell in contorted perspectives. Sometimes stellar sometimes serpentine. To swish and intertwine with tentacular facility under paradoxical projections of spick and span light.

WOMAN—the big Review—still inconsummate.

* Oscar Wilde

11

The Outraged Womb

When Freud opens his mouth to speak that gash of Semitic acumen discloses a hollow so profound in comparison to all other mouths, which, when parted for speaking, hardly remind us they are cavernous at all, one seems to get a glimpse of the dark prenatal cavern of his theory. And it is uncanny to hear an intelligible voice leap from its depth when one is almost expecting a throng of neurotic manikins to issue from it.

A man may have the impress of his idea so strongly marked upon him that our subconscious detects it as clearly as if it constituted an additional feature. And, could we discern the esoteric traits of his character, they would form a new pattern of him superposed on the person familiar to our senses: a cryptogram of the psyche that will have its place in the spectacle, of which the mind in its moments of greatest clarity begins to be aware. As though some universal metamorphosis beyond range of our present vibrations were being prepared by the long and seemingly patternless activity of Life.

But if beyond us the sum of our aspirations transposes to transcendental phenomena for consciousness to move among when it shall have torn down the three-dimensional environment, there still lie behind us the urges of nature of which we are vehicular. They have each their organ in the remote vicinity of the body (for is not consciousness a watcher leaning out of the tower of the body?): an organ which exercises its own particular consciousness to drive us or serve us.

This consciousness, or genie of an organ, subsisting from generation to generation, has acquired a sort of eternalness through transmission which haunts our entrance into and habitation of the flesh and, counting on posterity, at last, destroys the flesh. - - -

This genie is more persevering than we, for at the touch of death our essence diffuses and the proletariat of our organism immediately "lay off," whereas the genie of an organ survives in our heirs for the same circumscribed ends while their intellect starts out afresh with the old views at least tipped at a new angle, and with a growing conviction that the Will and the genii of the organs are dissociable.

The womb, the lobate organ of the Sphynx, is the medium of elaboration. Closing on a nucleus shot like a meteor into its extensile hollow where inertia whirled to vertiginous gyrations forms annular vertebrae, the womb will patiently let grow within its cavernous apathy the unconscious foetus; will organize it, conserve it and cover it with all the manufacture of flesh it needs. Although the prodigal multiplication this process incurs is a petty function in comparison to the creative impetus from without which incepted it (as if the womb received from an engineer the project for a mechanism to be worked out by one whose time is less precious than his). Nevertheless, a miraculous affinity drawing the *spirit* into the meshes of microscopic tissue also makes use of the seed of the Sphynx; thus when the spirit scintillates human eyes it is not only the impregnator but also the one impregnated who, in the infinite variations of heredity, look out of them—

Curious cavernous subcarnal events set in motion by aerial fatalities such as the chance proportions of a particular face impinging on the reflex of another being who, while abetted by the genii of the organs, is unaware of their existence, as they are of his. They are even, these obscure dwellers in the body, stirred to strange effervescence by the light reflected on a dead planet which, as if in ghostly protest at its own passing, will veil the aforesaid face in unearthly phosphorous as a sign that the hour is at hand to entice a new creature through the gate of the body into a living crowd.

As the genii of the organs associate with the intellect, the wand of Eros invades the cavern of anticipation with the same incisiveness with which the masculine brain invades the world. Both world and womb by virtue of man's passing are left fantastically modified. Yet the eternal purpose of the genii of the organs is continuate, as is the racial memory which holds us to our type.

Is the genie a medium for the desires of the being of whom the organ forms a part, does it impose its own desires on him? Or, intermediary between a cosmic reservoir of sentience and a finite receptacle, is the genie the accoupling and germinal throb of the corporeal world?

The response of the womb to the sentient urge is less conclusive, owing to the intervention of fecundity which involves it, after intake in a long biological rumination that is duplicated in the female brain, in the same way as the male initiative is set to the tempo of the phallus. Hence the female intellect seems to function in the post-creational way as the womb when it multiplies the initial cell it has had to borrow for the creation of that which it is unable to originate. Yet all the same this organ of asylum is as much the home of a genie as were the elements of Nature in mythology, for although the womb may lie void and quiescent awaiting a meteoric semen to set a molecular system in motion, and although it may flower and fade without fulfilling its destiny, the womb with its ageless instinct never ceases to ideate the concussion of ecstasy which is the sole aspiration of the genie—

* * * * *

Man, making part of a pattern formed by the outside of finite things and what may be paradoxically described as the inside of an infinite thing, lives in the interstitial arabesque that is his universe, while (like the child blockaded by psychic projections) he is pressed upon by a crowd of phenomena surpassing his senses. His consciousness is not only anchored to his body, that island in the air inhabited by organic genii and a slaving biological proletariat, but it is also haunted by an indefinable oppression which may be due to his being incommensurate to some vast organism of which an atomic sprinkling forms his solar system. Looking out from the world within his body which he cannot see on a world only partially revealed to him, he exists among convincing illusions that result from the interrelationship of the two.

But woman, in addition to all this, is subject to invasion by ego-universes that, entering her microscopically, emerge as something almost greater than she can bear. She is the vehicle of worlds which agglomerate within her and (as it is said did the earth from the sun) break loose from her, leaving the cavernous womb-brain to its everlasting dream of ecstasy in an extra-creational chaos. It is a dream which no awakening can ever efface. Keeping only its ecstatic end in view, while serving involuntarily as the decoy for reproduction, the genie of the organ which in man is so nicely synchronized to his instinct that its exigencies are gratified without undue complications, has in woman been disjoined at some obscure stage of organic construction in the past, as if on the evolutionary journey the genie had left a part of his instrumental paraphernalia at half-way (in accord with a theory which may have survived that the female is an undeveloped male: an anomalous incompletion allowing for sufficient supplement of function to mature the fruit of a race). So that which has long been known as the "pleasure of the flesh," a magneto-electric phenomenon in which the stimulation of one nerve is transmitted to another, whereupon the concordance of both effects an electro-sensory release, is in woman, as a result of her organic scatter, an uncertain eventuality, even in the most yearning embrace. For, owing to the structural interruption, that has in her parted these communicative nerves and left one of them at random (and, in different individuals, variably placed), either nerve requires a distinct stimulation and sometimes, moreover, responds to a different rate of vibration, so that in many cases the Sphynx's secret would never be solved were not Eros inclined to become engineer. Eros was hardly so inclined in the days of the bird-cage - - - - - - . Incidentally, the mechanism submitted to his solitude revealed no indications as to how it should be dealt with.

As if there were in the universe no small thing that is not the re-expression of a greater thing so that as each man, being a unit of mankind, mankind in time may form but a unit in some paradoxical dimension of an ultimate reality in which the solar system that reigns over us may share a unique identity with each molecule within us. According to ancient philosophy—"multipleness being merely the intellects' construction of the absolute"; so in some way all wombs are one womb; the eternal cavern from which Life issues, a temple whose facade is woman, which being very often empty would seem to give out a strange impersonal invitation to all irrelevancies - - - or a *terrain vague* that invites the dumping of all irrelevancy—the detritus of logic—debris of Ethics.

For woman, created so fragile in the design that she be torn, whose nerves are so strung the more easily to snap in constant over-tension, whom to be loved must be shattered, dripping with blood and shaken with earthquake parturition, is pinked up and painted to look as much like a bon-bon as possible. This surgical exhibit of the ages flirts her invanquishable coquetry as a spangled fan to hide her seismic body and smiles the outrageous smile of her unwarranted delicacy.

All this is true as it is false. We cannot sort out this woman of crude reality from among the multiple reality of the "social surface." Jigsaw gestures of living disintegrate her and put her together again in more pleasant patterns, so that the melodramatic crimson she contains "in the tube," which as raw paint in itself is as valueless as it is indispensable in painting a picture, exists only as transformable material which loses its identity when mixed with all the other colors in the kaleidoscope of civilization. The gory giantess, prop of our genealogical succession, is so sublimated that whenever it would seem that her disguised protagonist must for a moment become identified with her, the occasion turns out to be Doctor's business. An eternal river of blood is so successfully deviated from the social landscape that even advertisements for Kotex less than remind us of it in pictures of pale clients whose appearance of super-carnal delicacy suggest their being slightly disgusted with God.

A scientist must accept biological fact as tangible reality. It is a reality which hardly enters a woman's life; so that in the end she retains but a vague impression of having "looked away" from a pack of cellulose, or having, in a concussion of agony, glimpsed for a moment a partly raised sheet while an unseen drama of obstetrics and travail takes place beyond its immaculacy. On the volatile tissue of her existence that billows so capriciously on the breeze of her allure there appears no stamp of the factory.

Indeed, woman's life is so unreal that melodrama is often true of one whose misfortunes are so general and irremediable as to be disavowed by the intellect as cogitable matter and are tossed onto that *terrain vague* for their seasonal reflorescence. Nor can we catch her at her martyrdom as dupe of the universe, for the more tormented, the more she considers herself to grow in virtue, as if she dare not accept her helplessness.

She rises as the sun, smiles from her beads and sets on the hither side of love—to rise again—? All in a strangely squandered day, whose morning is anticipation and afternoon disintegration. As if the creative moment she had missed were the equivalent of eternity she moves outside it in an erratic Time which comes to a stand-still while she accomplishes twice the work it should be possible to do in it, or ceases, between her effort to realize herself and her effort to escape from herself.

In hoards as dense as the dust that drives them, myriads of aching marionettes positively embrace their burdens and perform their enervating duties with the common sense that solves all problems by ignoring them, and that economy of energy achieved through allowing no pause through which it may run out.

It is such indispensable toilers as these patient patching provident creatures, miraculously endowed with astral extra hands to wipe the nose of the universe and push it out to play while they attend to infinity in detail, who—like the minute organisms which, dying in their multitudinous similitude, form the coral substance of a habitual island—raise the family institution above the wave of indigence by keeping in condition the carnal spring-board from which the creative activity of man takes off. Still, in a spiritual survey this sound domestic rock of their minute achievement is again but the eternal *terrain vague* littered with the pitiable tokens dropped by deserters from the docile ranks of a scavenger army.

Here on this *terrain vague* lies the embroidered cigar-case which inspired that admirable example of idealist womanhood, Madame Bovary, to trail the provincial finery of her responsive soul through the mud in which so much of feminine aspiration founders when it sets out in search of a little "color." And here we can pick up the very eye of melodrama shining with that masculine avidity the woman of temperament is so liable to mistake for the brilliance of Paradise. See how her parasitic emotions dart in and out of the gates of its heavenly expression to gather sustenance. And see how unexpectedly it shuts. No stage, of however vast dimensions, could accommodate the beat of her flabbergasted heart, that, fallen into her high-heeled shoes, goes tottering in all directions, to dash itself against the sudden dark.

The eye has shut, and in the melodrama its lids have clanged upon her as the ghastly gates of the "Lying-In." It is only fitting that when she comes out the snow is falling to cling to her with the soft spineless persistence of that imaginable purity which insists on Life being cleaner than it looks.

Now she lifts the worn-out shawl of tradition that covers the bundle in her arms, and behold the living, lasting load she is carrying; the child who clings to her with the flesh of the father who has forsaken her is the same old eye of melodrama in whose inherited heavenliness she faces the irrealizable reality, that the valuable soul may be begotten of a cheap lie.

Before such terrific irrelevancy it is her emotion, not her reason, which founders, for her reason must be so averse to her destiny that it would seem to refuse acknowledgement of the plot of the play in which she takes part. Enfeebled by the eternal wound of her disadvantage she ignores the trajectory described by the weapons that inflict it. Transfixed to the pillar of Time, she is the target of arrows shot from paradoxical directions. Her essential quality lies in "being at the mercy of," for the values of her status are so extravagantly incongruous they make of her a sort of sane lunatic whose asylum is marriage.

In this institution which is based on his desire to count so much of his offspring as is compatible with his patrimony man binds himself to accompany woman further than she can go: woman whose spirit, when momentarily released from preoccupations that interfere with self-realization, cannot help but retrace its own tracks in an effort to locate her pure incentive only to find that she has none. To whom the most drilling introspection reveals her mind as a quick-sand circle in whose central lacunae all the material it gathers and brings to a condition in which the creative residuum should logically accumulate sinks and is lost.

So let her throw her amphora and her pearl into the quick-sand, her womb with her brain onto the discard area of unconsummated things. In a sufficient mist this *terrain vague* with all its litter may even become confused with those cruelly geometrical acres of crosses that spring up in the burial grounds of interrupted warriors; for it is nothing but the common plot whereon those women lie; shrouded in the teeming silence of their history. Of an eroticism seldom discharged, an idea that is seldom defined, an outreaching seldom taking hold— involving the nervous system of half humanity.

If an act of violence was perpetrated in the unaccountable past of the differentiation of species and determination of sexes, it is an act of violence which, undenounced, nevertheless in the dark of consciousness breeds revenge; for all the pained dismay of that certain percentage of women who have suffered the initial injustice favoring man in an automatic nervous recuperation that she so much the more requires to compensate her for the exhaustion of giving birth. So, at some time, at some point in the melodrama that has no denouement, one woman too many looks into that eye of mystification, all-promising in its covetousness, and finds something wrong with its expression.

The genie of the womb which, if more devious, cedes no whit of instinct to the genie of the phallus, aspires to have its dream confirmed. The colossal dam of a collective abnegation breaks down, as if after all its ultimate resistance consists in only one frail body and this frail body is after all the fearful giantess. So, in the everlasting cavern, vast as the cave of the four winds, a cyclonic voice in vengeance of the mute forbearing multitude of misspent women blows up the dusts of life; the debris and detritus that man, in helpless emulation of sadistic nature, has tossed there of his ethical logic, in vertiginous spirals of recrimination.

The rubbish of centuries crashes into words as the volume of all women's silence, become audible, rolls upon us.

For the womb is built of a long patience, but when the genie of it at last is weary of bearing together with its biological load the ghostly foeti of unsatisfied desires, it rouses from its apathy. Loosening a two-edged tongue in torrential indignation that hollows its course through the lobes of man's brain and erodes the quick of his nerves with the acids of old agony, the genie spreads a lasting blight on the crop of life which springs from the womb.

This sonorous flood is also deviated from the social landscape. Woman's reprisals are uttered behind closed doors. Her "incantation for laying the blame," like malefic secret rites of destructive magic, strikes undertones in our social symphony omitted in orchestration. Only her intimates within the breeding zone may listen to her drastic endeavors to exorcise the headless spirit of her desolation. And for man the pitfall of marriage, that under favorable circumstances is so succorable an association, lies in the odd chance of its shutting him up with this one-woman-jazz-band of the female universe. She makes a preposterous music.

As if in a fugue of irrefutable illogic a dormant volcano would rid itself of unformulated contents to get to the bottom of a smoldering unrest, she retrieves every note that Life has played upon her, complaining that each one, even from the beginning, has been struck out of tune. Her audience, however attentive, can never make out her leit-motif, for, chasing up and down a scale that has no key-note, she seeks to fix upon man a responsibility he has not incurred in failing to educe from her the harmony of a chord she does not spontaneously compose.

It is a long plaint, resistant as is negation. For she is unaware of her own meaning while the average man fits his significance to himself. Hers is an empty tirade which, as if her desperation were as unreal as her argument, never wears her out. She persists; unanswerable. Her echoing indignation flows on and the sentient wreckage in its wake, her family, is absorbed by sanatoriums and asylums with the connivance of official discretion which never listens behind closed doors.

Yet this parrot of the womb is innocent of evil, being only the unconscious medium through whom the outraged spirit of the weaker sex pours forth an automatic monologue. And at the menopause regains serenity, when, having forgotten the very sound of her outcries, she washes her hands of the psychic doom of her husband and children as being again but doctor's business.

It is a vulgar thing to dabble the fingers of the intellect in that which for a polite society does not exist. And extremely improvident, for were we to countenance the reprisals of the outraged womb and combat their insidious influences on the human psyche, or above all were we able to furnish a solution to the secret of the Sphynx, a fair proportion of our money-making concerns would disappear, with the substitution, for unrest, of equilibrium.

Yet, all the same, when this genie of the fruitful organ opens her mouth to speak it is pitiable to see a throng of neurotics issue from it, when one is almost expecting to hear an intelligible voice.

12

Interlude

Being alive gives us the sensation of using an infinitesimal amount of an infinite potentiality, of having an incalculable force driving through us into blocked-up channels: of being a semi-paralyzed Hercules.

It gives us the impression of being the witness of our own experience, of witnessing that witness and of witnessing that witnessing, until there is no end to the multiplication of the witnessed witness within us; sentinel of that mysterious reservoir of consciousness where there is no point at which we come to a halt and declare, "Here my being conscious *of* begins." Thus we are never entirely taken up by our "events," there being always something of us left aloof from them.

Being alive is a "walling in" by our blind back, a convenient housing of our biological perceptions, for otherwise who can tell but that we might be looking out of front and back windows at once.

Being alive is the loneliness of the multitude, similar in their helpless parasitic lascivity, distinct as each one crying alone and forever - - - "I - - - I!" That individuality which, like a phialed viable explosive, is conditioned by each man having, as label, a face which he alone among his fellows can never see; even as he has to compose his own psyche with the experiences of the human race. He exists to the extent of the general understanding of him unless he can make a personal contribution to add to this human experience of which he is composed.

He has no concrete proof of being other than a soft machine that moves in a landscape, and thus we see him, when looking from long distance, where he first appears as a pale creature stirring against a wall of green and later as a clothed creature surrounded by erected stone. But taken from close-up, he forms a covered entrance to Infinity. It is for this reason his strange intuition of the illimitable "presence of himself" survives a racial experience that should by dint of repetition minimize him; in such incalculable flux of similars does Nature spawn him - - - - does the world receive him.

The world of a juggler - - - - For one it will open out, spreading a vast plenitude before him. And the more he delights in it; building it, mining it, sailing across and flying over it; in growing familiar, the smaller it becomes and the greater is he in proportion. While on another this same world will close in until it is nothing but hostile walls and barred doors backing him into a gutter. And the less habitable area it allows him for his disgust, the larger it becomes, the more foreign are its resources which recede from him and the smaller is he in proportion.

But behold! The universe itself is a juggler's trick. Each of these men exists at the center of the universe, for only from this unique base can he command full radius for the exercise of his selfhood—. While, again, this selfhood all men recognize as having the same origin as their own, in spite of the apparently complete detachment of their mechanisms as independent beings. We are like nothing so much as a multiplicity of tinted tops, ornate with ears and toes, all spinning on an omniprevalent axis.

Time and space are only different modes of separation. As a remote star which, travelling a million miles might seem from our earth not to have moved at all, both these men—the one in his hospital world of many facets, where, as if living in a diamond, he may be grieving for primeval swamps; while the other is let loose in his sadistic world where shops, like blazing butterflies, jostle the eternal chrysalis of indigence, where the skies are lit with civic invitation to lie between the lips of a cinema star, when his only possession is a handful of mud, and, the unearthly colorings of neon signs leading him on to some sublime assembly-room, he is brought up short by his shoe-string dragging . . .

Both these men—and it matters not that the one be roaming; the other static; in as much as being alive is a gesture of destiny—the lasting hieroglyph describing individuality—as seen from sufficient distance would appear to have fallen from the mother's womb to their distinctive attitude; stricken statues in aerial molds infusing their pre-destined posture.

The one is commanding, the other cringes; others like limp contortionists as if ill-contained in their aerial molds reduce to uninterpretable ciphers, all like Aunt Sally in a fair at whom the World is shied, while here and there we are surprised by unprecedented gesticulations of the creative.

It matters not that in their own location each may have travelled a million miles in that desolate dimension inwards. Their apparent person—which marks the confines of the ego, though seemingly what each must *be* in his entirety is actually where each "leaves off"— their apparent person remains a changeless manikin arranged by an accident.

If our potential consciousness is drawn from an infinite reservoir, our restricted and utilitarian consciousness, into which our blind back pushes us through the window of our eyes, is a little front garden for us to potter about in—it is being alive. An exceptional gardener will succeed in advancing, ever so slightly, the fence that hems his garden in, to enclose a hitherto unfound flower, and revealing it to his fellows he gives them some seed. This is the act of genius.

While others of opposite destiny will have all the rubbish and filth from surrounding gardens dumped into theirs, until they are choked with a miserable refuse from which no man ever emerges except for an occasional Jew who turns it into transient gold. No flowers can grow out of their bare experience whose blossoming they may announce to their neighbors over the garden wall. They have no means of self-expression. Yet the infinite potentiality, the incalculable force is inherent to them as it is to us all, only in them the "witness" is comatose, aware of nothing that goes on. The infinitude of their potentiality loads up against the back of their mind which like an idiot stuffed with shadows lies monstrously asleep. And this is their immense distress; that all of us are served from the illimitable reservoir of potentiality but some of us are soused by it. Their racial concepts they scarcely acquire, and if they have any personal concept it is inarticulate as is the negative in the dual value of silence. And the advent of Death sets a seal on their secret that had found no confident, even in themselves.

It must have been for such as these that faith prescribed a judgment-day, which, degenerated to an inhibitory threat, originated as an encouragement; a promise that the horde, the load, the unreapable harvest of human existence which never became clear to itself, should at last find the Ear that hears everything, the Voice that elucidates, so that finally shall be alleviated the innumerable inconclusion of shifting human sands.

Being alive from the inside feels like having an open window where others see our solid face. We stare across the ocean of phenomena while it washes away the facade of our torso and flowing into us is dammed by our blind back which, like a shell with algae cleaving to it, throws up our arms, and our restless hands ride into our view like ships against the clouds.

If being alive is having a face, that window which is identical with the being who looks out of it, one can imagine a man who had never seen his own reflection even in a pool as remaining one with the air, or being stuck in an impersonal scenery as part of a back-drop from which he was incapable of making a conscious advance.

Whereas we who are familiar with a mirrored man who looks more or less like us, once we find out we *have* a face must endlessly project a self out of Ourself to run on a short way before us, and wheeling round, constantly recognize us in being, as it were, brought face to face with Ourself. How else could we maintain that self-assurance which depends on never losing sight of our own presence? This involves a perpetual holding in mind of the mask by which our fellows distinguish us. We are bound to constantly visualize *what* our vis-à-vis is looking at, or else we were in danger of disappearing from ourselves and leaving him to an intimacy, in some cases dear to us, with an entity non-existent for us. We should not know what sort of creature he is showing interest in; and above all, if we are beautiful we should miss the conceit of looking upon ourselves together with him and in line with his eyes, of judging our effect, until at last our facial awareness is become like a driver walking backwards holding a bouquet of carrots to draw the ass of our self-esteem on.

I was seven years old when I found my particular face. Before that winter evening my being alive had consisted entirely of emotions. I had no identity until, wandering into an empty, ill-lit room, I came upon my appearance in a towering triple mirror.

Drenched in those depths and distances of interreflected glass which are endless in having no existence, even as in the beginning I had attached my leg to my locality, I found the image of my covered body surmounted by my naked face.

Like a dead pearl in old dim seas adrift in an aquarium of mirrored fog and incandescent gas that appeared to draw back all the Life that wanted to look at itself into that ocean from which originally it arose. Or like some marine bloom aslant from a maroon rock, its contours formed that scribble on the air that is a profile, as if it had been cut in its shadowy cameo with a musical instrument; so much do some things plastic look melodious.

Awash on an unaccountable current, stirred by invisible incentives as I moved, my own face filled me with the instant sympathy one might feel for an exile recognized as a compatriot to whom one is powerless to attain. I was excited by a premonition of future meetings under unimaginable circumstances. This mirrored face drooped in its semi-luminous loneliness from the rock-like distortion upholding it and into which it seemed at moments to subside. Surprised into unwarranted recognition, I stood as if being mesmerized by a face already held in trance by myself, to at last describe in the maroon base it attached to the preposterous proportions of my winter coat sleeves. Sliding my hand down the side of the face I should never see, to "prove" myself in the mirror, "That's me," I thought—and it's got such a "different" expression. The unreal distance between myself and "it" disquieted me.

This fitting incident of hazard having picked that proper partition to fit me to my face, I, according to my kind and to be seen of them, walked away wearing that disastrous veil which falls to pieces before we have worn it out. Or otherwise topped by that inconsiderable structure flanked by temples, yet limitless in letting in the overwhelming light of the whole world. So we, provided with our ocular scoop, go forward mining the spectacle confronting us, while behind us, situate as we are in the atmosphere and our activity causing a constant emptying of our aerial mold whenever we move, the impalpable matter into which we are packed rushes in to refill it.

Our every advance sheds trails of vanishing sheaths of us, instant reoccupations of our evacuated space. A dissolving diagram of fading arms and hollow legs flutters from our proceeding, a frieze of effacements to follow us wherever we go, the slide of the air being forever at its *business* of refilling our contour of a moment before. The travel of our being alive overweaves the earth with a scurrying mesh; for the antics of our intervening atmosphere, if visible, would reveal a dizzy rush of intrication which the clairvoyance of cubist art has only partially indicated.

—o-o-O-o-o—

Being alive is a rectangular recurrence of waking up to the dilation of the same white ceiling, of often rising from a wasted bed, of shutting secretive closets and being swallowed whole by yawning doors. Of treading quadrate pavement as if the soul's adventure were an attempt to square the circle through a four-cornered invasion of the mind. Again our being alive impresses on some subtle medium more tenuous than air the stuff of the irrevocable, effigies of our earlier selves.

Gauged by our isolate exploration inwards the effigies of our past have no essential identity with us. So much do we alter. Yet, to an outsider they appear as the same symbol of our good-and-evil, we have never ceased the simple being of ourselves so that our present self almost evaporates to merely the future ghost of our past actuality, as if once having been defined only in secret may we evolve.

—o-o-O-o-o—

Being alive is anticipation of perfect arabesques formed of our fellow creatures' communion with ourselves: until we make out the formal pattern of the human bars to our cage.

Being alive is a Siamese twin-ship, in which to ourselves is attached the embodiment of all the rest of mankind, and our discomfort together, awkward as the entanglement of accidents, hurts us.

Once in a while this allied double shrinks to but one representative of our obstructive fellow beings; a unit of a diplomatic corps; the sweet ambassador saying, "In me you will find all you would ask of the world, lit by the tempered light - - - - - These your bruises are become kisses - - - - - - -"

Yet our utmost response to the alleviating presence of our companion, besieging that breach in the human fortress, the opening of the eyes, fails to save us, on entering, from losing our-selves in the endless quiet open of that dimension inwards, the corridor to the soul which is inviolate even when of being alive all that is left is a soft ferocious longing to unlock the center of one's self with the center of someone else.

At first the enticement of being alive is so intoxicating we can hardly hold that elixir of adolescence: the whole of Nature is our narrow blood. The sap of all verdures swirls in our arteries and the scented pollen of the punctual spring blows divine dusts against our eyelashes.

Our gravity earthward is a leash so slackened that our dancing sensibility would seem to suspend from some angelic gravitation tugging inflated youth toward the birds. And all of this so often discomposes initiative that for many of us, once having been over-alive, the rest of life is a hangover. For we are but a ramshackle edifice around an eternal exaltation; a building in which the aspirations are a flight of stairs whose base dissolves in the wake of our ascension; and at last our foundations sag heavier into earth; the whole of Nature withdraws to an impersonal distance and, left unrecognizable and alone in the undying conviction of our perfection, we wonder if Life is fleeting and escaped us while we essayed to reason it out, or whether Life is static while we absent-mindedly shamble past it.

Being alive is a long time while so little comes within reaching-distance.

But, more than all, being alive is a queer coincidence.

Islands in the Air

1

Hurry

As I arose from the spiral staircase to the top landing a door stood open. On the floor, abandoned, black as hearses, lay a pair of shoes. Thrown in the pattern of a T-square triangle one walked straight toward me, the other set out on its own at right angles.

Something remarkably sinister in their impursuable vagrancy brought me up short. That dead-lock gait come to the parting of the wayfarer took shape as a sign-board on my private road. Mine had been a dislocated journey, every step I had taken resulted in a jam.

The scenic dry-goods surrounding the foot-wear presented the cubistic hay-stack of a recent "School." Countless segments set at a various subtlety of degree and a wild diversity of direction piled to overlapping strata in the center of the room and started from corners to spear the eye at every point on the ocular periphery.

So acute was my sensation of having "irrupted" home through a paper hoop, the torn edge of the picture-plane framing a littered perspective, I felt myself drop . . . into the deadlock of those halted shoes . . . . awfully in my appointed place.

Here and there among the random of tossed objects, crumpled cleansing tissues with their lip-stick corollas blossomed indecently. My eyes oscillated between untenable foci in the confusion and sagged.

At five o'clock in the morning I had tidied that flat and on coming home – –so had life in its dire disorder crept up upon a visionary Distance.

Tonight my encounter with those shoes precipitated the crisis in a long realization that detail in deterring me had curtailed time. The panic of postponement which seizes those who suddenly conclude their temporal resources are irrecoverable put me in a violent hurry; a resurgence of zeal which by reason of its repeated arrests in the past now appeared useless.

Hurry, confounded by the extreme disparity of the only destinations left for its choice, separated from me on the spot: antipodal to the exciting display of a dreamy Distance stood a comfortable gas-stove with its benign assurance of available liberty. Also I offered this Hurry, with its sense of enterprise, a poor support: the weird vacuum of an exhausted body topped by an aching head.

A kind of short-circuit of being alive occurring in woman when she simply *can't* go on set my nerves quivering so intensely they inscribed a diagram of their system on my inner sensibility. The light that shone in the Distance fizzled out. Through closed lids I began to see more than met the eye in the immediate disorder.

Fallen upon the carpet an old idea showed up as a mere anxiety complex, on a sheaf of circulars in shadow lay all the advice I had ever offered, out of it, towering, hewn from stone, grew a Deaf Ear.

In a freak continuity the Past lay before me, behind me lay the wastes of Time strewn with an astral litter. The accumulation of ideas. Ghosts of manuscripts written at odd whiles, they had waned to inconclusion on subversive interruptions. Faded piles of ivory paper, with the passions of the years their rhythms vary. Half one volume had gone to the mice . . . . they leave a pleasing *débris* of a flaky, somehow oriental outline, fretted to the measure of a nibble.

The book I had felt impelled to write! Tentatively assuming that what seemed likely to me would seem likely to others. Intermittent . . . unfinishing, I saw how this Book in itself constituted my inhibition.

Had early preceptors' insistence on unconditional confession complicated by the shame they had heaped on all forms of self-expression brought me to the conscientious pass of a woman anxious, under the onus of revealing her whole absurdity, to preserve her incognito?

Meanwhile in misanthropic readjustment of the comparative a minute roach turned into an omnibus loaded with humanity in search of food in the sink.

Several years since I had, for no apparent reason in view of nature's vast example found myself unwilling to kill an insect. This had nothing to do with the injunction of a Seventh-day Adventist from Antofagasta, "Mustn't kill pig. Pig was once a Christian."

I shrank from loosening upon the ether the vibrational shock that occurs on concussive ejection of a life from a body; a shooting pain returning on the air as increase of a general anguish tapped by the human race. I had imagined a universal radio receiving and broadcasting something unlike entertainment.

Now, tossing all such irreal valuations on the present heap, circumscribed by the shoes I had landed in, I decided to crush that roach . . . While moving toward it I caught fleeting sight of a faint yellow patch out in the night.

Hanging in an Actual Distance was a line of windows where, lit with a human mystery of strange rooms, the aspect of solid beings dissolves to a surplus shadow among the slight gradations of a pallid illumination. In place of the "washing" taken in at eve they shone side by side across the flocking dark.

My mood changed.

His passengers restored to their rightful proportions, the roach, having discharged them in those luminous rooms, crawled over the edge of immunity.

As a child in the belief I could create flawless people I attempted to hatch them from a dove's egg concealed in my armpit, but the shell was over-fine. At last I watched them come to life busied about diaphanous tasks in these few back windows seen across a roof. The lowlier the interior the lovelier, shrouded in the phosphorescence of a dusty pane.

A little way off the commonest conditions take on grandure. From where I stood the behavior behind those windows appeared aloof as the planetary drama. Devoid of detail the underprivileged floated like angels in an ideal estate; their uncouth homes become opal shrines in which the solitary were surely illuminati, the married in their lofty eyrie concording sublimely with the pulse of Eros' wings.

The scattered currents of my mind diverted from uneasy channels united in the expectant peace of concentration when the ray of vision is about to fuse with the waves of sound. Given a sufficiency of leisure those windows could be set to words.

This glance out of doors was typical of another form of distraction leading me off the single track. Assured I had a precious knowledge to communicate to my fellows, whenever, having rid my mind of concrete nuisances, I prepared to write it down, just then, the least thing I caught a glimpse of however casually or even a vestige astir in memory would dilate to a dimension of beauty defying rational analysis.

For this it is that in moments of reflection a life which, lacking this magical quirk, would have looked, in retrospect, so discouraging, almost intoxicates me with the glitter it has left in my brain.

No longer in touch with the world at all I was left to bear singly the undistributed weight of my *communication*. Should its erratic parts be brought to-gether as if rolled into a ball to be thrown to a recipient, how light it would grow describing an arc, in transit.

Two generations have evolved while I stood at the cross-purpose of the roads, my mouth open to speak or rather my pen dipped in air.

When one is bound to write of things which while observed long ago have as yet barely come into existence, Accepted Reality may parry one's move with an inexistent public. The procedure under such circumstances is to create a public to mold a generation but the final output of my observations is tenuous stuff at most, to be cut to the contour of an electric spirit. To bring into view this fitful glimmer which is all one sees of man at a distance is a more speculative undertaking than to marshal a bodily generation.

. . . Bring into view! . . A lot of foolscap in a closed valise . . . . . . The Hurry catching up the tail end of time as a lash to drive me to a last exertion, was upon me again . . . . To gather up, to put together, to elucidate! . . . . To what end?

Perhaps the relief of a not uncommon anxiety to produce proof of having, oneself, existence?

Moreover, discerning in these tenants of a sheet of glass a public to my contact I must hasten to complete a message orally impossible.

Apparent only in a primary effulgence of Being as bare of troubled incidence as the area of perfectibility I would point out to them, this audience at a distance would wear whatever transparencies I chose to clothe it in.

My tenuous stuff is not all of a piece one gathers the meshes for its manufacture at intervals—wherever the dense material of life wears thin, letting through that little light which is always so surprising; to reveal it, yard upon yard of heavy dark must be unfolded. A life for a life. My experience to yours for comparison.

But listen to me, O Islands in the air, I have made even of your biology—a lily.

. . . . I ran to the closet and dragged out that valise. It was easy to pick the first chapter: "The Bird Alights." Here is no mysticism. I have simply used a traditional symbol as an aid in describing a unique registration of consciousness in infancy. When I became aware of what was then my state of Being.

Distinct to myself as limitless and reactive to a flux of light exceeding the normal; the fraction of a second to allow of this entire realization as I have described it covered the strange expansion of time that occurs on the outskirts of the third dimension. Concurrently—experience being ratified by remembrance, an as yet inoperative power of memorization functioned for a precocious flash.

In my investigation of first impressions one fact stands out, that however early they may be experienced reactions are always ripe. No less rich in import than those of the adult, it is never too late to resolve their significance to terms of the intellect.

Whether this preliminary illumination has any bearing on the origin of the idea that a transient body is animated by a "spiritual" continuum I cannot say; at least it justifies the high lights of grandure common to saints and the schizophrenic.

2

The Bird Alights

My first impression of being alive retains a certain distinctness as an infantile sensation of having come under a spell.

I found myself in an anteroom to the physical world filled with extraordinary light. Matter scarcely perceptible and the ether not entirely invisible together formed a cosmic vapor that was slowly taking shape.

My sensibility loose as the air extended indefinitely or dwindled to minute foci as consciousness unfettered, on an introductory flight, established that intimacy with subjective and objective on which the intellect eventually relies.

I felt no surprise on becoming a clock when my attention was touched by a striking hour, or a crystal reflection in my own toe-nail.

A conviction of having been everywhere-at-once while definitely aware of my *self*, survived my discovery that something I since have known as space intercepted my relation to other contents of the nursery.

This infant consciousness, that circles and darts and alights on its bird-like survey, soon ceased to actually amalgamate with chance phenomena, whereupon the blossoming-into-view of the objects of sense (which, for the mature, is a process so discreet they always seem to be here to meet us, or hang waiting around the corner of our eye) rammed my gaze so suddenly a flower would "go off" like a firework.

The give-and-take of consciousness has something of the mediumistic in the facility with which the parties to the contract "appear."

When, in the jugglery of birth, the Infinite performs its impossible stunt of omniprevalently "remaining" while infinitesimally "passing" through some seedling point within itself to emerge as a human entity, a jot of life is introduced to three dimensions, while that Inquisitiveness sometimes called the soul receives an impression of having recently been "drawn out" of the world around it . . . . of being both liberated and trapped in a sudden, ambulant individuality.

A winged perception, snared in our atomic mesh; like the Infinite from which it emanates, and whose omniprevalence it briefly continues to share, it must, in order to identify itself, first drift through the identity of all things.

During initiation to its environment, conceiving no distinction between the thing to be known and the knowing of it, this "inquisitiveness" becomes in turn everything it encounters, the while remaining "at large" and the last thing to be located by it is the center from which it diffuses, the *body* of its pending individuality.

The roving passage of the intellect between the known and the unknown is not unlike a bird in flight. I have often felt an unaccountable pang of recognition in coming upon that stucco dove which, since an alate ghost signaled the girded loin to rise from baptism, is splayed on holy ceilings.

Seen from beneath, the soles of its claws are like coral stars stamped on its useless underparts. The unsullied abdomen of the Third Person in Whom the whole hush of the altar concentrates above our heads showers down from the arches its ethereal influence.

If life, after all, should prove to be a divine emanation, this dove presents an image of our animation, and as we look up at its everlasting descent in a puff of gold to serve for the Breath of God, we may wonder whether this secret hovering over the centuries, if seen from above, would be revealed as the spirit of man suspended in intelligential ether . . . . . .

..... Yet this predecessor of my calculable self, a bit of cosmic consciousness in process of isolation, could have looked like nothing but a clot of flesh in a soft cradle .... kicking its legs out of curve to oppose the girding of the loin .... A bird dodging the cage ... the enticement to belong to itself only succeeds when the "bird" being dumb realizes the advantage of association .... the flesh has a voice ......

So the bird alights. We can catch its ecstatic throb in the cooing throat, recover the flap of its wings in a fountain of arms conducting the fanfare of self expression; and the child appears, an aerial infinity from which a body of grace depends as a plumb to hold it to the level of phenomena.

My concentrated effort to make this briefly enormous episode clear was often incongruously broken in upon. I recall so well when I was writing "we can catch its ecstatic throb in the cooing" the yell of calamity that shrilled through the corridor;

"Mamma! Come quickly, the cat has vomited in my bed."

3
The Beginning of the World

At the bottom of the valise I find "The Beginning of the World." Obviously a continuity, it describes how the cosmic reserve of an initial consciousness cedes before objective centers of attraction. Far from being fantastic interpretations of half-forgotten infantile responses to the commonplace with their queer resemblance to ceremonial magic, these analyses are as painstaking in their accuracy as a blue-print.

As though I were a nomad atom of a measureless giant from whom I inherited a serene cosmic continuity, to my natal preparedness the state of pure apparition in which the "world" at first revealed itself was not of newness but rather, a reconditioned state of something having part with me in an eternal Presence familiar to itself.

Thus the world retained sufficient continuity to make it appear indestructible, for whether it is significant or no the initial concept of the budding mind is perfection and the first demand it makes of perfection is absolute duration, an illusion which lasts until "Fact," in founding our suspicion, transforms the perfect to the seemingly impossible.

This was an almost increate world where hearing and seeing interchange and stationary bodies give chase to words that materialize. On entering it I made advances in a fairy air to communicative furniture which joined me in a veritable dance of consciousness the mature can no more move in than they can hob-nob with a micro-organism in its universe of concentrated distance.

In this incipient world I possessed the ability to animate ideas. Actual objects hardly convinced me; at most suggesting their immediate transformation, as horsehair sofas turning into ships. My improvements on three-dimensional conveniences being almost invariably their conversion into engines of escape.

Perhaps in that transcendental factory in which the "Word" is made "flesh" there is no inertia. The child's astonishing mobility suggests that radio-active onrush which comes to comparative standstill in our reality.

When I was twenty-three months old I had my first concrete impression of phenomena^^^^^ even then it was not so very concrete.

A row of glass bottles filled with colored liquids standing behind a fanlight over a door. The late afternoon sun shone through the bottles, through the fanlight, firing the drastic reds and yellows in a triple transparency. The blaze exploded in me. I was riddled with splinters of delight.

Quickened by that fundamental excitement combined of worship and covetousness which being the primary response to the admirable very likely composes the whole human ideal, my arms like antennae waved towards the glitter of those bottles and, through a sort of vibrational extension, came into as good as bodily contact with them. As if I were capable of a plastic protrusion beyond my anatomical frontiers. Infants are always attaining things they cannot touch.

At the same time I distinctly felt something not far away being held in a clamp. But even though aware that "it" struggled I was not yet enough of a piece with it to find that this something—a body—was attached to my elastic dimension.

A vague unease in the vicinity of the clamp prevented further extension on my part. The clamp descended, the fanlight soared.

Consciousness constrained to follow in the wake of its body had no chance to determine the agent of displacement, for as descent diverted its course my airy consciousness was out in the glow of the garden while the clamp must bear my load—or maybe a bed of those pantomimic flowers called red-hot pokers was immediately transported to me on the staircarpet . . . . . . first impressions being unconditional.

Probably at that early stage a fleeting reality consists in very clear impressions made on natal mind-stuff about to fall into desuetude. Permanent reality is making very faint impressions on a more utilitarian mind-stuff which, as it gains in substantiality, shows them up more and more clearly. Thus it may be that when I was twelve at some mention of this my only visit to the doctor's home the whole event emerged quite clearly. All I was alive to at the time were the flaming bottles and red-hot pokers.

I was staying with the wife of our family doctor to be "out of the way" while my younger sister was born:

Dr. Monks, who had one of those bulbous purple faces which have practically disappeared with the caricaturists who exploited them (he had not at the time materialized as far as I was concerned), was carrying me down a staircase to a carriage waiting in the drive. I even recovered the softness of the staircarpet under the doctor's tread and I knew he had been taking me home.

It appears that in infancy "Reality" lies in the magnetic property of attraction to incorporate the chosen object with the choosing child while accessory circumstances print pictures, even maps, which are not, as it were, "taken off the press" until years later.

—o-o-O-o-o—

While I still possessed the mysterious ability to float around myself, although it is impossible to explain why, whenever my elders stressed a word in their educative way I somehow took it for granted they were expressly giving a signal for embodiment.

"Listen," said my nurse as my mother laboriously played a march on a grand piano, "that's the soldier's music."

Instantly, before my eyes a file of soldiers sprang from the carpet. All shining and alive they jogged across the drawing-room floor with a full-blown military swagger, notwithstanding that they grew like plants only from the waist up out of a soft golden yellow pile lying in the light from the French windows through which they vanished.

After they had gone, the room and all it contained resumed the monotony of practical conditions I have always found so unconvincing.

Such an experience seemed casual enough to one who, herself so lately embodied, took such senseless miracles as a matter of course.

On the other hand I was non-plussed as by an abnormity, when shortly after, I asked for the march to be played again and, on my request being complied with, the living soldiery failed to appear.

These magical embodiments are simpler than they would seem, being the result of the child's receiving such intense first impressions it is able to exteriorize memory.

Groping back in that haze of infancy for an explanation as to why my "vision" had no legs, whereas real people were only, when at all, tangible up to their waists, I dimly recaptured an impression of being so held (on a previous occasion in the real world) that I could see only the upper half of a passing regiment beyond a garden wall.

—o-o-O-o-o—

The most reliable milestones directing the intellect are painful realities that lead to decease. It may not have been a coincidence that my particular consciousness snatching at the air on its fitful survey should choose a slight pain in the leg from the tweak of a buttonhook as a signal to enter the sphere of adult reality.

Lifted onto the marble slab of a hall table to keep tidy for my walk, I can see myself now; a speck at the bottom of a well of light lined with the unfurled fan of the staircase rising towards a skylight in the roof.

As a patient inhaling an anaesthetic feels agony drawn out of the body like an elastic that finally snaps, inversely, I became aware of a discomfort taking place at some distance yet more defined than had been the doctor's grip. It drew nearer and nearer until in a last operation of my early detached attachment, I located the discomfort in a slim black object lying in front of me like an overthrown post, in an uncustomary sharpness of perspective.

The mind, in an effort to define the nature of anything it faces for the first time, grasps at comparison. I thought of the legs of furniture that pillared so much of my adventure. But this kind of leg, in spite of seeming rigid, was secluded from the insensate stuff of its surroundings by an aura of viability and a certain tenderness in which I was alarmed to find myself beginning to take part.

I tried to recede, but the space that had so far intervened between myself and such things as I did not *require* failed to expand. Bound in a new relation of inseparableness, I cannot get away. The pinch of pain, unhindered, darts from the protruding solid to my brain; and the world congeals in a clap of inertia.

The tempo of my consciousness, the hilarious riot of vibrant infancy slows down, the scene dims, as when the weather changes. Distinctly as if a film of radiance and velocity should transform before my eyes to arrested motion and monochrome; for after the violently superlative values I had been used to, I cannot at once make distinctions among a milder coloration, so at first the actual world presents its lethargic performance in photographic greys.

A woman, of the color of shadows and strangely slow, is pressed against and bending over me in an intimate partnership of my concrete plight.

"Can't you keep still," she asks, lifting with a long exertion the buttonhook in her grey hand, "while I do up your gaiters?"

There must be something ominous about a hue refractory to light that led our ancestors to choose it for the pall of death (often an infant in arms will scream with terror at widow's weeds). The sight of the matte black sheath of my gaiter with its row of boot-buttons, stirring an inherited reaction of the eternal subconscious, is my first alert of mortality; although it is incredible, unless the condition for entering the adult's world is the acceptance of finitude; Death is staring me in the face.

And the heaviness of the flesh incurs its psychic counterpart, an apprehensive sullenness, when by some sly, slow, three-dimensional conjury one finds oneself trapped in a brick box, caught by the leg.

"Now, Linda, don't sit there sulking, it's time - - - ."

The marked propensity, in children, to hop like broken birds - - - - - .

4

The Accident

Hopping about in my short embroideries I could not make head or tail of the furniture in the day-nursery; a wreckage piled on the site of a Perfection that had fractured to time and space.

There is no knowing why incipient life, when first it turned towards the light, should have headed for this particular form of civilization, and with an organism responding to only a limited gamut of vibrations it was hard to find my bearings. It looked pretty much as though an accident had happened in the dark, and crushed my companions against their heavy household Gods; leaving things in this commonplace room so entirely out of gear I could not be sure whether I was a hopping child or an old crippled instinct poking about among shadows for something to save.

A sense of disaster penetrated to that core of intuition where the subconscious of our fellows seems more present than their person, so similar to the physical is the intuitional impact with the thing concealed.

Repression musters a rebellion that packs the atmosphere. I was blockaded by the doubles of women sitting their patient sit or rising like armoured towers with lateral signals flapping and cuffing. The effort to reconcile their actuality with the pretenses they projected was so preoccupying it prevented me from communicating with them.

To my brain so sensitive in being new, humanity was broken in half. I was just on a level with the souls of their entrails. My mother was but a corset-busk giving out ominous creaks as if nursing resentment for some secret affront under festoons of silk. Her subordinates were legs hiding behind panels of cloth. My father, two tubes rattling coins in their summits; magical sources of the houses and provisions that poured from them.

These people in the concrete extended no further than the waist because their vibrations going straight through me conveyed solidity. I could look up into their faces but being so far above me they seemed almost visionary.

On my father's face was a smile. Out of the mouths of the women floated words and words, some addressed to me. Not yet knowing whereabouts I was, miscalculating their direction, I failed to reply. Then, from that uncontacted visionary plane there rumbled, "she's too young to understand," while subliminal selves made appalling confessions to me. The women of the eighties were filled with a different stuffing to the upholstery they resembled.

A psychic pressure hemmed me in: the blind emergence of inhibited lives.

Feeling depressed I decided to ignore it, only when I turned my back on it all I found myself face-to-face with the elastic ogre Time. A huge duration with which I was unfamiliar drew itself out to its infinite length and wound itself about me.

"Feel me," drawled Time . . . . "how endless I am, feel how I am all bare . . . . . count me," jeered Time.

To save myself in space I fell back into the room. Clinging to form I tried to balance mass, to rearrange pattern, but design on a scene of devastation is so unruly, everything fell back into the same wrong shape again as soon as I moved my mind.

Sanity may depend on a sense of proportion. In the "Accident" even symmetry had been seriously injured and enough of my natal illumination in its blatant beauty had lasted to serve as criterion for anything I should ever see.

A room composed in a quarrel of display and thrift could not hold out the arms-of-its-walls to gather me in as it should. Yet I would sit staring at it expectantly for hours as if I were sure the tawny excrement of color spread over so many homes at the time must be the matrix of a jewel.

The convinced are always confirmed. Fiddling with the high wire guard round the fireplace I pricked my finger. The lucent embers of the grate glowed through the liquid drop. I had come into possession of a living ruby.

The origin of symbols is not fortuitous. Destiny having also its subconscious whose seeming accidents are omens of its ends, modern story mirrors ancient myth. There may be something redemptive about a fabulous blood.

—o-o-O-o-o—

I was jammed in the conditional yet it took me some time to narrow down to myself or pick myself out from among other people. Muscular reflex to past illumination persisted. My arms would fly up to embrace a blaze hardly extinguished to a ceiling. They made a liveliness in the air annoying to an audience by whom, could they behold it, the revolutions of the planets would be blamed as fidgets.

This happened to me once when I had been playing with some heavy dominoes and one still lay unheeded in my unclasping hand.

There ensued a train of events.

Words instead of sailing off to unknown destinations descended, stinging me with a vocal shrapnel of "wicked temper" and "smashed window."

I perceived that when my arms assumed a vertical position other, horizontal arms shot out, from all sides, pointers like craning geese converged towards a large placard of light I had not noticed before.

Sound increased. The mystery of all things visible become audible culminated collision in a supreme Voice rising from the steelbound abdomen. A very echo of the "Accident." Trends of ideas rushing from opposite directions within the same confines, to crash into one another and splinter to bits. Although unintelligible it reached that understanding having no need of language.

Like an ungovernable wind it swept through me, crying.

"You—you who have no conception of evil, I will show you evil. Look! Doesn't it frighten you to death? And where do you think I found it. Right inside you? You never knew it was there? You'd rather throw it away? Nonsense! How could God chastise you, with nothing to chastise?"

It was a strange Accident in which the intellect colliding with the absolute split apart into good and evil. I caught a hint of its causation as the Voice summed up "original sin," puffing my future equilibrium to the devil.

Told not to move while everyone else went down to tea, I just sat pushing my fingers through the holes in the cane seat of my chair. At the same time I was tremendously engrossed with that placard of light set in the air, so surprisingly involved with a series of excitements for which I could not find myself responsible. It was the being there of its not being there that intrigued me. Only this was plain. The soiled light of these dim new days did not come in of itself. An implausible wound in invisibility whose zone was fine as a spider's line revealed a clearer distance.

"Never mind"—a pair of eyes like violets too bashful to fade stole into the nursery with their maiden-lady to look at the hole in the window. "It was an accident," said Miss Mary Maud.

5
Adjustment

Life is at least heroic in fighting against infinite odds in determination to make sense of itself, still I could not have endured in my almost sub-physical helplessness among the specters of other people's sub-conscious that crowded their company upon me when, like Lucifer from heaven "cast out" of Perfection, I was bombarded with "ideas" peculiar to the human race: those mental sparks illustrating reaction of which the first being a biological myth of Rise and Fall inspired by the unconscious effort of breathing to align the sacred and profane concepts in paranoiac alternation.

Nature takes care of all that. She stokes the sun to an intensity compensating for the sublime . . . . . .

I emerge into clarity once more.

I was as high as the hedge grass. An horizon of immediate sky descends to my estate of insects and undergrowth on the edge of an open country road, and the residuum of its azure splashes one blue flower against immensity. Isolated by this grounded perspective in which the tops of my parents vanish on leaning over a fence I saw nothing of the hills and plains spread out before them.

I urged my body through the lower bars of the fence to reach into the field and gather this blue "innocence," its contrast to the ruby blood. But even a flower held in the hand is not possessed. There is something more about it than itself: the aesthetic suggestion to make beauty one's own through some dimly conceived and incalculable transformation.

Flooded with sudden determination consciousness diffused. For a moment the physiological vehicle is wiped out. There is nothing "here" but infinity: where my body had been standing there is simply a nucleus of power.

Even as my consciousness had come upon my body I found my will.

When I narrowed down to myself again, something of that Power which had absorbed me remained within me. It is the Power that hovers over our eyes and through the eyes reciprocates the light. The light which makes the Inside and the Outside one.

Redeemed by self-sufficiency, I said to myself, I can know all things, achieve all things. All is in me, to emerge at a sign, on some reflection with little cooperation. What certitude of the future. There appeared no barriers to that solar golden future washed up before me on an ocean of clarity.

The relief of readjustment, of perfect equipoise, when I grasped my heritage of dominion over all things elated me. The regenerative intervention of the will stirred up a great bravado, as if, having been held in thrall by specters and providentially released, I should prefer to pretend I had overcome them myself.

It is the nature of individuality to look upon the rest of the world in the light of an audience. I got the idea that "an impression is to be made." Trying to astound everyone with my unexpected potency and as often happens with the ambitious, bluffing a little. I would climb tall trees or in the dark ascend that indoor tree the staircase. It is easy enough to be brave before you know what to be afraid of, and my elders praised me; but they were being deceived, I knew nothing of valor, I had only that intuitional trick of keeping the body of jeopardy in custody of the spirit. It seemed so easy.

Again as in the case of our doctor's bottles, my conscious dilation on reacting to the blue of the cornflower in the country was all I experienced at the time. Later on, doubtless owing to the gradual development of that utilitarian mind-stuff to which I have alluded, correlative impressions emerged showing me this as an event taking place on the only visit I ever paid my maternal grandparents. At that age, around thirty months, I was supposedly too young to "remember." (I calculate the age by the bulk of duration the baby sister occupied in my mind which I also came to remember.)

My grandfather is sitting in the doorway of his long low carpenter's shed of tarred board, like a tree barber; for a fallen wooden curl lies pale under a trestle. As I stood at his gnarled knees beneath the humble apron, it seemed I was not so near to him as our actual proximity would warrant; his timid benevolence conveying how useless he felt it would be to grow fond of me. A stillborn love kept us company in the interior of that quiet black hutch built on a plot of waste ground with the same wild grass as in the ditch pressing upon its threshold.

Understanding that all operative objects have magical properties for small creatures like myself, he shows me an enormous magnet. I can see the new vermillion of its lean horseshoe, how with the passing of years, its size has decreased and its symbolic premonition of what in human personality would most intrigue me.

This "instantaneous" of my grandfather blows out in a puff of condescension given off by my mother, and on that same puff his wife some months later settles in an incommodious posture on the apple green plush of a flimsy gilt chair in our drawing room.

Her daughter, as in those days was the style, "toys languidly" with an ivory and gilt paper-knife. In her fingers the paper-knife slips and twirls as if handled by one blind. But all the same I could see it was a weapon with which in some metaphysical manner she succeeded in skewering this shrinking grandmother, who was almost afraid to look at me, to our pretentious little gilded chair. I never saw this grandmother again.

As in ancient times sorceresses were accompanied by their familiar. The Will may be seconded by an impulsive genie who can, if he cares, direct all the currents of hazard to further its course, and who advertises his presence by the showing of signs.

It seemed for a while as if I had come under his tutelage, for like the aboriginal who, on issuing from his hut, encounters omens, I picked up a diamond and other precious things when I went out for walks.

"Gracious, Miss," said the maid, "you've got good luck." So this is luck, I reflected. Nothingness itself crops up as values that remain. I reveled in the promise of my luck, convinced that not only should there be no hindrances, but that all the hidden forces of fate would actually cooperate with me.

Being an optimistic throwback, I knew perfectly well what to do about luck, for I had just been taught how to count up to ten. In spite of the strain entailed in reaching the handle of the door, driven by some inner necessity to escape from the Victorian era, I shut myself up in an unpeopled room to enclose myself with "what has always been" alone with the "air" that is "knowing" what I really am.

Once alone, I would turn round and round until objective reality dissolved. I stopped when I found myself attracted in a direction. It was imperative that I should bow low in this direction while certain numbers I had learned made a great to-do in my brain. Numbers that are forces for my protection, at once very present and very remote. Numbers that must not only be muttered, but also spoken to. The awe they inspired was over-powering and only offset by the security they bestowed. They must, moreover, be bowed out to the measure of their own count.

However, my indefinite impressions of the solids and lights and shadows that formed my home could hardly incite will-power, they having in the period of magical play been drained of all conjurative properties except a lingering tendency to disappear, allowing the gradual outreaching of the imagination to superpose an inchoate facade of the future, built to the indiminishable perspective of curiosity; even as the natal inspiration had once masked all phenomena.

If the will is a force, it is so much the complement of curiosity that the call of the unknown most efficaciously stirs it to action. The unyielding limits of the home afford the most urgent pressure in ejecting it into a larger sphere. While I was yet nothing but a bud of animation, so exactly like a toy from its miniature face to the lace on its drawers, in falling after a rubber ball I decided to conquer the world. It did not matter at all that the words "world" and "conquest" were absolutely unknown to me. Concepts are embedded in the human mind long before they become communicable. Just as degrees of impetus are defined by mathematical processes, I intuited my impulses and their oppositions quantitively if not in kind.

According to the etiquette of mythology, the will must encounter a dragon, but at that toylike stage the parental, or counter-will is still lurking. Unconsciously it awaited the convenience of seizing its opponent on common territory. So the formless premonitions of a conquestorial future continued to hang about me undisturbed, like the lace that ambitious arachnids spin out of reach. Desire puts its own construction on emptiness. Yet nothing pertaining to my phantasmal conjectures materialized until one day I happened on a little door. Many thresholds may be crossed for entrance into non-existent sanctuaries.

It was a door that lay on a low table, prostrate for lack of any palpable jamb to support it. I opened it and found that this entrance gave onto another door; this one so flimsy that it fluttered back to disclose what seemed to me an infinite succession of white, four-cornered flaps. They were covered with linear conundrums.

This was the first phenomenon that had come within my range that had nothing about it of the "déjà vu" of natal continuity. These signs of signs that record centuries of intellection have no cosmic prototype. They mark a certain independence of man that did have a beginning.

As the result of many inquiries I gathered at last that such doors as these open onto the contents of time; that behind them is stored the composite brain of humanity as if preserved in microscopic slides; the final answer to the whole question. All that was needed for access was to decipher the unfamiliar markings. A challenge to the curious will. I became such a pest invading other people's occupation, pointing to mysterious pages, they gave me a fat book of rhymed alphabets to keep me quiet. Enormously I concluded I was holding the doors of the universe ajar with my hands. By the time I was four years old, I knew how to read, and my life as a scholar terminated at that age. I could not guess when I came to "Z is for Zantippe who was a great scold" that again the methodical accidents of destiny's subconscious had, through my first scrap of knowledge, predicted the death of the will.

—o-o-O-o-o—

Now that I had begun to show off, I was only an actor on the common stage.

But could we get in touch with the child microcosm while it is still something nebulous or absolute, we might find in this seedling of all evolution not only the reflorescence of the past, but also a germination of the ultimate blossom of consciousness, and that, in the cyclic manner of secret things whose end is in the beginning, it starts its unfoldment right under our unparticipating eyes in a flashing synopsis of the eventual illumination of man, as if Will were the urge upon us of Evolution, to arrive, through a patient voyage of elucidation, at the point of departure. Only this time by light of our own reason.

—o-o-O-o-o—

Why I acquired this idea of incipient perfection being common to all infantile nature, including my own, is unanswerable. Possibly the exceptional quantity and quality of the degradations to which I was to be submitted, as if in inverted illustration of the brightest light casting the deepest shadow, caused me, the more I was blackened from without, the more to exonerate an essential incorruptibility within. The contrast of what ignorant Christians, while proclaiming the ineluctable purity of Christ, made of the merely annoying brat I may actually have been, and His "suffer the little children to come unto me," with its implication that children alone were fit for His company, may have necessitated my assumption. Yet again . . . this glorification of the infant must finally be accounted for in that first incomparable moment of transcending the self I described in the bird alighting. Also it is exactly the intuitive value every true mother sets upon the babe she treasures with that unparalleled solicitude.

6

Disappearances.

Roads whose old walls have trees casting shade over them are hospitable; one's thoughts as one lingers along in their gentle dust are not returned to one empty. They bring in a branch, a moss, some bird's banter or a snail in the hollow of a shadow. Surrounded by trees behind an exceedingly high wall in St. John's Wood, North Hall is like a discreet lady, with its turret décolleté for the stranger's eye just so far and no further. She conceals her treasures as any home should.

Accompanied by a nebulous presence I wait for the door in the wall to open, but on the clang of the iron bell this whole house, with its garden, disappears forever, leaving me nothing to remember but a rustic summer house. The forked logs nailed to it for decoration are dusted with soot.

Inside there is a wooden seat. It is defiled. A hen's egg has been smashed upon it spreading a yellow murder in its viscous pool. I knew that chickens came out of eggs, but this meaningless contour of mislaid life my mind is unable to cope with. More "difficult" than death, for this had never lived. I yet felt constrained to stand before it with my head bowed in the sullen reverence one shows to funerals while the defrauded race of chickens pecked at the gravel unconcerned.

To leave it alone seemed so heartless. But if I tried to bury it, it would drip before I could. It seemed to lie there for a thousand years until I dared not go near that summer house again. It was haunted.

After vaguely intuiting a manner of battle between a woman and a building - - - the battlefield is littered and we move away - - - - onto a square of sunlight the window has laid on the nursery floor. In relation to me the window itself is high as in a prisoner's cell, but my mother has come down to me on the carpet. Absorbed in an act of creation, I hardly notice the unusual shape her figure assumes in sitting beside me. I am putting the finishing touches to an exact reproduction of my entire concept of my baby sister—a feeding bottle I had somewhere seen steeped with its India-rubber tube in a pan of water. Inspired and painstaking I have perfected it, molding it as it were out of the first material that came to hand, and am holding it out for my mother's admiration of its translucent body and snaky neck, when a loud rapping startles the trivial scene into permanence. The door in the distance says, "if you please mam, Mrs. Monks," and my mother gets up with some difficulty of creaking busks. There is nothing smoldering about her for the time being - - - - - - she is empty and innocuous now as people often are with infants. Two tiny windows are dancing in the glasses on her face. I am overcome by an acute sensation that she is helpless and foolish and as she rises in the air drawing this feeling of mine with her, it changes into a chivalrous impulse to protect this vulnerable being.

The door has shut on that audience to which a work of art owes half of its existence and I am all alone, when to my cruel amazement in the palm of my outstretched hand I find lying a queer abortion, a sharp needle (is not one aspect of life each one alone with danger?), the thread in its eye is wound round and around its middle like a little tough white belly.

—o-o-O-o-o—

The thread of memory, unwinding, draws out across my eyes and becomes a concrete layer of pure white objects suspended in mid-shadow of the night-nursery.

The baby's cradle is hung about with clean muslin and on the marble top of the wash-stand beside a monumental basin and ewer the rays of an opaline lamp relieve all the whiteness there is in the room, so that the smooth honeycomb coverlid on Nurse's cold bed drips light on its coarse cotton fringe, even into the deep sub-furnitureal darkness in which I lie in wait.

There is a black cloth column standing by the cradle that breaks over my invisible sister, and, hushed as the lamp-light, a voice speaks out of it, saying, "Iarrhea, mam—it is quite green." Immediately visualizing a cat's eye from my mother's brooch—a lucent iris shifts its irradiate interstice—glooms and relumes on an orb of verdigris—I crawl deeper into the shadows in a vain search for this—

- - - - - the layer of dark mystery whence anything may issue has risen from the region of human feet to those inaccessible plains where only flies can crawl, for the light from the windows, opening out like a fan, does not enter the angle of wall and ceiling packed with the slats of raised venetian blinds.

The trend of something tossed directs my eyes to that somber barrier dividing the bright expanses of whitewash and curtain with an impenetrable strip of shadow, and all in a swish, two slight silhouettes clatter down from the cornice, turning upon themselves, and flap onto the floor. "Oho," cries my mother, who must have come in through the door behind me. "The fairies have sent you a surprise. Let us see what it is."

Two cardboard valentines with sky-blue cotton satin banjos laid in paper lace stuck onto them. I had just time to see that the fairies had written "with love from Louis and Bertie" on the back before, for fear that we should spoil them, the fairies, this time, spirited them away.

The trees in the sun are all alive and the grass of Hampstead fields is like shiny hair dressed with buttercups. Perhaps here is the very site of the jerry-builder's semi-detached residence in which later on I shall come to live, but as yet it is a land of treasure, for a rigid and ethereal lace is lying at the foot of a poplar, I have found a skeleton leaf. Through its interstices of decease I stare at a disintegrated sun, until Nurse takes it away from me because it is time to go home.

Dawdling along the hedgerow I see a miniature tower crowned with white and every story composed of heart-shaped leaves. I am pulling it when Nurse, who is growing impatient, calls back to me, "If you pick *that* (it was the shepherd's purse) your mother will die." Too late! The stalk has already broken. "NO! No!" I cried despairingly to the mysterious Everything, before whom all vows are vowed, "May all my grandfathers and grandmothers die - - - only *not* my mother." I felt quite satisfied my prayer would be answered - - - after all I had not been "shown" my grandparents since I was "old enough" to notice things. The coincidence would not strike me until a brief period later. Within the year both my great-grandmother and my only surviving grandfather and grandmother did die. Ever since I have had the conviction that were I to wish evil to befall anyone, my wish would be fulfilled. All my life I have had to be very, very careful.

The disparity between this world and fairyland is easily effaced if we disregard proportion and transpose relatively to our convenience. The ribs on the leaded roofing that jut out over the stairs leading down into the garden are very far apart; but fancy soon brings them together as I look down from my window. They contract to a magical railway line—and taking an imaginary train which "gets there" in the time it takes me to run downstairs and out of the house.

I throw myself on a wooden bench set against the sooty trunks of elms at the end of the lawn. I have arrived to stare into the inverted depths of a sea of green leaves in the sky, where the sun, through layer upon shady layer, splashes upon the platform of the branches spreading their peaceful foliage higher and higher and the fairies are just about to appear, when my mother and the cook come hurtling down the iron embroidery of the garden stairs. It is as if feathers are flying off them as when the sparrows bickering in the elms - - - - - -

Father and his visitor are not sitting under the elms for fear of bird droppings. They have moved their chairs away. My impression of the visitor was the tempo of his running back and forth across the lawn as he talked while my mother with the irate dignity innate to her, her abdomen steering her fine draped dress, paced the lawn lengthwise. Each time she passed him I distinctly felt an electric crackle.

It seemed he had promised me a rocking-horse, and measuring on the air with his arms he explained how he had had to send it back to the manufacturer's at the last moment to have several inches cut off its legs, which had been made too long. From his interesting conversation I gathered that this horse had often "not been ready," although I had forgotten ever having seen this man, who was one of my father's step-relations, before (and from the way my mother ground her feet into the grass, I felt I should hardly see him again) or hearing of any rocking-horse. I found his present particularly satisfying with its tail that last time had been too short; its dapple the time before that too pale; with its stirrup too large, its reins too broad, for as it was *not there* it was as excitingly incompatible with reality as my own visionary inventions. But my mother could not countenance his cheating a little child. She upbraided him for his cruelty, and, lowering her deep upper lip on disdain too profound to express, she sent me up to bed and resumed her meditative stroll.

When I was half undressed, she came running into the nursery to show us "a dear little bird" she had found fallen out of its nest. "I kept kicking it along the grass," she said. "I mistook it for a bit of red flannel." There it lay, mauled to a pulp, of that queerly putrid quality that bird flesh has without its feathers, an ancient and sarcastic look on its dying eye and monstrous beak. "When I found it was a bird," my mother continued brightly, "I thought, 'Oh, I must take it indoors to show the children - - - How they will love to see it.' "

At the end of our street on Sunday the butcher's, Baxter's grocery, everything, is shut except for the little sweet shop. Its crooked door is sunk below the pavement and leans up against a bow-window streaming with licorice boot laces and overrun by sugar mice whose tails are wisps of darning wool.

Its unreal air of unapproachable things (for Nurse says only "common children" go there) confuses it somewhat in my thoughts with a shop in the Christmas pantomimes whence Harlequin, a pied audacity, steals endless strings of sausages, and Pantaloon lunges at the policeman with a red-hot poker, while Columbine twirls.

In that striking incompetence to which idols are restricted in regard to other creations of man, that almost illogical impotence shared by simulacres, the sweetened vermin may make no inroads on the pile of iced biscuits forming the central feature of the window display, any more than I can, standing helpless in longing before a pane of glass, that existence without presence which shatters errant gulls on lighthouses.

In the pantomime a beneficent apparition declares, "I am your . . . . . fairy God-mother." - - - "*Urgroßmutter,*" gasps the most crude perhaps of all realities, an aged woman, appearing as if from nowhere to totter towards me on superannuated tiny sinewy feet. She also has the starkness of images and is covered with black brocade and bugles, all fringed and lacey; a bonnet encloses her head in a crescent and is tied under her chin with almost that violaceous shrill proper to Episcopal silk.

She is so thin, so straight. The copious wave of her jet-black hair might be that of a doll who is kept in a drawer. Before her noble narrowness her tremulous hands, spired as if in prayer as she peers at me, unpoint and part to patter upon my face, and raising the vessels of these tears that fall on me, in praise to Yahweh, she chokes, "*Mein schönes Kind.*"

At once a bestowal and a reception the unctuous *schön* in the unvanquished croon of an ancestry over its foredoomed offspring soothes me and swathes me for once in the nomadic embrace. A fallen fledging I am picked up and the aching quills are redressed.

This single envelopment in my paternal great-grandmother's adoration bequeathed to me a strangely emotional phenomenon which I am sure must be what in the Old Testament is described as "his bowels melted within him," and that as there is an amorous orgasm which is the juncture of our sensibility with cosmic sentience, so there is a spiritual orgasm, the mystic's admittance to cosmic radiance, an intellectual one immingling with the intelligential Ether, an aesthetic one on our impact with any of the myriad facets of cosmic beauty, so there is an orgasm of loving compassion, the lust of the humane.

The eyes of my ancestress are swallows dipped to captivity under the arch of her brow. As I look into her face she bestows upon me an even greater offering than compassion: the right to choose; for pointing to the window of the little sweet shop she asks me a question I have never heard before, "What would you *like?*"

As I watch her sere beauty in return to a puzzling exile fade, retrogressive as age, into the fog, my hands are holding a bag of iced biscuits molded with rose and citron sugar stars.

My mother, who always seemed to lie in total and eternal disoccupation in some invisible lair of her own (unrelated to anything existent for us) and about to spring, was extremely vexed with my nurse, loudly reproaching her for "allowing that woman to come near my children." She dashed my sublime little stars onto the hall floor and snarled, "Great-grandmother is she? Well let me tell you she'll burn in hell, buying biscuits on a Sunday."

. . . . But only her nightdress catches fire as she reaches for her medicine on the mantel-piece. And the great-grandmother from Vienna who had already looked so startled living alone with her foreign language in the street at the back of ours, opened her window screaming, *"Feuer!"* for a fire engine while the draught flapped up the yellow flames as they fed on her hounded body.

—o-o-O-o-o—

Lacking the material for conversation one can imagine a rudimentary family only aroused to social intercourse by the opening of the front door. A face is lifted. A voice inquires, "Going out?" . . . . "So you've come in?" almost with animation, for a temporary escape from over-familiar circumstances favors the possibility that an absentee may, like the primitive hunter returning to his cave with a carcass, capture an incident to be shared with those who remained at home.

So Mother would always, when we went out for our walks or came back, appear from whichever room she happened to be waiting in, probably charging her batteries for her encounters. As little peasants who, espying unusual tourists at the turning of a lane, will jump out and mock them, she had always something extremely disturbing to say, thus adding to my discomfort, stuck in too many clothes all rammed into a coat that was rather tight for me.

Once, as I waited in the shadows of the hall, having absent-mindedly, in spite of urgent instruction as to macabre consequences, succumbed to the child instinct to reabsorb the "Everything" into itself, an accident befell me. I swallowed my India-rubber.

I was very frightened and, looking about me in hope of help, or at least some consolation on my departure from this earth, all I encountered was what looked to me, considering the circumstances, a heinous glint in my mother's eye. "What a wicked girl," she crowed, "crying because you've swallowed an India-rubber. You ought to be *glad* to go to heaven and be a little angel."

This was the only time it was ever suggested I might not end up in hell. But as my nurse (for it was quite a small eraser from the end of a tin pencil-holder) immediately pushed me into the street with her, remarking, "Satan finds some mischief still for idle hands to do," I could not distinguish a difference.

—o-o-O-o-o—

One afternoon, however, Mother was occupied and we were "taken in" to say goodbye to her. Lying on a sofa with a book, "Come here," she said, pointing to an engraving of something vague wrapped up in a sheet, "and look at Shakespeare. Hamlet, 'I am thy father's spirit.'"

There was nothing uncanny about this quotation at the time. All it conveyed to me was that my mother was pleased to disseminate information. A beam of light filtered through the meshes of a curtain and played about her head as she kissed me goodbye. But now, after nearly half a century, so many accidental recollections arise in turn like shades to an incantation.

Why that red drop of blood in guise of a jewel set against the holy blue cornflower?

Why alone of all my alphabet rhymes should Zantippe survive? And my consciousness, disporting as a bird, be kicked along the earth and that terrifying thing together with some sweetmeat pebbles from Brighton remain the only gifts I remember my mother bringing me. Why did not that great-grandmother burn to death before so forbiddenly finding me out to bestow upon me the sentiment of love and the right to choose - - - - something beautiful? And why again should my so mysterious mother, out of the whole Shakespeare and on opening it once and for all, intone with a voice I could not forget that awful prophecy of whom so much should haunt me.

The devout do often, inserting a finger at random among the pages of the Bible, find the counsel sought for in the verse thus blindly picked; but there for the religious is stored so inexhaustible an ethical provision, they are hardly taking chances. Whereas, amidst the exceptional emptiness of my early youth, how should signs and wonders take form from nothingness to appear from nowhere? Or the casual gestures of inattentive people make patterns precise as keys that fitted into *what?*

In a house filled with unrest the mistress of us all seemed not to breathe the same disquieting air. She moved immune among us. But once, but briefly, an unbelievable change came over her. As if caught in a trap. As if that front door, which framed not a few of my memories, were sealed, she now distractedly seemed to dash diagonally, hither and thither, her hair disarranged, rebounding in all directions on impact with unseen frontiers imprisoning her.

The muscular hauteur of a stubborn face had melted in a fever of apprehension to a limp mask sagging from the stark anatomy of terror.

Her lids, from which she eyed the world with a peculiarly blind shrewdness I have never seen elsewhere, were pink. She was spattered with tears. The sanguine flush (that so often crept up her throat from her poor rabid heart to splosh upon her cheek while the rest of her face, drained of all normal color, showed the same waxen lividness as that resulting from blood-poisoning) now suffused her entirely, as is usual with people swayed by a natural emotion unconnected with more mysterious neural cataclysms of the circulatory system.

Then she slowed down as if a different angle of her maddening concern were penetrating her—at last she clutched hold of my wrist, dragging me to a row of carved oak chairs along the wall in the dining room, knelt beside me, and pulling me down, "Pray with me," she urged, "oh, pray to God to bring back my husband." Wringing her hands in desperation, she cried out of a shattering sob, "Where would I *be* without money?"

So we prayed in line with the empty chairs against the dining room wall in the interior gloom of those days with their imitation tapestry draperies lined with sateen, their ball fringe, their baldachins and their thick guipure curtains that covered the windows while the machine-turned carving of the chair back confronted me with the likeness of nothing I could possibly presume to be God. Gaping dragons putting out their tongues at me.

After waiting obediently for something tangible to define itself in this strange undertaking, my patience under this fruitless suspense gave place, as usual, to "fidgets." But my mother did not notice. She was praying so hard, sometimes to God, sometimes addressing herself to me, as if in need of an ally.

Her anguish, so extrovert, yet this once so genuine - - - never again was I to see circumstances get the better of her - - - was so rich in action that, although I had scarcely an idea why she wept, I watched the unfolding of her martyrdom as if from among a crowd round a stake.

I remember having prayed with her before, "God bless my mother and my father" - - - "Why," I asked, "must I put my mother first?" "Because God says you must love your mother more than anything else in the world." So I loved her with a suspended love, expectant that sooner or later must be revealed in her its mysterious justification.

The bizarre commotions she provoked in me I ascribed to God who so evidently made use of her as His mouthpiece.

As we rose from our knees she clutched my wrist and hissed a command into my ear, "You must *hate* that man."

Up to a certain age all the instruction we receive from our elders must be what is loosely termed psychic. The words we are taught, which on reflection would seem to require a wide experience to reveal their full contents, must be conveyed to us on a sort of telepathic transmission of our elders' interpretation of them. How else account for my subtle and appropriate reactions such as the almost philosophical quandary in which I found myself on coming across the *slain* egg in our summer house when I could scarcely have been five?

Thus this word "hate." It entered me. So dynamic with its own significance that from the moment my mother's insistent fingers pressed upon my wrist a racking vindictiveness took course through my veins. Provided with this impalpable weapon, I straightened myself in readiness to redress her wrongs.

That day was long and high, coming down from the skylight in the roof led by a staircase backbone like a nervous system entirely deranged. At the end of the flight, the last stairs opened out and curved with the banister, which thus seemed beginning to curl round upon itself. If I clung to its support so often, turning and twisting myself with its incipience, it was because I found in it a central spool—a spool on which the nervous filaments that trailed their aerial poisons throughout the house I must wind up again; wind myself with them also onto a centripetal axis.

For as day grew stale the atmosphere so thickened with female vibrations, errant, irritant vibrations of a home full of women sowing the sodden inertia of my bringing up, that one moved in it with difficulty as though ploughing through a hostile wadding.

Till at last in the evening when I had once more sought the newel post as one shipwrecked clings to a mast in an unleashed sea, a key turned in the front door lock and Father stood before me.

At once the wadded air receded, packed back upon itself, as he approached me, leaving him immune in a clear square halo, projection of the pure expanse beyond the momentarily opened doorway. He moved erect and gracefully released as though he had thrown off a burden, and his smile seemed illuminated as by a solution. As if he had decided it were henceforth impossible to mistake nothing for something; realized how ridiculous "it" had all been. And the spark of logic in his brain reacted on that hate in me like a chemical agent.

Perhaps the only "feeling" I have never been able to lift out of the past and analyze exactly is the one that overcame me then; something no child should ever have to puzzle over. The psychic poison I had absorbed surged about my diaphragm while the "whole" within me split apart, the two halves turning back-to-back as he picked me up. —A Judas-Janus I gave him a shamefaced smile, conscious that he was holding in his arms, that which I had not exactly comprehended until myself became one - - - a lie.

And all this while the wadding in the air continued to fall away, leaving us more and more space, more and more lifting and concentrating until, ultimately contracted and condensed, it hung above his handsome dark-eyed head with an imminent heaviness of stone.

"Well, little wife," he cried, invitingly, as my mother, with her fringe all curled and in her satin bodice, descended the staircase like a wall that, although marching past us at an imposing distance, yet left us shattered as if we had crashed our heads against its blankness, as she remarked to her husband, "I wonder you have the face - - - - - -."

—o-o-O-o-o—

If the adult mind, at the mercy of mystery, fumbles with phenomena the child brings an absolute assurance to its enterprises of destruction. When I approached the ornament, the candle or anything else I was about to spoil it was with the virtuosity of a past master - - - - But in the name of Hermes—of what art?

The child seems to have a preconception of what it "wills" to create, which at a riper age remains only to genius.

Of what transformation of matter is the child prescient? What ultimate object is it sure of making out of almost nothing? This inverted creator who cannot let well alone. All its anticipations appear to miscarry in breakage and sudden mess; yet nowhere occurs a more rocketing surprise or deeper discouragement than that of a little child, who, when struck with an unexpected impotence, also begins to fumble.

Evidently it is not informed of the laws governing matter. But as we watch it we could almost swear it has been accustomed to a different order. It always seems to be seeking something that must have disappeared.

We may suppose it to be very much of a monkey; that all this is symptomatic of the riddance of atavism such as is said to enable the newly born human to hang by one hand from a bough. But what *is* this monkey bent on destroying the mechanisms proper to its own future as if it does not find them, perhaps, sufficiently convincing? The mystic tenacity with which it guards its seemingly idiotic treasures suggests that all religious wars and wrangles may originate in this infantile conviction of possessing the best magic.

To one who cannot find the way we point out the right direction, so this stranger is put through a harrowing discipline to eliminate the peculiar principle of its useless activity; an interference necessitated by some sadistic evolutional experiment to which child and preceptor are submitted alike. Its final reclamation from a pre-factual awareness coincides with the extinction of that indefinable luminosity distinguishing it from the adult.

Until the crisis in which it exchanges its universe for ours, the child is not only alive but alight.

Intact in its qualities; responding only to beauty, joyous without rhyme for its joy, heroic unneedful of arms for its heroism; its April dolors only real as rehearsals of a future it tries to postpone, the child is prompted by a clearer reasoning than ours to avoid the perils and disgraces we hold out to it, and to linger in an unseen region it inhabits staked beyond fear.

As soon as it gets into our real world, it is frightened, in the dark, of dangers threatening from the rear, and this may be in memory of primeval ancestors or the first remonstrance having sprung on it from behind. It is also possible that it feels hampered in its facilities for self-protection by its blind back that has slammed like a shutter on a lost dimension.

—o-o-O-o-o—

Probably my intention when I stuck my fingers into the night-light was to gather its flame as one would the bud of a flower.

Price's night-lights sent to earth in a heavenly carton covered with mystic stars of blue, were packed in rows like conic mountain-crests of mythic ice.

The remorse that overcame me was measureless when, the tiny stiff wick capsizing in immaculate grease, the light went out.

I had not only extinguished the illuminant of my toy-world but as a night-light has also its import in the adult world this accident would give rise to questions I felt myself incapable of answering - - - - .

Timeless night could draw out no more indefinitely for a contrite murderer trying to bring a corpse back to life than this lateness I had blackened - - - I had never before been awake so late - - - as, lit by the sparse filter of moon through the cotton blind, I attempted over and over to set that wick up again. All my efforts remaining fruitless, I set out to seek a burial place for the lump of white wax I had utterly mis-shapen with my fumbling. Strips of dimness from windows led my wandering perplexity along passages that, in the depth of shadow, stretched into endless corridors. Desperate at last, although horri-fied at so unfitting a grave, I threw the cadaver of beauty down the lavatory.

Shortly after this I began to walk in my sleep.

Anxiety is a circus-master cracking his whip, exercising the noctambulist—up to the roof, down to the cellar - - - to batter on iron bolts of entrances. The smallest children inhabit the greatest buildings.

Escape - - - not from danger but from the dread of it. Menace is po-tent to create that which is greater than itself, so many who have been put to flight are unaware of what they would flee from. I remember the unreal seeming of objects which, static by day, assume mobility among the shifty hangings of the dark.

Before the fixation of my eyes that are wide-asleep the hall lies in a pit of half-spent light. The fanlike edges of the marble stairs, a pale dissection of distance unfurling from the tessellated floor, lay their cold planes under my naked feet. Beyond an open door the deathly damask of a table-cloth is surrounded by ghostly chairs.

In my silent somnambulist petrified world, angles play acrobat on a precursory silver screen until the automaton, halted by the heavy bolts on the street door, staring up at an open fanlight awakens, for I cannot fly.

Whenever we took temporary quarters for holiday time the asphyxiating conjugal atmosphere would lift and, like a rift in a cloud, - - - arrival at furnished apartments would always reveal some object of unguessed beauty, or strike a note of the cosmic harmony that never penetrated our home - - - So I lie in my bed at sundown listening to the boats being drawn up out of the surf onto the beach. An effortless sound of the end of day, a crunching too compliant to be rasping, for the ocean had left something of itself among the pebbles that made their subsiding among one another so slippery, it eased the ride of the craft.

I am aroused from the spell of this unaccustomed lullaby when my sight settles on the curtain-pole above the window that, facing me, lets in the dusk. The end of the pole is ornamented with a glass lily—or trumpet. It is one of the very few beautiful things I have found in the world.

Glass is scarcely white - - - it is of a whiteness so tenuous as to have evaporated through itself, leaving transparency. As, since long ages crystal is pregnant with eyes evoking visions, this lofty glitter lures me - - - Wisdom effects the transparencies of all things - - - - - when of a sudden the lily disappears in a loud explosion - - -

"You clumsy slut! How did you chip the wash basin? It will be put on the bill" - - - - the very Voice of vengeance.

"Now I shan't give you the nice treat I had in store for you - - - - a ride in the chaise with the white goat - - - " And the coveted goat, laden with my sin wandering away into the desert of that which shall never come to pass, dissolves into the white dimity of the curtains.

On this punitive interruption, the sound of the beaching of boats ceases to be soothing - - - If the barque of the soul be drawn out of the ocean of potency, what is the chart of the voyage it shall make? - - - I am a radium becoming lead. Looking back to the pole for the transparent object of my wonder—I see it is cloudy now as if breathed upon by a wrong breath.

"This is the voice of the glass trumpet." I listen as it says its silence, and receive a sorrow.

Alas, this transparence is but the echo of light.

Receiving all things into itself for strange interpretations.

In this even the sun is become a contortionist and beauty, brokenness - - - - - - - .

Of itself only an invitation to a shadow. Its finale - - - - - to filter a blank wall.

To what can be likened this volume that is only to be located in its reflections?

The past is dead as an outgrown superstition, a mummy with a thousand features crumbled into dust of which every now and again a grain blows into the eye of memory - - - - - .

Our little "boots" I no longer "see" tells me in front of the fowl house how the mother hen feeds her primrose little ones with milk under her wing; while on this brief impression is superposed a penny pair of pipe-clay Wellington boots he gave me for a present at quite a different time. While again this coincidence of associated ideas dissolves into my long, long-ago sensation of having quite close to me an aspiration akin to my own, an innocence groping among nebulous conditions that frustrated the poor little boot-boy. Like a fruit whose flesh has fallen away, his kernel lies in my path.

7

Ethics and Hygiene of Nightmare

Father who *will* spend his time doing the same thing over and over, is reading *The Daily Telegraph* - - - Once a newspaper, always a newspaper. Why go on staring at it? *I* am after something new! His legs are crossed and the toe of one of his carpet slippers is pointing a woolen cross-stitch rose straight at a worktable. There is a fancy basket standing on it I have not seen before.

I find that this basket is filled with fat white glass-eyed fishes, their scales and the ribs on their fins painted aniline pink; soft as cotton-wool; they have a thin crisp surface - - - it is as if my hands were full of a light warm snow.

Father looks out from behind his paper and remarks confidentially, "We mustn't tell Auntie Mary you peeped at her Japanese fishes. She meant them for a surprise."

That evening when my nurse brought me into the drawing room, the powerful masses of Miss Gunne and my parents were grouped around the fireplace. The black bars of the grate withheld a pile of glowing jewels from falling upon their feet while I advanced towards a wall of flame. I could feel these great dark silhouettes as they sat there in the dusk to be concerted in an intention to spring upon me. They were flashing messages to each other in a code of connivance.

"Did you peep into Auntie Mary's basket?" my father asked me, and his eyes reflected a hot gleam from a burning coal.

Auntie Mary, with her finely plaited basket on her knees, clutched it with almost convulsive protection in her fingers. I answered, "No."

As if this "No" were a signal confidently awaited, the upper halves of their bodies bolted out of their huge arm-chairs. The rosy gleam on Miss Gunne's white hair, the copper edge of my father's crinkly beard, and the embers in my mother's eye-glasses hung over me as supernatural embodiments of destiny might lean menacing out of an incongruously low sky.

"That's a lie," my father exclaimed in a voice of chuckling severity, appreciative of a scene he had evidently prepared with his companions. "You know very well I saw you do it myself."

The word "lie" seemed to release their sonority, and the Voice I had heard for the first time when the domino miraculously flew through the window gathered in volume above the staccato of the other voices' chattering of hell. It no longer detonated on a lofty plane. Now it was hissing out of a real person while I was *quite really* a bit of a person and the fire was hot on my face.

A lie was obviously the contrary of what actually "occurs." I had said "No" in compliance with my father's request. If I did not remind him that he had arranged we should not tell, it was because I succumbed to their necessity to make something out of me that they knew how to "deal with." Or rather because their animosity always stabbed me in the solar plexus, causing a knotted agony that paralyzed self-defense. All I could realize was the impossibility of extricating myself intact from intrigues in which my situation was very much that of the foot-ball in a rugby scrimmage.

I must make my escape. So I merely told them I could stay with them no longer - - - that I was going away.

"All right, run along," they agreed most sensibly. "We don't want a liar here."

Obligingly, the front door was opened for me - - - I rushed out and ran along Melville Terrace. On the one hand stood a row of brown-brick houses. On the other, a demi-lune of thickly planted lilac trees hedged the curved drive that swept in and out of the gates.

As I breathed the drip of the lately fallen rain loaded with the aroma of the lilacs, its freshening of the pebbles in the gravel, the balm of earth had already begun to heal the concussion of my nerve centers in this atmosphere so different in nature to the one that filled the brown brick box I had left - - - - when a heavy arresting hand clamped itself on my frail shoulder - - - they *did* want a liar.

—o-o-O-o-o—

The ultimate difficulty of ascribing guilt to the proper quarter necessitated the conception of the devil - - - for however we may search for the inspiration of that evil which gets mysteriously mixed-up with so many of our deeds, we can seldom locate it. Seemingly it is the result of impersonal causes over which we have little control.

Thus the riddle as to how, at any time, and unwittingly, innocence may change into guiltiness came up again when one Sunday afternoon my good-looking father, faultlessly dressed, indulged in a much-earned pleasure of taking his dear little girl for a walk.

On our return, he complained of how I had laid me down on the pavement and, kicking and screaming, demanded to be taken home in a hansom cab. I took great interest in my father's narrative, listening open-mouthed as if to an account of the incredible performance of some stranger; I was quite as horrified as were my elders by this evil deed. I had not the least recollection of the hideous occurrence - - - did not even know if my father had succeeded in getting me home without a cab or whether he hailed one to bear him away with his utter confusion. Yet, contrary to the time when the window "got" broken or when I told a "lie," I was not bewildered by the accusation. It left me undisturbed except for a slight remorse. No stab of injustice wounded my solar plexus for, in spite of having immediately forgotten what I had done, I *knew* that all my father was saying about me was strictly true. So if my sort of extra-dimensional existence is a thing of the past, it appears I am capable of a new, strange automatism acting, as if beyond my control, in contradiction to the ethical consciousness I had supposed to be the only one I possessed, and that this unsuspected automat within me had begun to *sin*. It seemed that this sin was the desire to identify myself with beauty, the beauty of the jingling swiftness of a cab on two wheels. But what was the nature of a desire that could fling me down on the stone lid of a civilized earth as one possessed of a devil, a desire that could scream for a jaunty conveyance which, half an hour later, I could not recall having coveted, an impulse whose consequence must be related by somebody else for me to get even a second-hand spectator's impression that I had ever harbored it? The one thing I remembered, and that ineffaceably, was the way the hard stone of the pavement seemed to attenuate and fuse with the mist that lowered upon it, as if of itself giving off in a sort of static steam the hushed lethargic opacity of a respectable London street on a Sunday afternoon in late autumn.

Another problem in guiltiness presented itself to me when, owing this time to my entire mystification I felt neither the anguish of false accusation nor a blank conviction of my culpability, I was standing at the head of a staircase swinging my right leg like a pendulum in time to a tune I hummed. An esoteric importance so often involved in the actions of childhood, attached to the seemingly negligible detail that it was my right leg. As if to replace the subconscious doubles of other people that had early faded away, I now hedged myself in with inexplicable taboos I invented for myself, unknowing that human society had prepared sufficient for me. There were so many objects I must never touch without first bowing seven times to them, and I could not eat peas because the mark where the tiny stalk had been broken off looked like a mouth. They must be boiled fairies who, having been previously bewitched, might with luck at any moment burst out of their green shrouds in their veritable form. At first I selected only a few that had rolled among the gravy and potatoes "mouth up" so that the fairies positively pleaded with me to save them on the side of my plate - - - - but I soon discovered that all peas have mouths. Bearing directly on the episode of the staircase was the affection I had developed for lost causes. It seemed shamefully unfair to me, for instance, that such general preference should be shown for the right-hand side. I would pick up the left-hand side with my sensibility and nurse it in my astral arms like a doll, croon to it and make ugly faces on its behalf at the aristocratic right that gave itself such airs. For this, it was my right leg that swung in the air, I allowing myself insofar as possible the use of only left-hand things; it was wearing my left-hand shoe, by the way, for its greater humiliation.

I swung and hummed, watching the housemaid who knelt at the foot of the staircase "putting back the rods" - - - - when suddenly she clapped her hands to her face and screamed, "you wicked gal, I'll tell yer mar yer kicked me in the eye."

This was extraordinary, for I had had no sensation like the one I dimly remembered of being able to make contact with objects out of my reach, and I looked at that space between me and the housemaid to see if it had fits of folding up. It never budged. As for my leg, it had now for some time remained at the normal length of about one stair and a half. No, there it was, the same as usual, wearing a gaiter similar to the one that had brought me into the world. The whole thing remained inexplicable until now, when, some decades later, I write it down.

These different aspects of moral responsibility made me curious as to the laws governing the *fixation* of guilt. It occurred to me that if misdeeds I had not perpetrated could be ascribed to me, I had the right to lay claim to somebody else's guilt if it so pleased me.

I had a long and tearful argument with a nurse over a defective poultice she had laid on my throat, when, on discovering in my bed what looked like a remarkably tidy turd, I claimed the authorship of the most heinous of infant misdemeanors not at all of my habit, while she insisted on depriving me of a distinct satisfaction that self-conscious Christian hysteria, whose "mea culpa," at once pleasant and painful, is a compensation for so much inhibited normal self-expression - - - with the assurance that she had not folded the poultice properly and so some linseed had rolled out.

The early summer evening was so shiny, and, exceptionally, this nurse so tender and consolatory, I could not be sure if I felt impelled to enfever this serenity with that moral turpitude incessantly attributed to me, if I was making a noisy bid for further demonstrations of a rare affection, or whether, in consequence of my cerebral routine, my mind had already begun to conform automatically to a rhythm of recurrent culpability.

The anxiety of such precocious introspection, winding itself up until, as a clock, ticking uninterruptedly through time, it was to function continually - - - even through the occasional hours of relaxation and entertainment.

—o-o-O-o-o—

When I entered her bedroom to say good morning to Mamma - - - she lay in the shadow of a screen that was covered with a woven foliage of several kinds of nut-bearing branches. As I drew near she told me to bring her the smelling salts.

It was rather dark and on my difficult expedition I hurt my hand, exclaiming - - - - .

Instantly that dreaded Voice leapt out of the thick air conserved by heavy curtains, so like a lash it almost whipped me off my balance where I stood on a puffy sofa, my arm upraised to turn up the gas.

"You wicked girl," it cried, enlarging the "wicked" until it entirely encompassed me. "What sort of mind have you got? Using the language of a lot of low scavengers?

"I'm sick and tired of trying to teach you to behave like a little lady.

"How can I make a silk purse out of a sow's ear?" it inquired.

"You're a downright disgrace to me!"

While I was recovering from the stabbing surprise that distracted attention, the Voice leapt on, gaining like a mountain goat, successive footholds on various rocky themes.

I heard it say, "The eye of God seeth thee." Also, "Day and night it watcheth over thee - - - . It's no use trying to hide from it, you shiftless, good-for-nothing lazy lout! He'll punish you!"

Again, it was saying, "Nice children are born in cabbages. You were found under a stinging nettle!"

And again. "A good ducking in the horse-pond is what *you* require."

There followed a long analysis which brought up my "filthy hypocrisy"—.

"You're sweet enough when you want to wheedle something out of me. Cupboard love! That's what I call it."

And the Voice that edits private history set out on a new trail.

"You're just like the others," it taunted. " - - - his wretched relations, they'd eat me out of house and home, claw the rags off my back if I'd let them," and I could see how my mother drew close her comfortable wrap.

"Not me! If I hadn't my self-respect they'd all be living here, and I and my children out in the streets begging our bread, I *dare* say! No, thank you.

"But you're all alike—the whole bunch of you. Here I slave myself to the bone morning, noon, and night till I might as well drop dead at your feet for all the thanks I get - - - it would serve you jolly well right, too!"

Although I could understand enough of what the Voice was saying to gather its insequence, I was shattered, for its sound vibrations beset me with the rough-sheathed impact of a class whose loud self-assertion lifts them above the manual clatter of their lives, whose heritage it is to lack the mental leisure which alone, of all conditions, allows for the culture of such superficial graces as amenity, the expression of affection or the tempered rebuke, —a class so hard-driven they had no time for loving their offspring. Her parents were the opposite—outside the home she was the sweetest, prettiest-voiced woman imaginable—her raving stemmed from an unaccustomed pride—of having married more money than she was accustomed to.

In the years to come, I was to read in a newspaper what may have been a canard, that sound vibrations would be studied by some War Office as the most deadly instrument of collective destruction.

"*Then* you'll be contented," the Voice went on, still overcome with apprehension of being worn to death. "But never fear. I'll let the neighbors know the sort of life you lead me. The world will point its finger at you. You'll be an outcast!"

Then it continued, after a short pause for breath, "So sly, so under-hand, always whining around for something. Nothing ever satisfies you - - - you needn't stand there gaping. Why aren't you having your breakfast, if you please?

"But I shan't let your father have his way and buy you a mantle ei-ther - - - all decked out in your frills and furbelows like a duchess. And who are you, I'd like to know? A child who has no fear of God! It's not surprising you won't obey your mother. I wonder you're not ashamed to be so ungrateful."

On hearing these unexpected denunciations, my mind, which nor-mally should work forwards, reverted; set out on that endless intro-vert journey in search of the motive attributed to it - - - .

However, this preoccupation had not as yet entirely wiped out my interest in the ceaseless appearance and vanishing of green pixies and gnomes taking shape among the cretonne foliage on the screen beside the bed.

"Haven't you any conscience at all?—" asked the Voice, probing the ganglions of my nerves and setting them all a-jangle, " - - - with such a lovely home and kind parents to do 'everything of the best' for you - - - What more in the world could you possibly want to make you happy?"

Although ere this the problem of happiness, whatever it was, had never presented itself to me, I felt that this very moment it was being irrevocably solved.

"But no, nothing is ever good enough for *you,* my fine lady. Look at those lovely boots I bought you only last winter - - - pretending they hurt you - - - - you grow like a weed that is no good to anybody.

"What do you *mean* by leaving the room while your mother is speaking - - - have you *no* respect?" the Voice demanded, as I shrank towards the door - - -

"I'd dress you in a potato-sack, if I had my way. That'd knock some of the conceit out of you, you stiff-necked generation! And you needn't think anyone will ever marry you, either, for all your idiotic father's wonderful plans—You, with your foul mouth! I'll tell the young man what you are all right - - - though it would be good riddance of bad rubbish - - - I dare say."

Disintegrated by the vibratory flux, I was quivering as a heat haze after the flame that engendered it had gone out; only for having listened to the fluency of British lane and lowly hearthstone, a little sound theology and the philosophy of thrift.

Change is not gradual; it is instantly that transformation takes place. Destiny is a lightning calculator who will show how this sum works out, subsequently, at great pains, in the numerals of events.

Selfless, defenseless, abject with shame, I watched my inborn equipoise recede among the shadows wondering over the future of its sallow double, six-year-old me, left behind in life.

"Don't you *know* that Satan takes people who use bad language and throws them in the fire? You'll burn for ever and ever."

"Couldn't I die?" I inquired, anxiously.

"No, you won't be able to die - - - and the fire hurts fearfully so you can't bear it - - - yet, you'll *have* to bear it, for it will never, *never* end."

"But," I pointed out beseechingly, "I only said 'bother' because I hurt my hand on the gas bracket."

My poor mother's myopic eyes peer at me with a somehow thwarted suspicion. "Don't try to tell me you didn't say - - - - "

I could not catch the name of the crime I had been accused of.

"Mark my words," the Voice slowed down solemnly, "no good will ever come of you. Nothing will ever prosper with you."

There followed the supreme imprecation of heavy melodrama, "The curse of your mother is upon you."

Then, in a more familiar manner, "Get out of my sight!" shrieked the Voice.

If only I could. But it's just all this sight one has to live in, that, baring the spirit to the quick, leaves me defenseless. Another pair of predatory eyes is waiting for me in the dining room. Governess' eyes that have never been kissed.

"Now let me see," says Miss Ware, consulting a list she has pre-pared. "One mistake in spelling, four in arithmetic, three in history, two in grammar - - - that makes ten pieces of punishment bread."

She sets my little body up against the table and watches as I stuff it perforce with the ten tremendous slabs of Hovis. Aridity absorbs *saliver*. My throat contracts. My stomach becomes deliri-ous as the tawny pulp expands its way down, tedious as an inverted parturition.

When it is ended, my breakfast that has been waiting on the side-board begins. Lumpy burned porridge, milk, a cold boiled egg, the regulation amount of bread and butter.

With this ceaseless invasion of tepid volume, I swallow Miss Ware's desolation of a bondwoman whose primeval "aspirations" are lying in a dingle with a naked boy.

"That child is getting terribly anemic," my father exclaims catch-ing sight of me. "Where's her tonic?" They manage to pry my mouth open and pour down some cod-liver oil.

He insists that my mother take me to the doctor. So we go in a cab to visit Sir Edward Seivkin, the Queen's physician, his consult-ing room being as near to court as we can approach. My mother is rigid with reverence as this awe-inspiring personage orders my left lung, or what remnant he has found of it, to be planted imme-diately on a country farm. But having had our guinea's worth of so-ciety, all that the lung gets out of it is a stout push and "See what comes of disobeying your mother," as I bear it disconsolately down the front steps.

I must attend to it myself.

Every child of that era was aware of what it meant "to go into a decline" for they could not learn too early of the consequence of wet feet or sitting in a draught—and should you be caught in the rain, will not the very drops as they fall upon you arise as feathers? In a liter-ature of smug fatalism, the "nicest" children cross flickering fingers on a hollow torso draped in calico; and even longer girls lie out at full length on the first disappointment in love.

These recumbent beings waning beside the window among the hyacinth bulbs, breathing ever more faintly their genteel breath and about to fly to heaven, aroused my envy, I having caught onto the fact that - - - once in this world you have one way out.

Standing outside the housemaid's closet was a row of tall cans she kept filled with cold water - - - so much more water than could ever seep into a shoe - - - jugs just brimming with consumption.

It was easy to inveigle my sister out of bed. Warmth itself is excelled by the tingle of being naughty. So we spent the evenings on the landing and with the aid of a tumbler she pours the cold water all over my body under my cotton nightgown. How enjoyable it is to shiver in defiance. As I paddle in a puddle, death is become a practical joke on my elders.

I only renounced death when I happened upon eternity. One night when we were out on this quest of tuberculosis, we found in this same closet a ladder left leaning against the cistern. I climbed it, and peered over the edge of a reservoir so near the ceiling it hardly belonged to earth.

In this grey shadowy vat is a metal ball soldered to an invisible support - - - an eroded orb on a bottomless water, like a caviar speck, egg of some fish that is increate, afloat on the face of doom.

Scarcely a cosmic spectacle. Yet in this waking survey of my inanimate, silver, somnambulists' world, I see it as a timeless universe or a clinker of a burnt-out planet.

The cistern represents absolute depth, as I cannot see to the bottom of it. For me, the little leaden planet has the blind patience of "before life." I am looking at a universe that is not yet "alive." - - - - - - - or has it some kind of liveness in being immeasurably aloof? For me anything may "come alive" - - - - a doll, a picture - - - I often laid a colored "scrap" of a meadow under my feet on the carpet and went for a walk in the country.

As so often in those early years I could "remember" things unknown to me, this, in spite of the stark impossibility of its ever having been cognized by any circumscribed consciousness, seems nevertheless familiar to me. Yet my probable knowledge of the elementary fact that the world is *round* would seem insufficient for evoking so great a concept from so trivial an object.

Moreover this disproportionate disunited creation - - - a planet and its primordial aqueous surface—which was what I surprisingly recognized in the metal ball - - - the gray water separate and incommensurate did not make sense—unless it comes clear, when we consider the disregard for dimension and location shown in infant drawings in which a bird may be bigger than the tree it perches upon or rain more defined than a crowd of people watching a locomotive travelling in the sky.

The wet calico stiffening on my body clothes me in a dignity as cold as the dim vacuous peace of my secret planet in the upstairs cistern; and perhaps because simplicity allows for vastness, in looking at my symbolic universe, I feel I am external to that which contains me and that somehow thereby I become everlasting.

These clouds of cosmic fancy soon roll away, and this plumber's orb reduces to a virgin playground - - - void, - - - and volcanoes and kingdoms spring up upon it (cannot a child bring the whole of nature into the house with one sod of grass?). Now, it is overrun by a superlative breed of people - - - I am just about to leap upon that planet myself to make merry among them, when it strikes eleven.

Miss Ware, all this while, sits with her book after her lonely dinner in the school-room - - - How inexact! Is she not this very moment in Denmark - - - "There's rue for you," she reads, - - - - - "That liberal shepherds give a grosser name." Her cheeks are flushed because mankind was once so young as to collaborate with spring.

She has had her door ajar to keep an ear on her sleeping charges. But the queer rise and fall, the rumble and pitch of points of view as opposite as the poles of the earth, pressing their dynamic impact upon a closed drawing room door, have prevented her hearing our assassinative antics on the upper landing.

Peeping over the banister, we see her coming up to bed. And the blood-red splosh of her evening bodice mounts the stairs in the wake of the wet, white flash of myself making for the darkness of the night-nursery at the top of the house.

Poor Miss Ware! My younger sister, who not being in the habit of creating universes, sees so much more than I do of what is going on, pretending to be asleep, watches the nursery governess undress. She sees her looking at her own nakedness in the mirror, finding it pleasant. Was it her veneration of God, or Victoria, that withheld this irreleasable prisoner from murdering us?

My maternal grandfather and grandmother were devoted. When they died they did so within a week of each other.

I was told how "Grandfather"—and I could see him as the snowy white beard I remembered, bowing over his wife's coffin in refusal to let it leave the cottage until he should accompany her as he sat in his armchair beside her, immovable, unfed - - - - he managed to expire in the nick of time.

It was a double funeral.

Apparently red with fury my poor mother, whose emotive life was so rudimentary her sorrows and apprehensions unified in a perpetual manifestation of seeming rage, preparing to attend was trying to sew some black cloth on the machine.

It was not yet I should recall my vow when plucking the shepherd's purse which had she known of it might have justified that look of denunciation lodged in my mother's eyes beyond the hump of a mechanized animal swiftly nibbling the outstretched cloth.

Their observation twisted as usual my sensibility to a drill boring the depths of my consciousness to locate "what I had done." The original evil these eyes denounced in me—was indefinable but for its suffocating pressure - - -

Standing submissively beside her as she inoculated me with "self-accusation" I at the same time gathered that "Auntie Mary" would come for the whole day to look after us while my mother buried her dead.

This Miss Gunne we were trained to call Auntie Mary was a gentlewoman in reduced circumstances who had discreetly advertised herself in the *Lady's Pictorial* as a "Companion."

The mention of her name correlated a scatter of incidents latent in my mind.

It evoked a brief respite in subliminal warfare, on first being engaged to propound the ways of the world to my mother she infused our constricted atmosphere with a little of the fairy-tale inconsequence traditional to English infancy. Among other things she had instituted "surprises." My mother at first responded; hence her throwing of the blue valentines.

This romantic interlude dispersed. Like "real" relations she was "forbidden the house." Never would my mother, her self-respect outraged, speak to her again. Auntie Mary, the silly thing, had theories on family life. Within a certain period, Mary Maud Gunne provided my sole familiarity with culture.

Round the corner from the sweet-shop where I had met my great-grandmother, Mary Maud's bell was set in a gate post so low I could pull it.

Once I visited her. I was again running away. Set out to seek my fortune in a peculiar land I could see distinctly. Void as the desert for my lack of imagination two trees like planed poles, each bearing its single enormous fruit, the one a pear, the other an apple, were planted vis-à-vis without further incident. Fruit of an unattainable knowledge in my empty promised land. I had transposed them from the rosy branches of fruit dividing vignetted groups of Kate Greenaway figures on the same wall-paper in the night-nursery—wherein before daylight I had scooped out primeval caves.

The ancient things in the home of the Gunnes seasoned my fingers. Poking the patterns of the past I could feel they were on the verge of being recomposed in the future.

Before her window draped with Virginia creeper, propped against the back of an invalid's chair, was a ball resembling a rose petal. It was kept under a lace cap. Invisibly rooted in it, threads, clinging together for fineness, silvered to metallic whiteness, slipped into groups of corkscrew curls on either cheek of Mary Maud's mamma. I would have required a fractional definition to compare the whiteness of these two women's hair. Auntie Mary's was pure white, Mrs. Gunne's was whiter still.

Either a temporary reconciliation between my mother and Miss Gunne had taken place or merely that temporary truce warranted by tragedy. I found myself in a soothing presence dawdling along in the leafy shades of those roads of old walls.

Ordinarily we were taken for walks in glum streets between semi-detached facades in paralyzed regimentation.

As nobody took action when we grew out of our clothes or boots, progress was agonizing. At one time I must have contracted from some old bruise a thickening of the bone. Every step I had to take gave me the sensation of my shin bone having been sawn in half and the contiguous ends bumping together. Nowhere an ear for childish complaints—like soldiers on the march we went on walking. Conversation was desultory; once on setting out from Blenheim Terrace I remarked to my governess, "tomorrow will be Good Friday." —"Yes," she answered two hours later on arriving at the same spot on our return, "tomorrow will be Good Friday." After nights insomnolent for toothache, the days insisted on their duration.

This day with Miss Gunne was a transformation. It was spring. She allowed me to wear my slippers. She told us stories. In her comforting society my body lightened: the solar plexus unknotted as should an understanding saint, visiting a prisoner who has no comprehension of the criminal automaton functioning within him, through some sublime response bring momentarily to the fore that image of God submerged in him, Mary Maud without a wand "turned" me into a happy child.

An unimaginable aroma drifted through the air.

With the perversity of chance, I found in this very heavenly afternoon the occasion for my unique experience of what is now I believe discussed as precocious sexuality in children.

We came under a lime tree in bloom, under a flowering dome of pale green tassels raining a thousand scents.

In a sweet assault of insect orchestra a cloud of bees impinged their zumming chords on spurts of light. There was a sound of shuttles of mobile air weaving a fabric of leaf-bud and pollen to hold in suspension the travel of the sun.

This tree, alive with melodic fragrance shaken in interlaced shimmer of ivory-into-jade, turned to the pitch of deific nerves dropped in its manifold animation soft translucent caterpillars filled with verdant juice. Vertiginous, in falling they spun round and round at the end of invisible lines in centrifugal counterpoint to a collective undulation of sweetened rhythm.

As aesthetic excitement stirred in my body a faint electric nuclear response, a projection of the vibrant lime transplanted within me, branches of nectar dripping through my torso and my limbs - - - - in replica of the arboreal structure—the nervous system.

"Oh dear," I thought anxiously, "a caterpillar has crawled up my inside."

Even the prudery of the inhabitants of a brick box cannot prevent a little sex-enlightenment from creeping in.

I was a little over eight, sitting outside the night-nursery at dusk with a little girl I had brought in to play with me in our seaside "lodgings." Entranced in the fantastic intercourse of young creatures, we dangled our legs from a great big laundry basket we had preferred to the banal accommodation of the sedate.

"You're so silly," said my visitor whose interests had revealed themselves as more realistic than my own, "I bet you don't even know where babies come from."

The jeering reflection of her remark, together with its import, relating itself to an accusation often sprung upon me by grown up people, I answered, "They found *me* under a stinging nettle."

"Oh, you booby - - - " then she crowed, "I know how you get them."

"Well, how *do* you get them," I asked her listlessly, not particularly requiring one.

"Same as Christians," this child, to whom "you" implied "Jew," assured me assertively.

"What! Just by saying 'Where's Christians?' " I exclaimed, mistaking her words and confusing them with an occult invocation akin to "Open Sesame" gleaned from some fairy-tale I cannot recall, staring the while at the pale sand—to watch the baby materialize.

"No, stupid, I said Jews get babies the same way as Christians."

"What are Jews?"

"Well, we just *are*," she explained, and started out on my initiation. The copulative prelude was summarily dealt with.

" - - - - then the woman," continued my instructress, "gets most terribly ill and writhes in agony for nine months and then the doctor comes to cut her open and takes 'it' out." (Instantly everything inside me had congealed to an icy lump.) "But it hurts so badly that she almost always dies before he has time to sew her up again. You see," she hooted in triumph, "I know more than you do."

The effect this information had upon me seems, now, disproportionate in a child whose mentality was already stuffed with hell and annihilating duty: the proof of whose existence was a constant pain in my head.

But I got to look so very unwell that even others besides Father took notice, and at last, when terror became irresistible, I ceded to my elders' curiosities, but the matter being too miserable for speech, I wrote out a statement with the stub of a pencil. A child in horror of its origin begging for reassurance. Alas, I had given my mother the opportunity to draw herself up to the very pinnacle of her superb morality.

Asserting, "It's *not true*," she added, degrading me with her righteous eyes, "now you are like a leper. Never will you be able to look anyone in the face again."

Secure in her immunity to the anathema heaped on a child who by chance surprises an unclean knowledge of which, the monopoly being reserved for the adult, mysteriously endows them with superiority, she flaunted the anomalous comparison of her unassailable status that made me despicable. "Mind you guard your disgusting secret carefully - - - Never breathe a word," and I felt I must hug it hopelessly to myself, live with it uncomforted and alone - - - always while through the panic of my thoughts I heard the pitiless Voice grind out, "You are no longer fit to be left with other children!!"

At last the secret meaning that lay behind the ominous creating of those busks was revealed to me as the working of a relentless machinery, involving *myself.*

—o-o-O-o-o—

The strangeness of my early dreams now makes it appear that I tapped a psychic storehouse of other people's perdition—

They're only dead men's heads in a dream—I assured myself for it would soon be time to go to bed—time for me to encounter the jibbering decapitations of the prophetic dark. The hour when I must relinquish an upright realism for the horizontal surrender to an existence one cannot "touch" was drawing near.

In my dreams I am crossing a bridge with my German nurse, whose head is covered with short chestnut curls - - - - an endless bridge spanning a shoreless sea that is turbid with red clay—and Mathilda is pointing upward in the air.

Out of this terra-cotta-colored sea that it seems I must cross forever, there rises an interminable stake, out of the depths of the waters up through the foundations of the sky—a breezeless brazen sky. And on this infinitely unabbreviated totem pole are growing oracular shoots - - - heads of ancients, like mummified seers of a type I had never seen—their bearded irony drips from their salient cheek-bones. Deeply embedded fevered eyes survey their issuant edicts as words to be weighed as gold—Heads of patriarchs craning alive out of a world that no longer exists save for its axis. All prophesying at once, they conjure me to some obscure enterprise.

I was afraid of falling asleep, for the seers were recurrent; I knew when I should dream them, for as soon as the gas light was turned out, darkness showered red and yellow discs like gory and golden money before my open eyes.

There was a "different" dead man's head in another dream that terrified me - - - being unexpected in so usual an environment - - -

I would be opening the rickety door to the chicken-run when a drift of snowy beard on the hard earth floor barred me. Buried up to its chin, which moved with difficulty in mumbling, an old man's puzzled face stared up at me. Not so much coming out of the earth as sinking in, my maternal grandfather tries to convey some duty - - - as though he were drawing me into the ground with him - - - I awaken in apprehension—.

—o-o-O-o-o—

If my dreams were unaccountable, I also met with the monsters of daylight, for as if the perfect craftsmanship of Nature is liable to be taken too much for granted, her even process eliciting no gratitude for her meticulous conformity to her own standard, she will sometimes go on strike to give us a glimpse of the awful phenomena that ensue when she allows her attention to wander for a fraction of an embryonic second from her everlasting job.

Perhaps to remind us of this, Mr. Barnum collects the misshapen output of her aberrations in the sideshows of his circus, or to alleviate the discontent of humanity for their average shortcomings by showing us "something worse," or to mystify children allowed to take part in their parents' amusements.

Roped in by a crimson cord - - - an unfamiliar organization of living forms I am not prepared for presents an ill-assorted pattern that, to my eyes, looks like a bodily lunacy, and it requires some effort on the part of my unpracticed mind to see it as actual substance.

Freaks! Parading on a platform. —Human accidents dependent on the indelicacy of a crowd for bitter sustenance of their ostracized, incongruous life.

The skeleton dude, sporting the derisive emptiness of his conventional evening dress, puffs wildly at a cigar the thickness of his arm; while beside him, the bearded lady's silky appendage slides dejectedly down over the amber satin of her upholstered bosom. On a sign from the show-man, these two defections of the creative clockwork ogle each other flirtatiously, suggesting to the leering onlookers that, in defiance of fleshly standardization, grotesque inflammatory desires call from his atrophy to her excess.

Slowly we pass on.

A youth in ruby plush lowers his shame-worn eyes to his abdomen, and handles the rubbery legs of his unborn twin which tend to cling together because the cramped heels of foeti are crossed. Over and over again he pulls the creasy limbs of a babe apart to inform the ticket holders. To me, in my sickening pity, it appeared that this half-body had taken a premeditated plunge to stick midway in the process of becoming, rather than ripen for the butchery of conscious life. I ached with the fateful hatred of the Freak for those legs of annihilation taking their static leap into the lasting exposure of his modesty; the cleaving of his stricken abdominal muscles.

Still we pass on - - -

The air is astir with monotonous writhing. Four arms about two young and sorrowful heads, lifting enlacing, parting as they strain for ease from their convulsive nearness; enlacing, parting—lifting as it were, a pearly imploration for release to the tradition of heaven. Plush and gold galloon encases the inseparable torsos of the Siamese Twins.

Now, at last, this pacing of torture is over, and I return to the child-reality as we come to a great glass case whose support is secretively draped with velvet reaching to the ground. It contains a live lady with crimpy hair and bedecked with diamonds. She is rocking cheerily on her hip, for from her waist down grow the metal scales of a fish-tail cocked up behind her, a cold, hard, reassuring release from a surfeit of erratic flesh.

These peccadillos of Nature's moments of absentmindedness closely resemble deformations of the spirit - - - - - .

On a visit to "Venice" at "Olympia"—gondolas, the deathly black of pleasure-hearses topple across the oily waters of an artificial canal—succeeded by a vista of planked flooring, cleared for the passage of challenging feet—the swinging swish of tartan kilts.

Raising my head I saw they belonged to what now appears as simply a troupe of Scotch pipers playing a lively reel—but this is how they looked and sounded to me then.

These kilted pipers are blowing into the parched thighs of dead men, and have stuck hurtful wooden tubes into them; they have tied up withered skin round the one end of the tubes and hold the other end with the new clear skin of their cruel mouths. The souls of the dead men are imprisoned in their mummied thighs which writhe and swell as the living blow their devastatingly live breath into them and their souls shriek out in torture and terror - - - while the big bodies of my elders straggling around them impel me to this deathly orgy by my throbbing wrists held in their ineludible claws of dominion.

It has taken me some time to discover of what material I could have formed this ghastly illusion; but at last I remembered a fancied resemblance of bagpipes to—smoked hams, together with the somewhat human misery of their squeals.

Another entertainment to obsess me was an early electric power plant open to the public view at Earls Court Exhibition. That always only half-acquiescent participant, a child, I trail along behind my mother and the governess. Stirred to an uneasy premonition of the coming mechanized world by weird sparks and flashes flying from the slip and clang of enigmatic engines, I decide it is imprudent to expose the working of such magic to unprepared eyes. In the dream I shall dream that night, I meet again with that steel swish and arc-lit iterance of a nerveless automatism engendering exiled moons.

I drag at my mother's towering skirts to entreat her to come away—she takes no heed—Suddenly this dream mother comports herself in the wildest way—She is flinging her arms up, and at once they become steely arms—She is changing—turning - - - - changes into a dressmaker's dummy of ringing metal - - - with expansible bust - - - the abdomen full as the curving breast of Lohengrin's oncoming swan. There, where the skirts should have been, all that upholstery dissembling the site of sin - - - is a forbidding cage of iron wire. It rasps my fingers that have clutched at it for protection, - - - a protection I now require against itself, the very author of my being - - - being author of my fear—twirls from my fingers—twirls, spins, spins to a transparent bobbin of intense rotation.

This fetish of maternity gloats in preposterous peals of derision while her face dissolves - - -

And this was the last of my nightmares - - - asleep.

—o-o-O-o-o—

From among those authored odds and ends I pick a scrap describing an incident preceding the period covered by the next chapter—

I was seven years old when I found my particular face on visiting a tailor's shop with my father, in whose windows we had rented seats for the Lord Mayor's "show." The tailor being a friend of his, they were having a chat after business hours and the lights were low. Before that winter evening my being alive had consisted entirely of a narrow variety of intensive emotions. I had no identity, until, wandering into a deserted fitting-room where the lights were low, I came upon my appearance in a triple mirror. Drenched in those depths and distances of interreflected glass which are endless in having no existence, even as, in the beginning, I had attached my leg to my locality, I found my covered image surmounted by my naked face.

Like a dead pearl in old dim seas adrift in an aquarium of mirrored fog and incandescent gas that appeared to redrown all the life that wanted to look at itself in that ocean from which originally it arose. Or like some marine bloom aslant from a maroon rock, its contour formed that scribble on the air that is a profile. As if it had been cut in its shadowy cameo with a musical instrument; so much do some things plastic look melodious.

Awash on an unaccountable current, stirred by invisible incentives as I moved, my own face filled me with the instant sympathy one might feel for an exile, recognized as a compatriot to whom one is powerless to attain. I was excited by a premonition of future meetings under unimaginable circumstances.

This mirrored face drooped in its semi-luminous loneliness from the rock-like distortion upholding it and into which it seemed at moments to subside. Surprised into unwarranted recognition, I stood as if being mesmerized by a face already held in trance by myself, to at last describe in the maroon base it attached to the preposterous proportions of my winter sleeves. Sliding my hand down the side of the face I should never see, to "prove" myself in the mirror, "That's me," I thought - - - "and its got such a 'different' expression." The unreal distance between myself and "it" disquieted me.

This fitting incident of hazard having picked that proper partition to fit me to my face, I, according to my kind and to be seen of them, walked away wearing that disastrous veil which falls to pieces before we have worn it out.

8

I realized the arrangement of angles around me had undergone change on touching a pane of imitation stained glass; filtering a morning light a monochrome branch of apple-blossom that looked sticky and felt dry was baked onto its surface.

My contact with a meaningless decoration brought within range the whole of a semi-detached residence that was brand new. A serial impression of static furniture forced me to enter a devaluated time-interval coincident with a stretch-on-the-rack-of years, to be spent in the sanctity of the home.

On touching that pane of glass I turned into a commonplace person with average aspirations. Agog with expectancy of normal life. Of the Cosmos of infancy the Voice alone survived.

In this papered and enameled container prepared for my adolescence, the checkered routine of my farcical training as a social unit would at first seem to consist in my being flapped in and out of mobile and stagnant air, out into Clinton Gardens and indoors again.

My handsome father trimmed with auburn mustaches stalked us on stilts of ambition exhorting us to glory. An uppish bosom intervened with "over my dead body." For Father's consolation my sister was a musical prodigy, while I, in a spirit of obedience, had bursts of self-expression. Balanced on the end of a brown wooden bedstead while the governess brushed Ida's hair I wrote a "poem."

NAT and Daisy

On a warm afternoon
In June
A (G)Nat in the air did fly
Ever so high `∴∴`.. ever so high

I want a sweetheart was all his cry
Ah! all his cry,

I've asked the white Rose
But she's far too proud
To care for a (G)Nat like me

And what do you think
The other day
I asked Miss Lily to tea
But she like the rose did not care for me

When low near the ground I flew
Disconsolately . . . Disconsolately
Ah! What did I see? Ah! What did I see?

A demure little maiden most pink and white
The loveliest maiden you ever did see
And unlike the rest she said she loved me

And then came the wedding, What awful fun!
Our friend the cat
Stole from the kitchen a lovely iced bun
To serve for the wedding cake

And the bees brought much honey
The best they could make

I remember no more, save that the (G)Nat having found his daisy with all her petals shed, I ended up serenely:

So he lay down and died
At his daisy-stalk's side.

It was shocking to learn, on being knocked off my perch, that instead of a laudable poet I was somehow "a sly minx, trying to get round Father."

Day by day, drifting from room to room seeking for "something to do" shooed by a blast of "idle slut" past the towering gilded mirrors from "North Hall," I felt put out by their flitting amoretti's dimples of inascribable delight. Father had been assured these mirrors, now cut down to the height of our present ceilings, were loot from the palace of Versailles. At the base of one, in a spacious jardiniere, a few poor artificial plants fell upon one another. I found it useless to try digging the pointed sticks on which they were mounted into the metal bottom.

The houses in Clinton Gardens were all alike but on the threshold of ours stood a menace as ominous as Charon. The clap of doom was at my back as I passed through the gate.

Retrospectively the sides of that brick box which seemed so vacuous actually creak. Forced to bursting point by opposite pressures from within. At the time a steady inoperation dulled the interior. Bodies moved without aim. Tentacles of waste energy wavered toward inexistent objectives. Like machinery working full blast on the production of nothing, I wore down my own dynamism. The brain for lack of intellectual material exercised its ceaseless automatism upon the biological functions to abnormal extent—one always had some kind of pain, heightened by the spasms of the solar plexus on impact with the Voice.

Gentle Jesus meek and mild, in my babyhood I conceived of as a mouse, would he "come out?" I had wondered, if he knew I wouldn't hurt him.

Now, with a private vow of atheism, I countered my mother's vicious pinches on our way to church.

Monday morning I fought my first ethical battle. While rattling my hoopstick along an iron fence I denied God; at the age of nine.

In a mobile pattern of alternating streaks of brightness and blackness, the fleeting palings rippled past my eyes coinciding terrifically with stripes of fiery hell and dark oblivion as I ran. I could not be *sure* the everlasting flame was bluff. Yet to the Voice I had such antipathy I could not conform to its precepts. Asserting a tremulous heroism, I decided to risk eternal torture rather than resemble the people He approved.

Hardly had I become an atheist when my religious education was reinforced with the cooperation of the only governess my mother never quarreled with.

Out of a flat-fronted woolen bodice of amber plaid with velvet collar and reveres rose the flesh and lashes of a swine. Beneath the cuff of a sleeve too short appeared a rosy wrist sown with glinting hairs.

The nearness of this pious governess added to my ills a perpetual nausea.

"Mamma," Miss Nickson had a habit of saying, her somehow accusing eye upon me, "never cared if her babies were pretty. All she asked when we arrived was, 'Has it got the correct number of fingers and toes?' "

A golden tassel on her watch chain dangling against my ear, her breath on the nape of my neck, merged in my subconscious with the horror instilled by my first information on procreation. In the pathological vortex she aroused in me spun a black Bible "cloth boards, 2/6."

Hour upon hour we looked up texts, compared references under the awning of her white eyelashes.

Aversion to her, obstructing my senses, deafened me to her lessons. To relieve my tedium I would investigate the Old Testament when Miss Nickson wasn't looking.

My mother's assertion that intercourse "isn't true" somehow rendering anomalous her condemnation of my hideous "knowledge" further confused me when I read in the Genealogy—so and so went in unto so and so and begat. For a while I was drawn into the obscene undertow of religious mania. To vent the uprush of sadism associated with it I turned (imaginatively) upon the physical repulsion to which it reduced in the person of the governess.

Nicky should be mated with a lion and *beget* cubs, whose manes inherited her sandiness, to lacerate her with *claws*.

Frequently I have sampled the emotive imbroglios underlying lunacy; that I never got "stuck" in any one of them I owe to my latent preoccupation with beauty. To the fulminating "wish on" Miss Nickson the level of my consciousness sunk lower than it ever would again.

Two years our overseer remained with us. From morning prayers until, having put us to bed at six she sat outside our open bedroom door still pouring her freckles over the Bible. She was there to insure a silence in which no original sin could rise to the surface. What Evil—somehow originating, I felt, in my father—were these women bent on driving forth from the young in those days of drastic watching and waiting?

This governess, poor thing, had one attraction, enticing me sometimes to approach her. She could sharpen a pencil to a finer point than seemed credible. Then shade the Narcissi she knew how to draw till they shone like lead.

Her sense of righteousness braced by Miss Nickson's acquiescence in purging me of my shame, my mother exhibited a modicum of calm during her residence. When the governess left the house this calm broke down completely. Father blasphemously believing in educational subjects, supplementary to religion. He had us "sent" to school.

The pitch of the maternal sound-track during the ensuing years could only be given in terms usually signifying wild exaggeration and the bias of a liar read into them. Not infrequently in the sheltered homes of the nineties, daughters were bullied to maturity subject to prohibitions unmodified since babyhood. Their only self-expression: to watch and pray.

I watched the startled groups of new servants listening in the hall.

Under the metronome, running scales, my sister sitting on the piano stool in that kernel from which all sound is centrifugal, herself unrung.

I watched my father's vitality congeal to a heaviness of the brow only to be supported in two quivering hands.

All the keys had been taken out of the doors by my mother except, in regard for decency, those of three lavatories on the different floors.

One above the other they stood, our ivory tower. Here I had knelt in bewilderment praying for God to "make me Good" while an opaline vase left on the washstand peered at me, a blind eye, through its lovely cataract of lacteal blue and rose.

One above the other in sanctuary we could hear our baffled foe shriek for us to come forth. As an atheist I sat on the heavy mahogany lid, my own eyes held by a mosaic head of Medusa, as the last limp trails of Virginia creeper waved their shadows through the narrow window across a polished paper tile turning me to stone.

Going to school I anticipated as joining an opposition club of youth combatting the mother-myth. I had stood up to God alone. Mother love was beyond me. I had urgent need for that exchange of confidences in which the helpless asses of misfortune appraise each other's loads to lighten them at least of bearing in silence.

"Do you love your mother?" I asked with significant inflection upon absurdity of the first little girl who wanted "to make friends." We were putting our books away on a lower shelf. Had I had any opportunity to observe the portents of normal human relationships I should have been instantly informed in this bobbing together of topknots, should have recognized in the hair ribbon a vane indicating which way the maternal wind blows. That other child's in its cheerful cerise lay caressing with a pair of orderly loops her formal curls while mine like a flag vanquished in some unfortunate engagement started ragged in asymmetry from a crippled knot in which some random hairs of my culpable head were caught to an agonizing tension among the overloose mass.

The effigy of vengeance is not sufficiently envisaged in the ramp of frog-like furies clawing the air. The poignant effigies on whom vengeance is brought home to us, are stuck all over with its trophies, in their general appearance of having been covered with the final detritus of any social cataclysm. The shreds and rifts in the clothes of the poor, the tired mud that cakes upon the patriots who have marched too compliantly, the indefinable collapse of child bodies whose covering is not civilized with the detail of affection.

Horror leapt to that other child's eyes. Involuntarily she looked upwards expectant of something to fall upon me.

"But of course," she answered, her voice almost drowned in the din of her disapproval.

A face expressing emotion from within is a bountiful face even if pouring out dislike which is also acceptable and of common traffic, but the horrified face that like a faulty mirror distorts its vis-à-vis . . . . the horror on that small girl's face is a reflected horror. So even outside the home, I am not a nice child. And now I perceive her hair ribbon, it is all tied up with love.

Original sin, where does it lie, in the process of logical thought? The problem wearied my mind to the exclusion of all further operation. I spent three years of education washing the soot from the ivy on the garden wall beyond the classroom windows with my wandering eyes.

As it was a moral impossibility to arrive in class without bringing one's homework, and a physical impossibility to concentrate at home, I copied my exercises out of the textbook. In order not to cheat the other girls I wrote in sufficient mistakes to place me permanently above the defective child with an oyster eye who sat in unassailable simplicity at the bottom of the class. Beside her I pondered that eerie hitch in a psychic mechanism rendering the defective so "differently" incapable of concentration to myself. Had she had for daughter that imbecile child would even my mother have spoken in vain?

Until that time when we must fizzle out like squibs in the damp, we glowed whenever we had company. Visitors aroused in us that over-animated gaiety of people who must ram their need for pleasure into brief occasions.

One of my father's step-relations who enameled his outdoor cistern vermillion had a paying guest or perhaps lodger he often brought to our house to dinner. A Welsh musician, he played us all he composed and Ida would join him in duets. My father relaxed in an armchair of lurid satin, melting in relief, let a few pure tears trickle to his beard. "I love music in a minor key," he avowed wiping his eye with a bandanna. "It makes me feel sentimental."

If I recall his face accurately, Edward German dominated the show of gas on our drawing-room with a distinct Celtic beauty.

I stood apart from the initiates gathered round him. Even the "step" was a music addict. Multiplied by the mirrors they made a crowd among the reflected ebony, gilt and alabaster, moving their laughter round an early gramophone as they recorded Ida's precocity on cylinders of café-au-lait-colored wax. My mother wearing all her diamonds assumed the smile of a diplomat who, assured of attaining his end, is not for the moment giving his policy away.

With Ida, my father's unaccountable presentiment of future glory seemed secure. Almost as a baby she moved her fingers on ivory and harmony was the result. As a girl she opened her mouth and emitted a "lyric soprano."

Her itinerary I could see so clearly marked. Already it had led her along a straight route of practicing up to a certain musical soirée at which, in Hamburg, Blanche Marchesi exchanged confidences on a sofa. Each had a star pupil. "There she is," they cried simultaneously as Ida entered.

Meanwhile on leaving school one morning, among a group of pupils, I noticed standing somewhat apart two tiny sisters waiting to be "fetched." One, a trifle taller than the other, so stringy their drab striped coats were outstanding as raiment on puppets, each had a perfect head of Osiris. Intrigued by the almost invisible molding of their oval faces, the idol-flatness of their noses, I lingered to admire them. Their name was Hesse. "Myra, the smaller one, plays the piano," an elder girl remarked. She had none of Ida's "advantages," I was given to understand.

While for my sister the divine penetrated to her environment, in mine the walls were hung with pictures from the Royal Academy.

Music, intangible, speaks for the dumb soul; other arts have too articulate audiences. Ida, as if her curls had condensed to minims and crotchets, still moved serenely to constant applause. I was confused when anyone inquired of me, "I hear you draw. Can you draw a cork?"

Being the elder was also a strain. Paternal benevolences incident to different stages in a daughter's development naturally fell first to me. Experiments ending in catastrophe.

"You're getting a big girl now," said Father when I was fifteen, producing at the dinner table gatelinked bracelets of plain gold. "I thought you might wear a little quiet jewelry."

His wife turned red, flung away her knife and fork, crying on Heaven to witness the sacrilege, wasting money on an undeserving . . . . . She made a dash for me, my father averted her hand.

Squatting slowly, cautiously to the floor she lay down flat with her head against the fender and screamed . . . for the servants to be her witnesses . . . "Fine bracelets you'll both get, handcuffs is what you require" . . . her husband anxiously explaining he did not knock her down.

"Father," I implored him, "how can you go on arguing with her all these years, listen to me, she's putting it on. Pour some cold water over her."

My father, who is quaking with nervous shock, stiffens.

"Now what sort of girl are you turning out to be, have you forgotten she is your mother?"

"If only I could."

"Ah, I'm afraid your mother is right about you . . . you're heartless."

"Give me my cloak and bonnet," my mother declaimed, probably taking her cue from some old melodrama, as everyone now wore hats.

"I leave this house forever to put myself out of my misery . . . Murderers both of you."

The servants huddled together in the hall argue with the kitchen maid, who is crying.

"It's not for us I'm crying, we're leaving; it's for that wretched kid of a Miss Linda as does no 'arm to nobody and can *never* get away."

"Go," said the father I have antagonized, gulping a stiff dose of brandy. "Go and take care she does herself no harm. I should never forgive myself."

Too young for stimulants, having had no dinner after similar inroads on lunch, I crept upstairs to hang limply about the keyhole in my mother's bedroom door until after midnight.

I see her arrange herself serenely on the sofa; her body entirely relaxed, directing the pitch and toss of her sobbing. Hearing no sound of having been followed, she stops dead and listens, narrowing her crafty eyes. Has she no audience?

Somewhere a door closes, she starts afresh, baying (on principle) as a dog at the moon.

In the face of such monstrous opposition, my father had performed heroic acts. When first he noticed our danger of going naked, he drove us to Marshall & Snelgrove's and had us "fitted out" in the delightful fashion of the period. To the same imprecations, he sent us to school, committed Ida to her professors of music and, later, enrolled me, with the best intentions, in an art school.

As things got worse, he could take little fresh initiative; his "health," which was behaving queerly, became his major concern. Haunting Harley Street, where specialists repeatedly decided there was nothing the matter with him, he could not believe they were right.

At last when the density of sound vibrations blocked up space while disintegrating the compact of my identity until I seemed embedded in nervous rock, on the brief occasions when I drew myself out in my original form I could find myself closeted with Father, both of us white-faced and shaken, conferring as to what "could be done."

Despite a domestic chaos steadily precluding us from any "mode of life," vital necessities would confront us. Predominantly my peril of becoming unclothed.

It is often the case that although a problem shared by two may be obviously insoluble for oneself, one has only to put oneself in the place of the other one to see it simplify. So before the problem of how to address my mother on any subject whatsoever without bringing down the rain of her abuse upon us, Father, although he no longer attempted to come to terms with her himself, would meditate on my behalf, then with a knowing smile:

"Coax her," he advised me. Such inadequacies were native to that generation which "clung on" long after the bough of its fixed-idea had broken. But this was not the only reason that, loyally my father's ally throughout my purgatorial apprenticeship, I had really no ally of my own. His solicitous confidante, I yet perceived, beneath his need for commiseration, downright suspicion of me. He shared with an almost total majority of men at the time a somehow subtly obscene aversion to any female who used her mind. If he could shut his ears and invoke the quiet I guaranteed would heal him should he cut his marriage in half; the more plainly he heard the "opinion" which the middle class lived to propitiate, of a "society" for whom that class must exist incognito. "Never," said my father, static as a fakir, "it would harm you children."

His visions were his own however. My harrowed entreaties for even minor respites he parried, "It wouldn't do," gravely shaking his head, "no daughter should ever leave her mother's side." How far his voice receded, measuring the duration of this vision's tenacity with a sob. "It's *so* beautiful . . . the bud beside the rose; men like it," he consoled me.

The bud. Patched to distortion under the elbow-length bell, the tight half of my sleeve often wearing thin had been recovered as if by an insane upholsterer with so many layers of miscellaneous stuff it had grown to a shapeless bundle. Discouraged, I let my forearm, like the incommodious appendage of a crustacean, drop to my side.

All the while I had been growing up, becoming a woman.

"Someday you'll be a mother yourself, *then* you'll understand," says mine, pushing me violently in the chest. This *névrose* body is developing and for thrift she is making me a dress from a pattern with a child's flat yoke. "How can I fit you? You nasty girl. Do you think at your age it is decent to have a figure? Your vile flesh, you'll get no good out of it. Curse you. Curse your father . . . I'm going to crush 'it,'" she screams.

Having seen little except for machine-made furniture, the subjects I found appropriate to art were cupids, peacocks, cypresses, and swans. Ah swansdown, swans neck condescension in curves, against sunsets of jam.

To what most sweetly could I make flesh compare? Fondants. How idealize foliage? As emeralds. And eyes to be fully orbed? Would not sockets or lids detract from their astral entirety?

I imagined creation to be an intensification.

Uncultured pilgrims to the shrine of an aesthetic leap at the superlative only to slow down to analysis on reaching a senility of ardor.

The night before I entered the Art school, I could not sleep. Visual excitement hung on the dark pictures I longed to paint as soon as the professors showed me "how"; a pair.

The one "in the treble" portrayed a cupid having no joints whatever, his fondant face flat as his brassy curls. Added to his grace was a swan with nothing under its feathers. Of a whiteness on which the slightest shadow would be a pollution.

The one "in the bass" portrayed a "bronzed" cupid. His curls and eyes of ebony. He leaned against the outspread fan of a peacock glowing with unsullied color straight from the tube.

As I lay there planning the response of the multitude to my lovely boys, my brain suddenly aware of being led along by an intention dropped that intention as it was trained to do. The effect upon me was of an abstract blow. In a flash of darkness, the mental scene-clouding filled with a sense of shame. I automatically reproached myself for my presumption.

Expecting the study of Art to be a participation in something familiarly resembling the transformation scene in a pantomime I was ushered into the Antique room through a leather padded door whose swing back sounded at once a groan and Hush! A place was assigned to me among a line of students along the wall. Rows of miners in the galleries of ignorance. Scritch go their charcoal sticks and the black blastings of their emery blocks strew their voluminous grey pinafores, leave chimney-sweep smudges on their anemic features as they push the English wisp of hair out of their plodding eyes.

In Italy, three centuries ago and yesterday, to displace a block of enormous marble doubly blanched with alabaster dusts, the haltered oxen with their hooves of slaves labor the white road from Carrara.

Hanging from air inserted in it, David's nose emits a plaster clink as I set it straight. I am ordered to reproduce it exactly. The rounding out of the wing of his nostril was effected by rubbing a hard Conté crayon on the sandpaper until it was pointed as a pin. You came to a pore on the Whatman paper, you jabbed your Conté into it leaving there, like a fly, your minute speck. The speck is too black, you pounce upon it with a sharpened eraser . . . it pales.

After several weeks of persistence, the area thus covered may be smoothed to perfection with spikes of coiled blotting paper called "stumps" and twiddled bread. You are "stippling it up" among the dry and dirty crumbs fallen into the rack of the easel in which lay the hallucinatory white feather of my vanished swan.

Next to me a zealous young woman has detected in David's mouth a non-Buonarrotian addition. A startling line dividing the lips, because for some accident of labial obliquity the dust does not settle there. Her determination to reproduce this intrigues the masters. Approving, they linger to bring a male ingenuity to bear on a still finer tipping of India-rubber.

As Father looked so important, the expression of his top hat so harmonized with the rest of him, and I being only fifteen was the baby of the school, to palliate the nostalgia of a first day, I was invited to a tea in the private studio of the elderly monitor. I found myself among her friends in an atmosphere unaccustomedly kindly.

"You must feel rather unhappy," she inquired of me, "away from home?"

"How should I," I answered warmly, "among such charming people." Evidently this put them in a new light; they pealed with laughter.

To relieve my bewilderment as to how I should paint beautiful pictures from soiled casts, they assured me I should find all I needed in the evening life-classes.

That was where I came upon the poor bare man with the eyes of a lizard who had known no sun. Because the studio dust was somehow similar to the jaded hair on his body, that body seemed fearfully deprived of a divine right, while the professor cocked his eye at a plumb-line appraising the proportion of a lamentable being who hardly seemed able to hold together. I heard him discourse on sensing the bony structure beneath the masses, noting how the leaning torso sagged into the pelvis. All that was clear to me was how the excrescences of the model's unproud knees confounded his symmetry.

Not being sufficiently developed intellectually to guess that facts can be supplemented, requiring Adonis, I repudiated the model.

Why draw the head like a square block, why dash a line where the eyes should be, I would argue with the students. Construction? Where was the beauty in that?

Soon I could depict to a nicety, detail almost scattered about as leaves without a tree.

Invited to little teas by the more high-brow pupils, at one such tea, intimate behind the gigantic cast of Hermes, I found myself listening to the headmaster Brand—who gnawed his mustache—

"Everything here," he said pointing to me, to Hermes, to the tea-tray set on a wooden stool, "all matter is composed of atoms. Nothing is solid, each atom is surrounded by space . . ."

It flashed through my mind that this was an explanation of how the man in the Bible got out of a bolted dungeon. I could *feel* there was some "control" in the brain with which he, knowing how to use it, could pass his atoms through the spaces between the atoms in a wall of stone.

I had never been the least intrigued by this biblical episode I barely recalled, yet I welcomed this sudden solution as if it were one of importance I had long sought.

Although at the studio I was removed from immediate terror, I found it a haven of disappointment. In a clap of astonishment rolling its echoes of anxiety along the empty channels of an excitement which for want of concepts takes the place of a mental process Art had faded; leaving me to the house-paint.

The sequestered wound of Beauty revealed itself in the color of dried blood. On door and wainscot, the bases of casts, mounting the stairs along the gallery, even the oil-cloth. A wandering mind is one so feverishly preoccupied it will seek a sedative in anything. — Off the maroon obsession spread to the ladies dressing room floor I picked the fallen printed page, by which that very wound was to be healed.

From that moment I began to have a life. I read in a scrap of book review that a certain Max Nordau considered the refrain in poetry to be a symptom of dementia giving as an example the works of one— and it was at this time I passed into a condition of elation—Dante Gabriel Rossetti - - - The name! Smelling to the ear as to the nose an orange stuck with cloves to temper dried rose petals in the more sophisticated "pot-pourris."

Not seldom an aesthetic springs from the spirit of contradiction that instigates secession, and anger which dare not aspire to a physical outlet supplies the substratum for an intellectual pugnacity.

How could a man named more ornately than all other men as far as I could know be mad?

Being myself to the eternal assailant the assailed, I was biased as to the relative merits of the critic and the criticized. Even as I had espoused the cause of the inferiorized left hand, I condemned Max Nordau and all his works.

Why this particular combination of syllables should be more conducive to spontaneous veneration for an empty mind than, for instance, William B. Cadwalader, is mysterious as the fixations of allergies.

Father, on my entreaties somewhat against the grain, for, observing in his portrait on the frontispiece that Rossetti's trousers bagged, he concluded this must be a trivial artist, brought me home the volume of his complete poems, reproductions of his paintings and, for full measure, Christina's *Poems* bound in red morocco containing his illustrations for "Goblin Market."

Poor Rossetti cooling your Italian nostalgia in an alien language, your passionate brush to tentative British technique. Of the Latin spasm disciplined to retention, a pomegranate mildewed in the mist of the Thames, you concocted in your poesy so powerful an emetic of the spirit as to relieve a middle-class visionary of her adolescence and clog the gorgeous rubber "crops" of your wide-eyed women stricken with fried hair.

The acoustics of our unlovely sitting room attenuate to the echo of you. The dye stuff of your luscious gloom has come off on the air - - -

I was tented in visual arras like a medium emitting the pneumatic lips of your Sidonia and Proserpina to float through my mother's irate pince-nez listening only to a silent ventriloquy of your refrain:

O Mother, Mary Mother,
Three days to-day, between Hell and Heaven!

The enormous cavern the mind can scoop out of the smallest sod where man may infinitely haunt himself with any ghostliness he chooses, this psychic retreat, this area of perfectibility hitherto stored with emptiness, Rossetti filled for me.

Under his influence, I began to "furnish" England with a small pattern, an incipient rhythm, a wisp of Folk-lore. A poppy head, a knight errant, and, later, something from Liberty's in Cymric silver, with a covetous eye on a "greenwood tree" or rather a simple wooden bedstead stained to a violent emerald by Ambrose Heal in the Tottenham Court Road.

My fancy pottering around this "soul shoppe" with a candle on a pricket, I beheld that art being "spiritual," the highest function of a maiden is to yearn, of a young man also if he can be brought to it.

My outlook having brightened, I wished that others might share in my relief. I pondered on the maternal face the cause of its sullenness. Then coming to a lightning conclusion, probably stimulated by the gas illuminant burning up the air that always excited me, I stretched out my hands to my mother:

"Oh, won't you realize that there's nothing the matter with any of us," I begged her. "Imagine how charming you would be if only you were not forever so angry. Everything is really all right, only somehow or other you've just got into the habit of *thinking all wrong*.

"There's no reason why you should not start afresh this very minute. We can all be happy *Now*.

"Why shouldn't you smile? Just one little smile. *Please,* quick before you have time to reflect. One—Two—Three—"

"Have you," she asked, drawing herself up, "*no* respect for your mother? You shall go to bed without your supper and I hope you will awaken in the morning a sadder and a wiser girl."

Seemingly it was I who was thinking wrongly. My mother was thinking "straight"—directing her policy of *wearing down* the imagined opponent - - -

Tipped off as it were by the poet I preferred, I at last began to function. Having found something to love—love being the mechanism of talent—in the English, almost nursery, medievalism of the day, I discovered that if my powers of concentration flagged with a model before me, I could fairly draw anything I longed to see provided I had nothing to look at. While much that is learned from the study of models seemed to have registered on some unsuspected plane of memory.

My first entirely independent work executed in the shade of that same Hermes stirred the wrath of Brand.

"Wasting time," he grumbled on espying me.

"I am joining the 'sketch club,' " I clarified.

Brand was about to expostulate when catching sight of what I was doing he goggled - - -

Amid unprecedented astonishment that first drawing won the prize and established me as one of the outstanding students of the school.

Composition I determined by the fitness of the "expression" induced by the relation of parts. My standard for faces consisted in an egoless purity brought about by the harmonic contingency of their Celtic features. Once one of my women was so lovely that the visiting Royal Academy judge practically licked his chops.

This instantaneous liberation of my self-confidence diminished my subconscious anxieties for a while—until my mother in one of her accesses of outraged morality tore up my drawing of a bare Andromeda lashed to a rock.

As "Vile, debased," she rated my mind of a "vicious slut—'marking the division.'" Trying to make out on following her thick accusative finger what she, whose powers of observation were so rudimentary, might mean, I at length concluded in a blush of violation, that she had mislocated a shadow line as marking the spring of my innocent-eyed Andromeda's virginal—thigh.

Thereafter the lack of keys, making it impossible to protect things from her, allowed for incessant raids on the work which had for a time so comforted me. Drawings and poems became the prey of her disoccupation.

Infantile apprehensions revived in me.

"Shocks" having hollowed out pockets along the mental route the mind trained to drop into them did so independently of impetus from without. These periodical plunges into a depth of shame lining the constructive impulses had in the long run the inexplicable effect of forcing me to deliberately ruin a beautiful drawing in some single spot—very much as warriors surrender. At present, the interference in my work took the form of violent depression, and soon of terror, on receiving praise, of never being able to produce anything again that could merit praise.

I do not remember the exact relation in time of my impact with the Pre-Raphaelite and my second sex enlightenment, when my friend Evangeline came from Edinburgh to stay with me. My moral leprosy become stagnant was revived by my mother.

"Mind you," she whispered as we said "good night" rolling her eyes in her usual savage directive hints in the presence of guests, "if you breathe a word - - - "

The rise in psychic temperature was immeasurable when, as it seemed, immediately, from her pillow on a bed beside mine, Evangeline gurgled in derision.

"Confess. You can't be so 'green.' We went into hysterics over you when you came to Scotland.

"You *don't* know what people do on their honeymoon? You're jolly well going to find out."

The buzz of innocuous pornography darkness generates in the young rose in crescendo to—

-— " - - - then the man - - -

- - - - "Suddenly," Evangeline assured me, "you are overcome by the most marvelous sensation. It is just like being in heaven."

The orb of consciousness reversed in my brain. The illuminated side fallen into contact with my senses on this only intimation that there is such a thing as "pleasure" in the world I had ever received.

"But," Evangeline amended, "it can't last more than one second because the pleasure is so *intense* that if it lasted any longer it would *kill* you."

This unprecedented shock of antithesis knocked me into a coma of delight—probably what is known as daydream. At once I understood why love stories stop short of marriage, there being no words designed to describe it.

I shut my eyes but I slide off the track in my daydream. What I had got hold of is the ascetic trance of illumination. No crisis of the flesh or is it a mingling of both? Is there perhaps little difference? Or has my imaginative sensibility, so crucified, in a psychic haste passed its destination?

Evangeline prattles on of ways and means. All I caught was cold cream.

My mind conforming to a fairly general fallacy scraps all that. I have learned all I need to know. A momentary, a magic contact. Such is marriage. *Un effleurement suffit.* Having as a child devoutly accredited fairies, I retrieve the wand for the immediate, the immaculate transformation.

Of the millions accepting, in that era, existence as a vacuum surrounding the Three Events the majority were by nature so well-adjusted to inhibition they appeared to have exteriorized it to wear as an armour of agreeable inertia. The rest, ill at ease in such intellectual depravity, exhibited every gradation of a domestic fever whose crisis was reached in homes such as mine.

Most of the people I chanced to associate with functioned contentedly within the boundaries of their domestic interests. These, being, unlike my mother's, in their case long standardized by a tradition of social pursuits, composed an adequate program for their meagre dynamism. Leaving them, however, uniformly flat. What imagination, emotion, apprehension they could generate, they summoned solely for Birth and Marriage and Death.

The torture of girls to make them fit for marriage became a chimeric affair in homes so nicely guarded that parents must have supposed marriage to be something fateful striking unannounced, like death.

The girls were torn with anxiety between the appeal of a sole liberation and the paralyzing certainty that the very torture of their isolation rendered marriage unattainable.

A family of average tepidity might never have mentioned this restrictive fetish. But my father, despite the din of his wife's remonstrance, must go about marrying off a daughter even as a domesticated cat goes hunting "after dark"—a streak of fur across furnished apartments flooded with electric light. He can't make out why this terrorized child in his desolate home isn't on the way to making a good match.

"Sixteen and thin as a rail. An old maid already."

From the accustomed dual opposition, I gathered that were I not "dressed" I should resemble "bad women." Unless I turned out to be a genius I would never "appear." That were I to express an opinion, I should fail to find a husband. If I as much as spoke to a man I would become ineligible.

"Can't you fatten yourself up a little," Pappa asked anxiously.

The young are seldom aware of their privileges. My unique opportunity to experience the eroding discipline to which the offspring of the lower classes are submitted together with middle class morality amid the larger advantages of civilization I could hardly appreciate at the time. My parents' eternal exhortations, from their opposite standpoints:

"What do you *think* people will think of you?" inspired me to project into the minds of others an uneasy mental inquiry inquisitive as a probe. So incessantly I endeavored to read their thoughts that in the end I was able to. However, the psychological material thus gathered, under the pressure of my induced complex of culpability, sank into the subconscious, to accumulate for years before I was free to bring it to the surface.

Meanwhile as the majority do I shoved my observations of actuality aside lest they encroach on the type concepts impressed on the mind from birth.

The insidious element in rebellion against parents consists in your inability to detach yourself completely from the basic mesmerism of their ascendency.

Seeing my mother fall by the fender purposely, hearing her sob at will, served merely to render paradoxical the initial imposition of filial duty. Behind her tantrums loomed the collective maternal heart given into the keeping of the doctor of that era. He pronounced it so weak the slightest emotional stress must cause a devoted mother's instantaneous decease. I lived like my father in breathless apprehension of committing an astral murder. There appeared to be no way of averting it. This feeling of culpable responsibility toward other people lasted the rest of my life.

She had a knack of emitting invertible accusations in lightning sequences of transposed logic which revealed an unparalleled self-protective agility in the female running to waste in consequence of her anomalous relationship to Nature.

I have heard it again—in modified form—from Mr. Guffy on Eddie Cantor's program in March 1939.

I suspect that collective heart aliment, coddled by countless distracted families, of having taken the doctor for granted as an accomplice.

According to my parents, all spectators of that suspect showpiece, myself, must inevitably receive impressions to my disadvantage. Sometimes this had the effect of my injecting into those ransacked minds the very conclusions I was warned against yet only after so long a siege by my unnatural anxiety that their primary genial acceptance of me wavered.

The extremes which marked my to and fro between world and home were those of a pendulum endowed with consciousness swinging beyond a calculable range.

The reactions I evoked outside the home staggered me more than those within, where the very sight of me stirred up fury. At first I accepted as practical joking the rush occasional acquaintances made for me as they twittered:

"You're the loveliest thing I have seen in all my life."

Neither of these valuations of my physique assumed significance in my scheme of things, where the maiden who lost her eyebrows in Burne-Jones's *Love among the Ruins* fixed the standard of beauty to which alone I should, at the time, have been proud to attain.

My trouble was the friends I made so easily urged me "to do something about" myself. Unable to explain my situation which didn't make sense, I formed the habit to avoid vain regret of paying no attention to what they were saying. With the strange result that whenever I asked a question I neglected to listen to the answer.

Sculptured by my parents' thought, England agglomerated to an omnipotent adult of dual embodiment—female, endowed with a divine right to insult me—male, endowed with a similar right to ruin me.

Nothing has more amazed me than the idiotic apprehensions of the moralists that the world had lapsed from the purity of the pre-First World War era.

Preoccupation with the still somewhat unformulated concept, sex, permitted expression, has become intermittent. "Putting it into words" supplies sufficient egress to allow of average individuals' entirely concentrating on other interests for considerable stretches of time.

At the close of Victoria's reign it formed an incessant obsession of the respectable. They never ceased to be aware of "not doing something" and the necessity for preventing others from doing "it." The striking characteristic of the early years of the post-war era was a pronounced purification revealed in its concomitant, a marked, although unfortunately individual, abatement of sadism.

9

"Men"

Where the "forbidden" suggests escape from a narrow misery and that discrepancy, "love," offers the only alternative to a rabid inertia, the captive anticipates *man,* the scarecrow on the parental landscape in the ingratiating guise of an Evangelist.

I came to imagine his recuperative gentleness, my crushed mouth filled with the acrid taste of wall-paper, when in the early morning hours my mother at the height of conjugal recriminations had burst into my room and bearing me out of bed dashed me against the wall as she screamed, "you *horrible* children I could *kill* you." I sensed to a nicety the point at which, even in the phenomenal force of fury, an ingrained fear of the law curtails spontaneity.

Entering upon the truly amoral period of life, to my lasting disgrace I actually laughed about a silly young thing because her swain at the art school transferred his attentions, which consisted in a lingering beside an easel for the giving of advice, to myself. This period of thoughtless sport in the normal adolescent, when the feelings of others, one's own being so superficial that a joke appears the supreme indulgence, are not taken into account, was of necessity with me of short duration.

One concrete—if intermediary—event could be added to the Three on a maiden's cursory program. Birth, marriage, and death ceding importance only to the acme of the wedding cake was the experience of becoming "engaged."

My relegation by my father to the status of "old maid" for lack of obesity, my mother's prediction I should die in the gutter because, as a student, I required more than one pencil at a time added to a terror whose only let-up was total boredom had thrown me into a panic of yearning for concrete experience before it should be *"too late!"*

With such ease I forget how it happened I got secretly engaged. As this event took place on the hackneyed plane on which I outwardly evolved according to program it was not long before this led me into a jam.

In the jocular prelude to conscious adolescence one not unfrequently "falls in love" with something "funny." I picked my young man because he smoked a curved pipe which hanging over his long chin made him easy to caricature, having first consulted with my girl-chum before clenching my choice.

Above his cherished briar appeared incidentally some extremely good facial sculpture, a pair of deep-set clearly lidded long dark eyes overshadowed by an ivory brow. His oval lips become somewhat constricted from clutching the tubular decoy of my attention. He was always excellently tailored, oftenest, at my command, in brown "to match his hair."

The nearest I could get to my ideal of "Love in the Mist" was to sit leaning against his arm on a damp bench on Primrose Hill, when I ought to have been in life-class. We stared straight before us into an uncompromising fog. There were no primroses.

Hunched in inhibited ardor, paralyzed with "respect," he did not say very much. It was not long before I began to chide him gently, bidding him reflect on all that Dante Gabriel would have been saying under the circumstances.

"I fancy the poor brute would have been just as dumb as I am when Miss Siddal was actually there," my fiancé countered.

I must have been, sometime, very fond of him. Once when we "gave a dance" my mother postponing all arrangements with daily pretense of calling the whole thing off owing to our "wickedness," leaving the last-minute hectic preparations entirely to me, I remember the sympathy of his pectoral muscles under the dress shirt whereon I laid my tired head to be soothed by his long, kind fingers.

He had one idiosyncrasy that disturbed me. The ladies he drew among domes and minarets of extremely able penmanship had each a queer kink under the nose slipping into the mouth. Some years later I heard he had married and his child was born hair-lipped.

He read me *Lorna Doone* in Devonshire where through arduous plotting our families happened to spend one summer holiday.

Saying so little of note himself, on looking back I am surprised he did not virtuously jilt me, my random remarks being for a "maiden" positively alarming.

Inspired by a light lady wearing plaid bloomers in the chorus of a travelling company, her face smeared with red, her frowsy hair jammed into her eyes by the exaggerated vizor of a cloth bicycling cap—we were in the midst of a discussion as to whether *all* human beings had souls, " - - - - most people appear to be only 'half there'—do you think," I inquired of him, "they would even want to do 'it'—if they had not been told they mustn't?"

His smile clenching the briar tighter, "I shouldn't wonder a bit if you're right," he assented.

Yes sometimes on that holiday I would win free. There were frequent storms and my mother had to retire to her room and hide under the bed; so terrified of thunder even propriety must go by the board.

At the end of our stay she allowed us to go for a row, taking my younger sister along in the boat as chaperone. I wore a light cape and, zenith of romance, Lucas had his arm "round my waist."

My sister watched us balefully, then infinitely malign she sprang forward—"Let's have a look under that cape," she exclaimed lifting the hem gingerly, then drawing back in a kind of bland triumph sneered grimly as one who uncovers a louse.

Perceiving he was unlikely to grow in poetry while my consideration for others was beginning to evolve, I pondered some means of breaking off this engagement I had most likely induced without "hurting" him.

Due to the violent primitivism of my parents' ethics my trend was inevitably towards melodramatic expedients. In chastest terms I allowed him to infer I was no longer a maiden.

Lucas, an agonizing mule, opposed my infallible panacea: "That's no reason for throwing me over," he implored, "the way I see it if you'd *loved* this other fellow you'd have stuck to him—there's nothing to prevent your marrying me," decided this precursor of modernity who, however circumscribed his power of self-expression, was surprised at nothing I said. From his remarks on some best-seller I had read on his recommendation I gathered his idea of the acme of sentiment was to have me for wife and feel terribly nervous while the baby arrived.

Unsuspected an inner self which picks and chooses, wins or loses, unhampered by that program of the practical, began to have its own subconscious reactions to which a pale stranger, broad-shouldered, narrow-hipped, lifting his arms in a white shirt, is a lily on the air of spring swaying from a dark stalk.

"Pull down your skirt chick-a-biddy," said an older girl as the students grouped round the courtyard took their tea out of doors watching a game of tennis.

That sensation in my knees of being exposed to Röntgen rays whenever I sat down was irremediable, however blushingly I tugged the dress I had outgrown. My mother, whose ideal of propriety was a state of living-death, herself imposed upon me an indecorous condition harrowing to my modesty in those days of blue serge bathing suits flopping round ankles.

The head of the stranger under his volleys leaped forward from the lilac tree surrounded by bees ahoneying to drive into mine a pre-impression of that same man in the *men* I was (fated) to love.

His—their—eyes were grey diamonds, the form of irises and lids making them both round and square gave these eyes a superfluity of expression permitting infinite interpretations. He who operated them, as though many faceted they reflected some glow from within, could throw them at will into a dither of benevolent amusement.

The stranger of intense eyes from where I crouched on a stone coping in an effort to telescope my legs under that inadequate skirt appeared from my shame-faced situation ethereal in his height, as someone soaring in an inattainable "beyond" pursuing a planet. Yet in those preliminary years of youth, as in infancy, nothing was out of reach. In the usual way all wishes had of coming true for me he soon became my constant companion.

Irrevocably he drew me as if to a fount of compassion when sauntering along the road I came upon him, his arm again upreaching - - - among the branches of a tree in his front garden.

"That damn dog," he explained, "my cat is in a delicate condition." With an innate gentleness he lifted down the feline body throbbing in its distraught fur.

Holyoak wore a look of mystic dissipation. Ploughed in his army exams, an ex-actor, he had now, on a threat of an aunt to cut him off if he didn't do "something," taken up art photography and rented a studio house to work in near the school. Across the threshold of that little house, through a glass door, I passed into my "other life" of the intuition, whose motivations one never associates with circumstantial reality.

A girl who had been studying so long at the art school she had grown old—Anne was thirty!—at last launching on a career "did" his retouching—a very good sort, she brought to the place a good deal of laughter.

I hung around disoccupied. Capacity for creation steadily drained by the Voice, I was in danger of becoming a chronic onlooker. Over the wall of my rising inhibition, I observed these privileged to be care-free. Yet Anne had a cross-eye, Holyoak constantly gave vent to a comic condemnatory sniff: his comment on life in its essentials.

Not being entirely supine I would try to take council. It was useless. Even a modified allusion to my quandary struck as fantastic those who, whatever their preoccupations, had no conception of what it was to live continually terrified.

"You," Holyoak decided assistingly, "seem to be waiting for something to happen; let me assure you, dear, nothing *ever* happens." My fancy fell to planning government supervision of domestic interiors.

When sympathy did come my way it was for so paltry an assault it did not seem to call for condolence.

It was at a Royal Academy ball. Her perfect skin of a fair rose, in the creamy dress I had bordered with a Greek key pattern in gold, Ida, to whom I had introduced all my friends, bore herself as a slightly cocky empress, bestowing on any man she danced with a smugly disdainful silence.

"She *looks* so magnificent," one confided to me, "I could almost risk another waltz."

I was about to dance with Holyoak. My father, who had accompanied us, approached under his educative scowl.

"Now what sort of a girl are you turning out to be?" He gave me a "dressing down" for taking all the partners for myself and leaving my sister without any.

Holyoak procured a man for Ida and drew me away. He no longer wanted to dance, only to seek some nook of privacy.

"Oh Linda," he said, "my heart aches for you. What you must go through is too horrible, and I mistook you for an unruly daughter— rather talking through your hat; I offer you my abject apology."

Rid of his idea of me as a rebellious adolescent he became associated with me in a tacit affection. Except for the blank intervals when he disappeared into his dark-room, his nearness made the light grow lighter.

For this dreamy kind of man-about-town, the shilling celebrities exhibited in stationers' windows came to life. Marie Tempest with lace parasol sailing into the "photographer's" on the foam of her skirts. Her strict features pearly as her dog collar had an almost superhuman éclat in those days when few but actresses wore cosmetics.

Constance Collier eyed with the centers of sunflowers curtained with lashes, wielding her Greco-Roman curves with slothful graciousness.

He took my photo too—staring at a straight iris. My mother consequently rushed to the art school staging a scene because my shoulder "showed." Brand, a friend of Holyoak's, explained it was only a study in drapery.

It was not only in Holyoak's friends that I caught glimpses of a world which unlike mine did not exist incognito. There was Lawrence Grossmith who had a mind to study a little art appearing round that same Hermes, with the chic negligence of approach then common to characters in musical comedy.

"What a pretty dress!"

To his voice of flippant sophistication I flushed, raw as a wound to a probe, then I noticed he wasn't looking at my dress. So we made friends. At a party for his brother George I met a girl of thistledown, probably his wife, whose incomparable name was being celebrated in a current ditty:

Oh Lydia Flopp, my darling
All the boys will say then
. . . .
Dance and Dance away then . . .

What else remains are the lean lines on the comic-sensitive face of George and Lydia Flopp's squeal of incredulous modesty at a "study" of the model I had first deplored, his virility crammed into a linen bag.

Men proved to be exactly the antidote of misery I had supposed. Beyond the matrix home whose unease was sensible as a prolongation of the crucial vibrations of parturition, one passed within their stabile aura as through gates ajar on liberty. A little breathless with escape, a girl in their company achieved an illusion of sharing in that liberty. It seemed so clear that life for them entailed no anxieties. I was wistfully stimulated by their glorious irresponsibility.

I spent more time alone with men than was compatible to that era. No ruin befell me. In fact the general attitude consisted in an innate assumption of our liliaceous superiority to the soulless Mrs. Grundy's base obsession. Tête-à-tête was defiance of her aged depravity. Of course connected with that group of pals who, though accidentally thrown together might have been assorted by fate for the unity of their deportment, there were men to whom one said with the perspicacity of youth when left to its own initiative, "I should not be *allowed* to sit for my portrait without a chaperone," whereupon beauty would lose its allure.

A swerving sail attached to the skimming acuteness of a steel dragonfly flashing back the sun, Holyoak guiding his bicycle around a curve . . .

Holyoak raising the stoic irony of his face in wonder to a cumulus cloud, the piled anomaly of an illusional massif, its seemingly immovable dominance, the strange conveyance of the eternal in its unlastingness.

Conversely to his descendant softness with the cat a shaft of basic strength ascended from him as he shared with me a half-recognition of supernal forms in this aerial phenomenon.

Aping the enormous beauty of the cloud with the tenuous kaleidoscopy of its myriad whiteness, its occasional arcs of gold, grew an apple-tree laden with blossom; in comparison bleak as china yet of an odor intangible as its prototype above.

I was exalted by my first intimacy with anyone who ever looked up at the sky and only less by the lore he displayed in making an unknown definition with the word "cumulus."

From the brow of the hill road where we stood we descended side by side, still somewhat awed to a valley of big stone-fronted houses. Holyoak shared his with an actor and his wife.

Without entering the house, we passed under the London trees through a gate into the back garden; at the end he had built himself a large music room where he played the organ.

On first arriving, as if the apple blossom showered over a wall, he covered my face with rueful kisses, then dashed to the organ and began to play music I could not yet interpret, so probably Bach. Later his actor tenant came in and on seeing my slowly fading blush the arc of his eyebrows became that of a man whose interests are involved.

Thousands of miles away in a warehouse is stored a cabinet containing a secret drawer. There lies a small snapshot of a lean man on an organ bench. His eyes almost white with a dreamy dilation, seated the way he was when he veered round to talk to me. Holyoak appeared to me at the time to emerge from a far-removed Merlin forest of reed pipes uplifting the ceiling.

"Queer, the things that happen to one as a child," he was saying. "I used to lie in bed staring across the room at a speck in the air; after a while it began to rotate, grew larger, drew nearer and gathering terrific speed dilated to a whizzing planet of luminous fuzz until on reaching my eyes it burst . . . ."

The tacit implication of a separative wall became so embedded in our native unity, we waived all further kisses as irrelevant. For me unquestioning, untroubled by it, the vaguely intuited barrier was abstract as an Euclidean theorem.

A supreme, an ultimate kiss I only took part in by proxy. A bunch of us were twittering "at the photographer's," youth on a glorious early summer day setting out from the city. Holyoak and I were cycling down to lunch with the actor's wife, who had taken a place in the country. Before we left I almost came upon him sitting on the edge of a medieval chair, his feet stretched out before him doing an ecstatic little tap-dance on their own as, looking like a puppy who fancies he is worrying an angel's wing, he kissed the lining of my jacket.

In this man's presence my surroundings resumed their erstwhile aspect of the miraculous. A setting for an absolute contentment happened to be the parlor of a wayside pub where we stopped for refreshment. The confining expanse of marbled yellow wall-paper, the vinegar moat of a glass fly-trap became Empyrean, whose sublimated glow gilded an all-inclusive precinct of quietude.

The invasive hush of the hot sun heightened by the aspiring buzz of metallic blue-bottles passed for the cumulative "music of the spheres," the very fly-blow on advertisements for ale formed seals on a pact of peace.

House-flies drowning in the acid deception of their ideal did not disturb the equipoise of my serene emotion. I would not fathom their pain. They dropped. Struggling illustrations of the words that died on Holyoak's lips.

I was not to recover the happiness attained in this bizarre harbor until seventeen years later, riding a wooden animal on Coney Island.

Pleasant reception by my hostess, Mrs. Peck, was of short duration. Chatting amicably on our arrival she suddenly changed to an alarming replica of my mother when Pappa brought home the bracelets.

"Who gave you that?" she screamed pointing to a blue bead I had laughingly attached to my person when Holyoak had handed it on to me; one of a scatter of surplus relics some professor returned from excavating in Egypt had divided among a few friends.

Entirely bewildered I recognized the splotch of purple creeping up her jaw as she turned on Holyoak. His brother, Ian, a house guest, drew me by the sleeve. "You and I are going for a nice little ride," he explained as he shoved me through the door.

So it turned out, in that era, men also to a certain degree could be ruined, by getting too inextricably involved with another man's wife.

This I was learning from Holyoak's brother, fuming on a stile in view of a meadow of blazing buttercups.

"There's nothing to be done," he raged, "we, family, friends, all of us have moved heaven and earth to get him out of it. With no effect. It's his damnable notion of chivalry 'the horrible thing' whatever it's called," hissed Ian, who, famous in the world of art, insured his bachelor-hood with transient retinues of professional beauties.

Ian calmed himself it seemed by laying one chaste finger on my throat, which may have been cool to the touch, and keeping it there. "Of course," he mused, "you're divinely lovely but what can that mean to me, Linda? You're one of those girls strictly reserved for marriage . . . . poor dear," he chuckled in commiseration.

The clang of sunshine on the golden weeds ringing in the brain, he again became restless on Holyoak's account.

"The pity of it," he muttered grimly. "Do you know how they get them?" inquiring of me. "They *nurse* them.

"Hol fell ill . . . 'Oh woman in our hours of . . . . .' a man's pretty helpless pinned down to a bed . . . . . and Peck's so noble! Believes in letting everyone live their own lives, just for the sake of appearances he's got half Hol's home."

Mrs. Peck does not reappear and how we fed or returned is a blank. My mother received a letter from her asking if she was aware of my visit, she being the last person in the world to encourage a daughter to do things "behind her mother's back." Amazingly she saw nothing odd in this communication and, delighted with an audience for a "gesture of dignity," replied with "surprise" and the assurance I had had her permission. It would not occur to her that a Mrs. Anything would have male guests to lunch.

The next time I contacted him, once more at the curve of the road, Holyoak as he floated off his bicycle said:

"Linda, I have something to tell you."

I could *see* the barrier overthrown. His voice was weary with liberation, an unfathomable gravity took the place of the quizzical fatalism that had marked it hitherto.

"Linda, my dear," he said, looking as if he had by superhuman ordeal recreated this world, "I have left Mrs. Peck. I didn't dream a woman could be like that. —And you were so kind to her."

Jubilant on receiving the abstract impression of the barrier having vanished, "But Holyoak," I answered, clutching at the first words to rise from the subconscious, "that is of no interest to me."

Queerly enough it was true.

I might always have known from that "talk," which for self-protection I had formed the habit not to heed, of his so sturdy liaison; yet my heart in electing him, somewhat shopworn among other men who were fresher, younger, responded to the nameless essentials forming the structure of his gracious spirit; this, the faint bestiality of Mrs. Peck's underlip had never entered, the contents of her corsets dissolved on its frontiers. It was common in that "suggestive era" for the lure of the flesh to be baited with some reminder of its purported vileness.

So of that nucleus in Holyoak to which my affection was grafted I was stirred to not an iota of jealousy; he existed, for me, bare of entanglements as Truth.

His announcement, drawing her for a moment into relationship with himself, overwhelmed me with a sudden modesty. Holyoak being the man to the latent woman in me never invoked the spontaneous improprieties I had voiced in my neutral association with Lucas, with whom I was free to use the little I had of analytic brain. To Holyoak I reacted in unadulterated maidenliness, of a maid who flees in confusion from a man about to "declare himself."

Only on reaching home did my consciousness develop a fleeting impression of a Holyoak struck by lightning, apparently mumbling, "and you of all women—you were so kind to her—"

Conversantly enfolded in their lining I had been incapable of apprehending the surface effect of words which common sense on coming into action reversed to a callous snub, unwarrantable from a girl who had so obviously to Holyoak attained in his companionship to the sumptuous well-being of "affinity."

Remorseful as a pugilist who should unwittingly hit below the belt, I decided in a flash of anticipatory "feminism" to make amends. I confided to my girlfriend Eva Knight, who quite agreed with me that the only thing left to be done was to march bravely in upon the shattered Holyoak, who must have deduced from my seeming volte-face I had unpreparedly discovered him in the shocking light of a "fallen man," and explain how, in spite of verbal discrepancies, loyally I loved him.

Her hair braided in a coronet above a complexion frequent at the time; it looked as if greasy glass let through the burst capillaries due to violent soaping; the pallid fawns and blues of a delicate constitution spread like a pale bruise over really classic features in the premature shrinkage of a woman whose glands have not been stimulated; Eva Knight had a fundamental bond with myself.

"It's fearful," she had whispered to me, tense with hatred, "sometimes I become aware of my own voice. It sounds like 'hers' and I want to commit suicide." Her mother also stickled for the moralities. She prevented Eva from marrying the man she loved, insisting she was forfeited to another who having been occasionally her partner at tennis she accused her daughter of "leading on." Eva's loved one went into a decline and died. Eva had "taken up art," living with the tiny fluttering woman, alone as did so many echoing their astral murderer.

An ill-tempered maid from a briefly opening front door informed us Mr. Holyoak was dangerously ill, the doctors forbade all visitors.

The Peck tenancy complication prevented any friendly assault on the premises, getting a note to the invalid or even news of him, all my friends having left London for the summer holidays.

Holyoak's front door closed on that period in which Nature allows innumerable maidens some inviolable appeal luring destiny to accord them whatever they desire.

"I'm not interested, God," one may say to destiny while it is still not too late for Love to antidote the parental poisons and misery appear from the sudden altitudes of liberation a bizarre ephemera for joy to laugh over . . . .

A hideous instantaneousness has marked the shuttle of my life between light and darkness. On returning from my frustrated pilgrimage, I immediately found myself imprisoned. My mother, who had staged her latest fall under a "marital blow" upon the cold stone of the hall floor, had miscarried her only child to be favored by fortune. The tradition of filial duty to a sickbed in spite of the hiring of trained nurses entailed hours of mute reception of violent abuse. Finally breaking down I appealed to the doctor, "If you could only get her to exercise a little self-control there would be less danger . . . ."

The doctor, taut in the usual reaction to my helpful suggestions, pierced me with a frozen eye, "*You* are *unable* to *appreciate*

your mother," and turning his back on me left me with that exqui-
sitely modulated voice of his patient echoing in his ears. So shy, soft
as a distant bird call, sweet as the breath of flowers. That voice of
an innocent caught in the talon of a monster, wondering what has
hurt her.

Although we were forbidden to leave the house, a widowed companion was engaged to chaperone us, presumably for our social en-
gagements with the walls. She required quite a lot of attention with
the smelling salts, subsequent to a remark made by my father to the
effect that "no man would want to marry a widow . . . damaged goods."
I noticed, during my father's disintegration, the occasional letting
through of an unseemly remark reflecting the unexpected agony of
his respectability and an increasing obtuseness to any sensitivity but
his own. This craven neurotic was almost impossible to relate to the
glorious enthusiast I had glimpsed in my early childhood.

In "cleaving only unto" his spouse, he had undergone a gradual
vulgarization in listening only to her discourse. I could not reproach
him for at length becoming something at sometimes rather awkward
to have for a pappa. Piquantly, neither he nor my sisters bowing to
her as a moral preceptor exceptionally dynamic, as they could see,
ever suspected her ultimate significance as a blast to caress. So Pappa
when he bullied me at a ball, functioning impartially as ethical men-
tor, did not perceive that Ida was "behaving unpleasantly," the pleasant having so long been hidden from him.

This form of ethical regulation of youthful error to which his wife
accustomed him . . . and he had extremely modified it, he supposed
must be native to familial publicity. Too deeply troubled he had not
noticed her meteoric morals only struck in the absence of any strangers whose approval she sought.

My parents' cross-purposes in regard to a match for me had come
to a crisis. While my father tortured in anxiety over the unprom-
ising fate of the beautiful daughters of a mis-polarized marriage,
Mother, strategic whenever she found an occasion, would make a
move. Fearing a possible denouement with Lucas, she had, he told

me phlegmatically, sidled up to him and cooed, *"You* don't want to marry Linda, you should marry a *nice* girl." Again, seizing on flowers he had sent me from his hot-house, with the flair of the sadist for involving the sentiments of youth in reactions of disgust, she sniffed in mockery over their immaculate scents.

"A cat's been on them."

At last Father, his opponent actually prone, gathered what wits remained to him, in a supreme effort to save me from "those good-for-nothing-artists." Having once espied me escorted home by Lucas, who compared to us was extremely wealthy though less so than the Holyoak set, he vented upon me his agony of apprehension with the inspiriting adage, "Give a dog a bad name and it will stick."

Subtle as a fox on its last run to cover, he wrote the British Consulate in Munich asking him to recommend a family who would take a paying guest arriving to attend the Woman's Academy.

The result sublimely resuscitated his initial ambition for us. The list submitted by the consulate was headed by the address of a Baron and Baroness.

My suggestion that any reputable family would insist on knowing who—whatever—I was, my father ignored.

I realize now that the fact of his being in trade provided his wife, once she received an inkling of social gradation, with an absolute warranty to martyrize us. Also she seemed to ruminate her own "rightness" like a sacred cow to whom alone were the theological mysteries revealed. She attained to actual magnificence in settlement of our discussions of an inscrutable God.

"Tosh," said she, "God is as easy to understand as this"—picking one up and tilting it to and fro on the table cloth—"spoon."

There are people who become important through wielding a censorship while cartoons of nagging wives are considered innocuous. Women whose appearance is so neglected it destroys, at *least,* the digestive system are presented as the protagonist of a little normal fun. Even as these my mother had made a clearance of Father's early friends. Their lavish sociability, their wedding-marquees, their expensive presents blushed out like transient fireworks in the chill of her unformulated unguessable social ideal until we came to a point where we saw no one at all.

From one of those light-hearted families she spurned because it was Jewish a brand-new Lord of the British realm arose. Whenever I hear a revival of "Ta-ra-ra Boom-de-ay" it recalls the shock of my return as a small child from counting the crystal buttons on the plum cloth encasing the wasp-like waist of a Gluckstein girl to the abominable bosom of Nemesis. Rebecca still leaned toward me out of that tune of elative stampede, her gentle oriental eyes under raven ringlets, a Victorian picture of the Song of Songs as the maternal solo, my first glimpse of anti-Semitism, leapt upon Father from behind our front door. Then quivering with a dashed-out laughter, sent up to bed, I passed at the turn of the stairs the point at which our good fortune began to dwindle. The following morning all that was left of Father— he was due for a conference on stocking the markets of the world with British cloth—was a scraped nerve. It impressed me as an interrogation mark tied in a knot.

And at the end of a week, we were left in the room of a sheeted survivor who had also passed a turning point of what Doctors diagnosed as peritonitis. There was no predicting in this system of lashing the emotions to serial crises, where, in congenitally healthy people, the bodily reaction would revolt.

That had been a good while ago. Now Father's social outlet was reduced to entertaining his loyal Italian barber; in the haven of the bathroom he chatted despairingly, draped in an enormous Turkish towel.

Set adrift from his concrete world of "business with a future" by his wife's ideal of ignoring it, "My husband is *connected* with trade," she would reply to all inquiry in a clearly regal voice, he endeavored to evolve, in void, a suitable impressionism of contact, arguing to himself thus: if Linda arrives with a paid chaperone, the Baroness will figure these are respectable people - - - of means.

The widowed companion became quite cheerful at the prospect of an unexpected trip abroad.

10

Along the broad white streets of Munich, the Baron's Vandyke beard opened and shut as he waved his arms about. In vocal frenzy, he rattled off the multiple titles attached to royal persons for my chaperone Mrs. Rayburn. Preceding them, his consort waddled along with me, pausing every time he stopped to point out a *Palast;* her alpaca skirt stretched to the limit, she was presumably on the brink of giving birth.

"My husband has asked Mrs. Rayburn what your father is, but—"

"Oh do tell me," I implored, curious yet going hot and cold at the thought of my mother's secretive disgust for the occupations of her whole family. "What is he?" The Baroness suppressing her surprise, "she could only say he directs numerous subordinates and is obviously a man of importance, don't *you* know?"

"My mother does not permit the subject to be mentioned"—I answered grandly.

The Baroness definitely confronted with a problem paused awhile. "Your Herr Pappa," she decided, "must be Purveyor to the Court, that comes nearest to an acceptable solution." "*Donnerwetter,*" she added, "and one would take you for a princess."

After the imposing Mrs. Rayburn returned to England, the processional grandure of our reception changed to family encirclement in which three or four anemic children struggled with life in the unpredictable shifty atmosphere of debt.

In his youth the Baron, it appeared, had fallen on his head. The Baroness had had a Mamma. She evoked her in brilliant vignettes, perched on four-in-hands being doused with champagne by swanky officers. - - - *"Reizend"*—she nodded reminiscently.

With this woman who equated her husband's unnatural excitability with an exophthalmic calm of China-blue eyes, I exchanged confidences. Her poker stare accepted all my miseries, while her own communications as to the nullity of conjugal bliss coincided with the outstanding opposition to the cheerful resources of life I listlessly attributed to adults in general. The story going round Munich at the time, of a lady who sampled illicit love only to exclaim: "Why it's just as dull as marriage," did not incite me to any heretical speculation; universally, human sentiment clings to implied mysteries in the face of factual report.

Going through the gestures of taking me to her imperturbable heart with the gentle sloth of a ruminant—caring for nothing, never did she show sign of rebellion—her voiceless putting-up-with-circumstances stilled me as if I had entered the silence after a storm. Adopting me as a daughter she was bent on spoiling to make up for my filial misadventures: "You shall call me Mammalie," she said. There was a certain pancake she would toss for me whenever I demanded. Otherwise, delighted at choosing my own delicacies, I practically lived on bread and leberwurst. Meanwhile my sentimental monotones on the piano changed from "In the Gloaming" to "The Blue Danube."

Before long I found her receiving the first of her very rare visitors. On entering the room I was eyed by a female with so exact a replica of Mrs. Peck's expression when she espied the bead, I retreated in haste not without subconsciously noting how the patient gaze of my consolatory foster-mother only slightly modified became hard-boiled.

"She called about her husband. He got involved with a very pretty nursery governess," the Baroness later announced, not explained. "Her parents who wished her to finish her studies sent her to us 'au pair.' The wife supposed you were her," she mentioned casually.

I did not make out why the complainant was kept in the dark as to my identity. It must have been convenient to camouflage the actual location of that mislaid girl.

That same evening a young diplomat dined with us. The following day I received by express from this stranger an offhand "command" to meet him at some notorious night restaurant. Utterly bewildered, I showed it to my hostess who, stonily placative, endorsed my resentment with the enigmatic remark, "Bad move. Too fast a worker."

Soon there appeared another young man, a student of law from the Netherlands; somewhat in the same capacity as myself—a paying guest - - - for dinner. A God-send I thought for Mammalie in the precarious state of her finances.

It was noticeable how little this "Alexander" had to do in the evenings when the meal was over; how suddenly the Baronial couple contracted appointments away from home. Left to entertain him, I was frightened by his crescent gallantry. I felt I had escaped Bedlam to fall into a trap. My ever-watchful mother desiring her legitimate share in the grandure Father had procured for me had written the Baroness at great length setting out in detail my disobedience, my strongheadedness. Exhorting her to exercise the utmost severity should I show the slightest tendency to behavior contrary to her wishes. A letter which cast almost a radiance over the inflated pink flesh and mouse-colored plaited crown of a petrified Gretchen, it placed me unconditionally at her disposal.

"What a woman," commented the Baroness—"only to complaints from her own child would she turn a deaf ear."

Horror of a calamity my parents, obsessed by morality, had tried to avert by frightening me into utter subservience to the dictates of others was steadily developing into a terror that if anyone I disliked insisted upon my doing anything I was averse to I would automatically comply; so systematically they had obfuscated my instinct of self-preservation.

However it was not yet I should reach the maturation of an engrafted anxiety. At first over-stimulated apprehensions disperse before the comparative insignificance of actual crises. When Alexander, acutely molded in evening dress, stood before me with a pistol, about to blow his brains out should I find no use for his passion, I said, "Shoot."

Anxieties flourished in my louche situation. Complexes were not yet public property. Neurosis, in those days, so very much resembled an unhappiness screwed to the pitch of pain.

Having been given some white liqueur which almost blew my head off, I sneaked the bottle to my room, supposing that should I swallow the whole contents it would kill me. But after a long battle of the breath with an explosive suffocation, although the liquid dynamite had blown my body to a numb rigidity, my eyes survived.

They did not look out of my head. In a visual advance to some distance before me they played in strange aliveness with my reflection in a mirror the other side of the room.

Over there my comatose face endowed with an ectoplasmic facility for transfiguration escaped the conventions of a normal retina in streamers of distorted flesh. Its structure accentuated to stalagmites of bone thrust beyond the glazy surface of the looking glass—it drew back its lips in the bray of moronic fiends—Poked and spread—dripped in self-dissolution from a thorn—recomposed as innocuous sleeping beauty, to burst and fling its India-rubber stuffing in a crescendo of grimaces to the corners of the frame.

Throughout the night the chameleon mime put on the illimitable rictus of human sensibility revealed by the fluoroscope of an eye in fixation.

In the morning there I was, safe and sound, my anxiety intact.

Utterly confused by the persistent evidence that all my parents feared for me, in their ignorance they forced upon me, a desperate sense of having no one to turn to had been a major factor in my uneasiness. Now, all at once, I did find someone to turn to: Alexander.

To my timely advantage the current distinction among womankind was clear-cut. Apart from the ugly and such as were carnally achievable there existed—angels.

"You are an angel," said Alexander when I saw him again; gravely affectionate as men were wont to be when they had just "found me out." "An angel," he repeated warningly, "who has flown into a wasp's nest. Linda look at this." It was the Baron's advertisement for male diners, in an evening paper, offering the bait of an "English Miss."

"Thank God you've got *me* to come to dinner." It was quite worth his while to watch over me he explained, "I'd rather talk to you than any man—you're so damned intelligent."

It was through this most unexpected comradeship I gained the experience of a continental "man of the world."

My association with a wealthy sensualist with that face which only takes form atop of good tailoring would have been the rather usual expedient of chance for lack of any social scope including anyone congenial to me had it not been for the unbiased Christianity of his attitude towards prostitutes. For this I found myself indebted to him for an ethical relief substantiating our intimacy.

—o-o-O-o-o—

Ever since finding myself alone somewhere around Piccadilly, I had straitened in an indefinable grip of conscience. It had been while looking for a bus after visiting a gallery with students who lived in an opposite direction that, halted by a tug at my coat, I made out, a little above my knee, an infant face.

Floated up from the shadows entangled with feet its unutterable beauty was strangely divided between the awful purity of undernourished babyhood and willfully applied daubs of soot. It was the fifth of November. The little flower of poverty held forth the cup of his hand and wheeled, "I'se de Guy."

Immediately after, I approached the only woman passing in the crowd to ask the time.

Her eyes were unmentionable.

"I beg your pardon - - -" eyes of defense expressionless as a barricade. Whatever lay siege to them from without was as nothing compared to her own brain battering on the back of them. Dead eyes promenading. Why, they are in hell, I thought, surprised at my sudden acceptance of that drastic locality. Not the time, but myself they measured as momentarily I came between her and the rest of the world.

"Could you tell me - - - " I smiled into those unflinching eyes of a lady ashamed. Her face soared. In a gust of glad excitement she panted the hour, handing me half past five as a precious keepsake out of the past - - -

"Injustice" kept knocking at my head on the rattle of the horse bus. "What's the matter with women—the matter with women that they *allow* one of themselves to look like that. How cruel that a streetwalker should be so pleased when I ask her the time." And these complementary specters of a London street fused in my indignation.

"I'se de Guy," said the prostitute.

"I beg your pardon." Oh, I beg your pardon.

So in Alexander, though I never surmounted my neutrality to the sophisticate commonplace of his *mondaine* features, I found a moral spaciousness soothing to my obsession of an enigmatic sex-class culpability toward that woman on Piccadilly.

Even now I would not care to have to look into those eyes of an English "professional" reflecting the sky-line of Victorian seemliness.

Setting out for the holidays with the genius of certain Teutons for putting one off one's ease my hosts found satisfaction in pointing out to fellow-passengers that I was English. At that time the *Buchhändler's* windows were decorated predominately with Queen Victoria's naked posterior. Throughout our journey personal insults referring to the Boer War mingled with something for which my father was paying heavily as it dripped down my skirt from the baby Baroness I had to carry.

In the Bavarian Alps where gathering thunders bowled the panoramic peaks—infinitesimal in isolation a stroke of whitewash marked the primitive hunting lodge in which we lived.

Crossing the river I spent my lonely time on miles of flowering weeds; discriminating among the various contours of their green leaves I drew only those which like beautiful bodies diverged from their structural similars in some esoteric ritual of line. The heraldic curves of giant dandelions, the crowded constellations of the umbel . . . . .

Spasmodically a rural social life, we had three scattered neighbors, dragged me in every direction through fervid sun and crushed pine by beaten tracks half breaking off the hill-sides to distant objectives of identical beer.

Seated at high wooden tables grey with dried rain on their atrophied legs, the Baroness, her stare become hypnotic, ceaselessly complimented me on being a lovely "vampire" fatal to men.

The Baron occasionally started shouting about crowned heads but nobody bothered to take him up.

His uncle, a bald eagle specimen of the *"vieux marcheur,"* came to visit us. Also hard up, unlike his nephew he was very much all there, punctuating with his flashing monocle stories which escaped all risk through their openness.

Entirely at home among the peacefully neglected children in the bare wooden hut, these Barons so "pot-luck" compared to England's were of historical lineage whose glory had lasted until so recently it must only have been cut short by that fall on its head. They reached the apex of their alpine enjoyment behind the terrace restaurant overlooking the Starnberger See. Creeping up on the line of "aborts" in the garden to guffaw at the ladies of the party as they stepped out. The cannonade that, to my English aversion, echoed along the serried enclosures of those shrines of Nature could only have emanated from the most martial of races, the chemical compounds of their very nutriment manufactured explosives from Pilsner and Sauerkraut.

The Starnberger See held the bluest water I have ever seen, an ultra-sapphire slab, after hours of our libations on its shores under a vast sunset of incendiary warfare in Heaven it changed in all its magnitude to opal.

"You're so sure of yourself," the Baroness was taunting me. "You think no man can resist you."

My only mention of men having been the sad exile from an idealist adoration of Holyoak to whom, I confided to her, my everlasting fidelity was dedicated, she must have intended this remark to be propelled in the direction of a feminine offensive in which she hoped I should be robbed of my defenses.

Following this invocation of an irrational vanity, my descent from the mountain was arranged.

—o-o-O-o-o—

A fair journey from our speck of domestication in an almost unpopulated valley, on a high road bare to the sun, we called on the heiress of a stone quarry. She was deformed. Had been married for her heritage. Somehow the Baroness conveyed me into her arid parlor, like a stick through bars to enrage a moping ape.

Prominent in the room, great and square stood an empty white porcelain stove reflecting the hot glass of the windows, equally unnecessary was our conversation; it seemed sufficient for the Baroness to have "shown" me to her . . .

Below in the quarry where iron bins ran through white grit on a little railway we found the Baron planning to climb the Krottenkopf with the poor woman's husband and his brother. Two short men with tepid blue eyes thrown up at the foot of boulders and covered with a froth of stone, they were baked grey in their scrubby colorless hair.

"*Morgen,*" gesticulated the Baron elatedly. "*Es ist erreicht.*"

"Hush," urged his wife glancing at me.

Preparatory to the ascent we all slept in another hunting lodge much higher up. At four a.m. we were ready to start. First the Baron dropped out. I had not wanted to join in an expedition too onerous for one whose brain worried so "rapidly" that it sapped my physical resistance; but the Baroness fortified with my mother's authorization forced me to "do as I was told." Pushing me out onto the mountainside in the pitch-dark after the quarry owners, and:

"I'm not coming," she told them, her eyes slamming with the door.

These strangers, awkward in their mystification, were yet very considerate. They showed me how to climb. Trudging, clinging as the air lit up, we rose and rose to, incredibly, arrive at the top of Krottenkopf.

Here as if the whole world had covered itself with ageless excrescences, sight was outdistanced by range beyond range of shattered multiple cones. Sharp as armament, caressed by mist aretes and crevasses glittering in the icy whiteness of forenoon heat. Recognizably populous with an unconvincing absence of mythical beings - - - - one could have sworn these inverted avalanches of eternal adamance were not inanimate, so irresistibly they moved in upon recesses of memory stored with mountain folklore . . . . .

The little husband mysteriously, I could not know what the Baron may have implied on the eve of our setting forth, seemed somehow to have been allotted a leading role, probably wondering what his wife would say, he appeared both desirous and sulky. Whenever we relaxed our strenuous progress, the brother would stand aside watching his indecision as to what was expected of him, in, particular for their class, this bawdy situation. They knew at least I had had no wish to climb a mountain.

Such glorious outburst of the Alps in a diamond morning, the comparative ease of descent, our relief at regaining normal levels after such unexpected elevation in isolation of the ill-assorted made us almost companionable, we returned with the triumphant yodels of accomplished mountaineers. Wistfully, as though in reparation of misjudgment, they bowed abashed over the formality of kissing my hand.

One other early morning expedition, not at all ambiguous, was our drive in the forester's two-horse brake to Oberammergau. After the hush of forest roads awaiting dawn. The modern sheltered pen for an international crowd was inconducive. The chorus of four cornered women stood in a row like Uhlans in curtains. The wood of the "policeman's rattle" used for breaking the bones of the crucified thieves in their rosy cotton tights was over-new as on a bazaar counter. "That rattle," the Baroness remarked, "is the most effective instrument of anti-Semitism." The show, to me, seemed preposterous. I was later to know what it should have been like watching a de Max miracle play on a laic stage.

That day in Oberammergau, Judas, owing to the intervention of Nature, turned out to be the hero, in saving the aesthetic situation. As he came on for his lonely act, the skies darkened, a wind blew up whipping his remorse to elemental drama. Tossing his full long hair and his Roman garment across his staggering self-accusation in magnificent accident.

Had it not been for this sudden change in the weather, I should have seen nothing to prepare me for my hallucinatory meeting with the holy family.

The Baron being the *personnage* in our district was notified by the "*Wirt*" that the actors in the passion play were stopping at his *Gasthaus* on one of their days off and he wished to present them to us.

To adjust my Victorian eyes to those passing guests restrained by heredity tradition to an atavism of handsome sanctity, I cast off centuries.

In the incomparable glow of oil lamps diffusing mellow clues to eroded wall and blackened rafter the jeweled flesh of their goodly medieval German faces leapt in defined portions from the bronze matrix of the profound chiaroscuro of an old master.

Leaning this way and that, spontaneously biblical in composition, they ate at a long narrow table. The parting above Mary's brow lay quiet as if smoothed by hands in prayer. Christ Jesus shred an onion with the gesture of sacrament. Above a virgin beard rested the saintly eyes of St. John the Baptist in humble tranquility. Nobly handling their peasant knives, they might have been hewing out of themselves cathedral monuments of those they represented. One even detected a grave angelic chord of their "*Guten Abend meine Herrschaften.*"

Christmas came, the Baroness in lymphatic calm, as if in mating she had contracted an opposite effect of that cephalic crash, came as near to her spouse as her belly allowed her; drinking together from a loving cup under the candles winking on the tree. With no emotion they observed their annual sentimental rites. Alexander and I were their audience.

Now mysteriously lightened of debt, daily they touted me to lunch at a fashionable restaurant. In we trooped. First the gesticulator—the belly—myself, blushing in the exhibition.

Poor Mammalie; her inflation was trompe-l'oeil. On my arrival I had shuddered at the thought of her delivery until she explained her permanent appearance to be due to the ignorance of a doctor who had "not" done "something" when the Baby Baroness was born.

In view of my childhood horror—and the fact that expectant mothers modestly disappeared from circulation, the corsets then in vogue boosting their generate load to an unshapeliness too awful to contemplate—going about with her "did something" to one's virginal aplomb.

Led to a table, the Baron, as was the custom, presented himself before taking his seat, "*Freiherr von*" . . .

Sword-slashed men who had acquired in duels of honor the faces of seamed potatoes clicked their heels before him. Then, after introducing his wife; with a flourish, "*Die Miss.*"

"*Gnädiges Fräulein,*" click, "surely this is Cléo de Mérode? Liane de Pougy?" they inquired.

Whatever my sponsors' expectations, the only person I decided to speak to there was a well-known waitress whose intimate tragedies I had learned from Alexander. Inwardly I was evolving a weird strictly personal form of feminism of which the militant aspect consisted in being peculiarly benign to any woman who had been "pushed." Mitzi, pretty and pale under her pompadour responded intuitively with sweet welcome.

Came Carnival. My faithful guardian, Alexander, initiated me to the celebration of *Fasching*. As we galloped along, the folded red of his Neapolitan woman's head-dress, the startling black of my velvet knickers had almost the same tone-value as Masqueraders the other side of the Platz, so clear was the cold atmosphere. The colored shower of confetti on newly fallen snow made game of the Impressionist Pissarro; providing a *subject* matter to *express* his technique.

For that long-ago Carnival, Munich seemed, in seismic festivity, to have thrown all its citizens onto the streets in travesty. The crowd was flamboyant.

We dined in the charming retreat of the Vier Jahreszeiten and ended the night watching the "live for the moment" turbulence in the Café Luitpold. In counter-action Alexander became seriously anxious as to his future. He asked me to marry him.

When I got home, Mammalie had retired. I sat in the dark on the end of her bed relating our adventures when, bursting through the door, loud as a braying ass, the tall Baron, beside himself with excitement reiterated, "Ha ha ha - - - ha ha - - -." He said they had been in the Café. *I* was there—they never stepped foot inside the door—ha ha ha!

"Hush," said the Baroness pointing me out.

"But Mammalie," I exclaimed, as he beat a retreat. "Whatever is he so happy about?"

"Na-nu," she answered patting my shoulder pacifically, "one pays no attention to him."

Drowning whatever cerebral harmony Nature had intended for me the record of the Voice playing on my mind periodically accumulated such confusion it exceeded my capacity. At this point in endurance, I would receive a blow on the brain and sink into a slumbrous coma.

On awakening—I felt relieved—as one beginning life afresh—Gradually the painful dissonance returned.

At last, receiving a peevish letter from my father, I discovered the cause of the danger I ran. He complained of my writing him nothing but nonsense, descriptions of Oberammergau "angels" tumbling in the hay. He sent the Baroness, at her request three hundred pounds to buy the luxurious outfit I required for the round of social gayeties I was now enjoying under her aegis—and I had never even mentioned it! My parents in their distrust of their offspring seemed to take for granted the blanket innocence of the adult.

I had only the vaguest conjecture as to how their getting me into "trouble" would have prevented my father discovering the deflection of his money. In those days a girl who mislaid her maidenhood was promptly let out on the streets, without a farthing, by her family—perhaps it would be presumed the visionary finery had gone with me. But how to explain the "showing" of me to the quarry heiress—obviously an angry wife had played a role in the episode of the student governess. The "good idea" stiffens with the backing of a precedent. Of course! She could be depended on to "publish" a downfall of which the Baroness must appear unaware.

Had Alexander not brought me the dinner ad and even at that been forced to delicately indicate its implication, my uneasy intuition would have sunk into the bed-rock of my anxiety complex, and becoming part of it, persuade me with that recorded "Voice" my suspicion of Mammalie arose from my own shortcoming.

Sharing with my parents the prevalent assumption that any couple of opposite sex, if alone together, must automatically come to a clinch, notwithstanding the large percentage of people in that era so fundamentally inhibited any primitive gesture was almost impossible for them; she might have spared herself her mystification as she watched Alexander come to dinner month in, month out with no dubious breaks in my unruffled catch and return of his friendly teasing, spared herself her inward exasperation when a light-hearted yodel concluded her desperate expedient: *two* potential violators on a dark mountain; if only she had reflected that *no* financial complications whatever could have induced me to cut short my year's respite from the Voice. Mammalie may have been "shady." Never did I hear her utter a violent word.

"We did not tell you," said the Baroness. "We thought it *better* so." She referred almost shyly to what she had accomplished for me in winning that cheque from my father.

"Indeed," I assented amiably. "You are now in a position to give me a latch-key."

My life henceforth could run its average course as a student of the art *Verein* which should have sufficed to rid me of a dejected sense of inhabiting a psychic house of ill-fame; of, wherever I went, being offered to the first comer. But a long fermenting urge to proclaim myself voluntarily unseductive came to a head in so clownish a gesture, that, had it not "worked," one must fail to attribute to it the sublimated rationality of most nonsensical impulses:

I bought a clay pipe.

The scandal invoked for me, unprecedently reformed, turned on the Baron and Mammalie. The consul who had furnished their address was hilarious to behold me, flaunting the outrageous purity of that penny pipe under *Bayerische* colors, the blue and white striped awning of an open tram.

The Baroness, I had demoted to landlady, the Baron, a cringy old man they had presented to me as (the then so youthful) "Marconi" and his huge beetle-browed wife who saved the lump sugar in cafés, stuffing it into her beaded reticule as she rose from the table joined hands and encircled me singing:

"Du bist Verrückt mein Kind
Du musst nach Berlin"

They threw back their palms before the impossible. "An empty pipe, between the lips of a raving beauty."

I preferred to appear as an amateur lunatic rather than an amateur baggage.

Trying to work I found myself incapable of sustained effort under the most efficient system. Angelo Jank had us draw life-size one's point of view taken from the other end of the studio; one had to carry each stroke of form in one's head while crossing to an easel placed up close to the model. At first go, intensely enthusiastic over what I was doing, he declared himself interested to watch what would be the outcome of such extraordinary talent. A new problem, a new environment could always stimulate me to incipient achievement. As I became "accustomed" the same obfuscation beset me. "It's like soap," Jank at last complained, bewildered.

Recreation—
Studios—rooftops—garden restaurants—Tingle-Tangles—at one of these art cabarets producing the compositions of the ultra-modern I heard a song:

"Ich war ein Kind von fünfzehn Jahren,
Ein reines, unschuldsvolles Kind,
Als ich zum erstenmal erfahren,
Wie süß der Liebe Freuden sind.

Er nahm mich um den Leib und lachte
Und flüsterte: O welch ein Glück!
Und dabei bog er sachte, sachte
Mein Köpfchen auf das Pfühl zurück.

Seit jenem Tag lieb' ich sie alle,
Des Lebens schönster Lenz ist mein;
Und wenn ich keinem mehr gefalle,
Dann will ich gern begraben sein."

Samovars—an island fête—drifting to music across a twilit lake under Chinese lanterns strung from bamboos on a great barge draped with rich brocades—the nocturnal picnic under the ilex and my glimpse of a notorious nymph—heroine of the shocking novel of the moment in which the complacent author *watched* his I seem to remember pregnant mistress sell his pregnant wife a hat. Today a lyrical family name recurring in the newspapers recalls that ostracized scion, the fair *Gräfin,* superbly wan, bearing back to the barge at dawn her love-child asleep against the shift of red "art muslin" appended to her etiolate skin. Its trailing hem was sodden in the mud of the shore.

The rehearsal of *Lebendige Bilder* at the *Frauenverein*—myself, picked as the ideal Madonna by the respectable against the Baron's Café acclaiming me as a reigning Parisian Courtesan, perched on a tall wooden structure nursing a dummy in my lap. The lamp lashed to my waist to shed the light of the Holy Babe from under my veils bursts into flame, the committee of ladies vanishes, the janitress in the nick of time cutting me free with her kitchen knife lifts me down, dashing the lamp into the courtyard as it explodes.

Reflecting on my extraordinary calm in this and similar tight corners, I concluded that as the breaking up of the normal condition, which for the average person is security, occasions shock, so for the habitually scared real danger in shocking them *out* of their usual condition acts as a calmative.

My pipe with the albino fly molded beneath the bowl introduced me to extremes of society—excentric starvelings among the "geniuses" of the *Verein*. —My first anarchist: Stephanie with her voice of inherited patience telling me how she had worked out emancipated love sitting in the *Englischen Gärten* with her sweetheart laborer on whose arm, his sleeves rolled up, she had planted a thickest row of kisses from wrist to elbow; the wide modelling of her pure pasty face suffused with an insufficient inner light as she sat in the deserted anatomy hall drawing life-sized replicas of the skeleton in lieu of lunch. —An elderly countess who having seen me in the street and decided "there goes *somebody*" insisted on meeting me—or the pipe?

German Art being beyond the pale of my shadowy Pre-Raphaelites, I was entirely without aesthetic allegiance to any trend among a Bavarian intelligentsia; handsome, warm-hearted bringing a comprehensive viewpoint to horizons vast in comparison to those of English students. Their international contacts adjusted to a nicety. Having no choice to make, I was left to the choice of others. Much as a flower might find itself picked I was drawn into an eclectic set principally of German men and Russian women. The men were grave and courteous, the women chastely *advanced*. Some were "well known." Common to all were their untarnished titles, these they subordinated to their intellects. In long-forgotten converse we toured the night dining beneath ceilings of foliage the lamps on our table hung with a screen of chestnut leaves.

Safely unchaperoned my year in Munich drew to a close. Father, entirely discouraged, allowed me to make the return journey alone. The only memory it leaves me is the bronzed symmetry of the tall youth trying to present himself to the averted brim of my hat as we left Ostend, the name of the place had a racy tang at the time.

Afterword

Mina Loy's Paris lamp-shop stationery features her name and business contact information in delicate, stylish lettering inked an irresistible peacock blue. On the back of one sheet she wrote a list of chapter titles (fig. 1). Because the piece of paper is torn in half, the book's title and part of the list are missing. What remains, however, will come to play a crucial role in the preservation of *The Child and the Parent* after Loy's death. On the front she jotted a note as if addressing future readers of these novels: "Twice everything has already taken place that our personality or destiny is like a roll of negative film— already printed But unrevealable until it has found a camera to project it—and a surface to throw it upon" (fig. 2).[1] Loy was a lifelong virtuoso of the material, and even mere fragments of her small archive are vitally charged.

In *Living a Feminist Life* Sara Ahmed writes of feminism as "a fragile archive, a body assembled from shattering, from splattering, an archive whose fragility gives us responsibility: to take care."[2] Her description fits the physical condition of Loy's papers, weathered by time and, at times, painful in their partial state. It also describes the greater archive of literature and art produced by women, and it is not surprising that even during Loy's lifetime her output was at constant risk for loss. Writing to her son-in-law Julien Levy from Paris in the 1930s on this same lamp-shop stationery, Loy recounts that

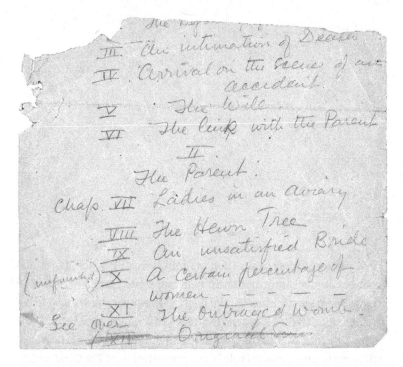

Fig. 1. "Notes: The Child and the Parent," recto (Mina Loy Papers, Yale Collection of American Literature, Beinecke Rare Book and Manuscript Library, by permission of Roger Conover)

while living in Florence before World War I she found her "natural rhythm of Expression—& wrote many things—most of which were sequestered by one of the poets when I went to Mexico"—a cache that has never surfaced. In later letters to Levy from this period she writes from Paris in repeated hope that the autobiographical prose manuscript she refers to as her Book, sent to him in New York City, might be returned. In an undated letter written to the New Directions publisher James Laughlin after moving to Aspen in 1953, Loy says about the manuscript of her novel *Insel,* "It is a miracle that the story survived—I found it once in the furnace room of an apartment house my daughter lived in—it had been *saved* by someone down there—who had stuck it carefully in a Bucket." Responding to Laughlin's interest

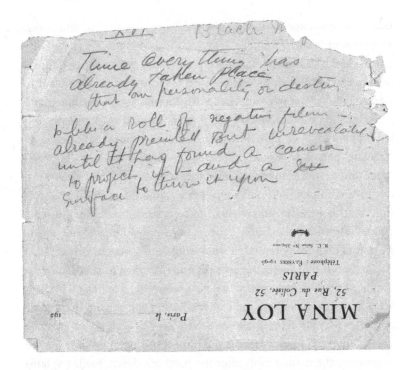

Fig. 2. "Notes: The Child and the Parent," verso (Mina Loy Papers, Yale Collection of American Literature, Beinecke Rare Book and Manuscript Library, by permission of Roger Conover)

in publishing what was almost certainly *Insel* or a larger version of Loy's Book in the early 1960s, her daughter Joella relates that Loy is "perfectly amenable to editing." Unfortunately, the copy they have seems incomplete. Joella, however, assures him, "I have received a box of her mss from New York, when her apartment was given up a few months ago and I think my next job is to sort them & file them—then I have to get her to let me go thru her house where she is living now and collect what she has there."[3]

In 1974 and 1975 Loy's family donated her materials to the Beinecke Rare Book and Manuscript Library at Yale University, establishing the Mina Loy Papers, the largest Loy-related collection in any public institution. It consists of typescripts and handwritten drafts of poems, novels, stories, essays, plays, designs, inventions, and notes. The content is extraordinary, and Loy's use of materials is striking. She drafted by hand on letterhead, plain paper, graph paper, address book paper, and even receipt paper to ensure that nothing went to waste. Typescripts watermarked with the names of European and American manufacturers are often accompanied by duplicate copies. In pencil, black pen, blue pen, and sometimes what appears to be pastel pencil or crayon, handwritten corrections scroll between typed lines, and drafts frequently incorporate sketches, anagrams, lists, word counts, and other numerical tabulations in the margins (fig. 3). This eclecticism reflects Loy's circumstances, her intimate connection with the material process of composition, and her capacity to find creative potential in what would otherwise be discarded.

Loy rarely dated her manuscripts and reworked much of her content across multiple projects. She also seems to have had an endless taste for revision, seldom indicating whether she considered a piece complete. A note from Joella housed with *The Child and the Parent* dated June 11, 1975, documents the impact this open process had on organizing the manuscripts after her mother's death. Joella explains that she previously assumed *The Child and the Parent* materials to be early drafts of *Islands in the Air* because they had similar chapter titles. After finding the torn half-sheet of lamp-shop stationery and its table of contents, however, she realized that there had been two different versions of the book, and she christened the earlier text *The Child and the Parent*.[4] Organizing the material this way revealed that except for the first two chapters, which seemed to be missing along with the last two pages of the third chapter, two copies of the manuscript through chapter 12 had survived.

Not until the twenty-first century and the archival research of Sandeep Parmar would *The Child and the Parent* recover its first two chapters. As Parmar relates in *Reading Mina Loy's Autobiographies,* while studying Loy's papers she found that these first two chapters were not missing at all: they were filed as typed early drafts of chapters 2 and 3 of *Islands in the Air*. Parmar noticed that by adding penciled lines Loy had changed the typed roman numeral of chapter 1

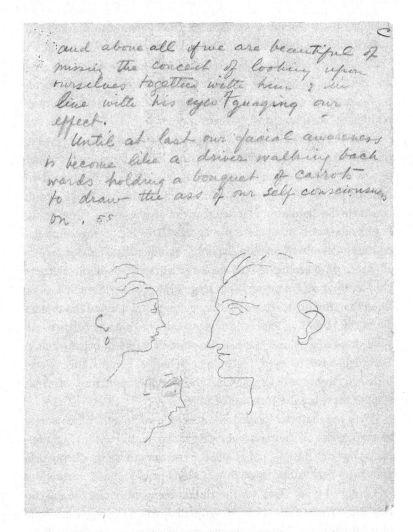

Fig. 3. "The Parent" (Mina Loy Papers, Yale Collection of American Literature, Beinecke Rare Book and Manuscript Library, by permission of Roger Conover)

to 2 and the roman numeral of chapter 2 to 3 as she began reworking the beginning into the later novel. As such, this material plays a dual role. It is the first two chapters of *The Child and the Parent,* and it is an early draft of the second two chapters of *Islands in the Air.* In addition, Parmar's analysis provides dates of composition for these manuscripts. The lamp-shop stationery and paper watermarked with a Parisian manufacturer indicates that Loy wrote and revised *The Child and the Parent* between 1926 and 1936: after opening her shop and before immigrating to the United States. *Islands in the Air,* in contrast, uses paper made in the United States and is dated to the 1940s and 1950s, when Loy lived in New York City.[5]

When I began editing *The Child and the Parent,* the two pages of its third chapter still seemed to be missing. But while reading through one of the folders of fragments of *Islands in the Air,* I discovered the missing pages. Incorporated into the present volume, they not only complete the chapter but also restore the proper name, "Goy," to the book's otherwise anonymous protagonist. This file of fragments also contains a handwritten paragraph that extends *The Child and the Parent* into a third section as well as part of a draft that adds an eleventh chapter to *Islands in the Air.* Both fragments are considerably less refined than the novels to which they belong, and none of the materials in the Mina Loy Papers provides evidence that she further pursued these extensions. Because they are valuable in tracing routes Loy might have followed, I include them here as an Appendix.[6] Never finished, faceted with alternatives, and eternally open: the two novels suggest these are the contours of a life.

With the material located and pieced back together, two copies of a typescript of *The Child and the Parent* through chapter 12 emerge. Each copy has missing pages and the two are otherwise distinguishable from each other through variations in Loy's hand corrections and color of type: black for the ribbon copy and violet for the carbon copy. While each copy is fragmented, when the pages are combined they create a comprehensive manuscript. In a parallel fashion, three incomplete copies of the typescript of *Islands in the Air* are preserved with Loy's hand corrections; when combined, they also create a comprehensive manuscript. These typescripts articulate the most fully realized version of each novel, often incorporating changes from previous versions and revealing an evolution. Each manuscript has been disassembled and archived by chapter, rather than by draft. To reconstruct the texts in this volume, I reassembled the novels from these chapters.

Loy's revisions reveal her to be an astute editor. Her alterations to these developed typescripts focus almost solely on the refinement of syntax and word choice indicative of editorial polishing. Rather than arbitrarily selecting one typescript copy over another, for each novel I incorporated all of her corrections whenever possible. When I encountered competing modifications, I opted for the edits that flowed most seamlessly with the surrounding language. Mindful that Loy was a visual artist with a deep commitment to the way words look on a page I usually retained her eclectic capitalization, hyphenation, and punctuation. Along with generating a distinctive texture, her stylistic choices are essential to the experience Loy describes. Her hyphenated compound words, for instance, evoke the flux of the physical world to which special modes of consciousness are especially attuned. Obvious errors and minor inconsistencies I have corrected silently. I also joined the typewriter's two short hyphens into a long dash and replaced her irregular ampersands with the word "and" but otherwise reproduced her unique dashes, ellipses, and use of the asterisk, which had a special place in Loy's imagination, to mark footnotes. I italicized foreign words not in the eleventh edition of *Merriam-Webster's Collegiate Dictionary* and substituted italics for underlines and double quotation marks for single ones. While I regularized the spacing between prose passages, I maintained the chain of five asterisks she used in *The Child and the Parent* to delineate sections. I also regularized and reproduced the necklace-like ornament she created out of dashes and o's to separate segments of the book's last chapter and continued to use throughout *Islands in the Air.*

Loy's original use of language is by no means restricted to typographical flair. She was an ardent nonconformist; her style reflects this. Fluent in English, French, German, and Italian, and with a smattering of Spanish and Yiddish, Loy draws on uncommon words and spellings. In a letter to Levy in 1932, she writes that while revising her Book she had realized she "was trying to make a foreign language—Because English had already been used by *some* other people."[7] Loy sometimes spells words phonetically. Where this appeared incidental, I took my cue from her other editors and made corrections. Following the lead of *Insel*, I standardized the mix of British and American English, selecting American spelling except in rare instances in which her choice of British spelling is both meaningful and consistent, such as "anaesthetic," with its provocative inclusion of "aesthetic," and "armour," with its ironic proximity to "amour." When Loy's uncommon spelling resonates with significance in English or one of the languages she knew, I let it stand. For instance, throughout the manuscripts she spells "grandeur" "grandure," an archaic spelling that associates the hardness of the French "dur." I also let stand the rare spellings of "antedeluvian," "nought," "operettes," and "tabu," which develop the ornate style of *The Child and the Parent* (she used the more familiar spelling of "taboo" for *Islands in the Air*). "Sphynx," which Loy consistently spells with a capital "S" and a "y," brings a touch of the antique throughout.

The survival of these novels unfolds against the larger backdrop of escalating anti-Semitism and fascism in Europe, as well as of Depression-era New York City as the United States declared war. While many other modernists' archives resulted from careful curation and planning, there is no official record of Loy's preservation of her work. It seems likely that instead of projecting a future legacy, the Mina Loy Papers harbors material relevant to what she was working on at the time, saved out of sheer creative necessity during her many relocations. Of special significance to the present volume is "Goy Israels," one of the other preserved autobiographical prose manuscripts and probably Loy's first use of material from her childhood in long-form prose. Highly fragmented and only partially surviving, this work is thought to have been written between 1925 and 1930 and features a young Loy-like protagonist named Goy. While it includes nearly identical childhood scenes to those explored in *The Child and the Parent* and *Islands in the Air*, Loy composed "Goy Israels" in the third person and amplified the parent figures to nightmarish proportions. As the writer Amy Feinstein asserts, "Loy uses the mixed

English-Jewish Israels household to demonstrate that the social pressures of minority status in England may be as destructive to the Jewish psyche as physical violence is to the human body."[8] This all but collapses any space for young Goy's development or survival, and Loy interweaves the book's narrative scenes with blunt, abstract meditations on race and ethnicity. The existing fragments are devoid of Loy's characteristic wry humor, and Goy's artistic formation is charted through negative, harsh critique. Torn, fragmented, and vigorously marked with cross-outs and circling, the physical state of the manuscript holds the traumatic energy explored by its content.

A thirty-seven-page holograph manuscript titled "Goy Israels: A Play of Consciousness" dated 1932 is nearly identical to the beginning of *The Child and the Parent*, and, as Sandeep Parmar maintains, the draft "suggests the abandonment of Loy's interest in the 'race drama'" in her autobiographical writing.[9] Loy's handwritten corrections to *Islands in the Air* show how she continued to edit away from a focus on her Jewish heritage as she developed the main character Linda's story. For instance, toward the end of the novel, after Linda's father has arranged for her to stay in Munich, Linda worries that "any reputable family would insist on knowing who—whatever—I was." Continuing this line of thought, Loy initially wrote, "I realise now that the fact of his being in trade & his having been sired by a jew provided his wife with an absolute warranty to martyrise him" and proceeded for two short paragraphs to detail the parents' volatile relationship. Although these paragraphs sustain the narrative's previous discussion of Linda's Jewish identity, Loy crossed them out with determinate pencil scrawls and modified Linda's reflection to read, "I realize now that the fact of his being in trade provided his wife, once she received an inkling of social gradation, with an absolute warranty to martyrize us."

In the next and final chapter of the novel, Linda arrives in Munich, circa 1899, and her Jewish identity is left behind. This abandonment is emphasized by the casualness with which the Baroness approvingly tells Linda that the bone-breaking "policeman's rattle" is "the most effective instrument of anti-Semitism"—a statement that Linda narrates without comment. Written during the publication in New York newspapers, newsreels, and radio broadcasts of the terrors of Nazi Germany, Linda's silence weights the moment with fear. For the remainder of the chapter Loy directs her attention to the way Linda's perceived class, British nationality, and feminine charms are selling points in the Baron and Baroness's attempts to turn a profit from her. Acknowledging a parallel between her situation and that of women who have taken up prostitution owing to economic necessity, Linda recognizes the "enigmatic sex-class culpability" of women, such as herself, who come from the bourgeoisie. "Inwardly," Linda states, "I was evolving a weird strictly personal form of feminism of which the militant aspect consisted in being peculiarly benign to any woman who had been 'pushed.'"

Although *The Child and the Parent* and *Islands in the Air* move Loy's Jewish identity to the background, her late, unpublished writings on the Jewish intellectual tradition, anti-Semitism, and the figure of the Jew in history indicate her sustained interest. Additionally, a practicing Christian Scientist, Loy wrote about matters of the spirit in letters to her family and friends such as Joseph Cornell, and in philosophical notes dated to her later years. Across her work her relationship to race, ethnicity, and religion is fraught, as is her approach to gender, and, as evident in *Islands in the Air,* to physical difference, which is made into a profitable spectacle by "Mr. Barnum" and "the sideshows of his circus." The descriptions of disability that appear in the novel were typical of works written in Loy's time, and they fit into the context of the book's Victorian-era setting, though today's readers are likely to find them disturbing. It should be noted, however, that, while not easy, Loy's engagement with socially and economically marginalized aspects of identity might best be described as identification. In a note scrawled on an early draft of chapter 6 of *Islands in the Air,* she indicates just this: "None of the people in this book have ever really existed—although if you look *into* them deep enough—they are all the *same person.*"[10]

Created from fragile materials such as cellophane, opaline, and parchment, many of the lampshades in Loy's shop were mounted on bases of shaped-glass liquor bottles she gathered at the *Marché aux Puces*. Upon its opening in September 1926, the business was a success, and Loy eventually employed a staff of six to manufacture her designs. She experimented with recently developed plastics to create organic forms such as calla lilies with illuminated filaments concealed in their bases and even invented a new synthetic material, which she called "verrovoile," a "glass fabric" suitable for detailed, delicate leaves. Prestigious French lighting firms expressed interest; New York department stores placed orders. Loy's contribution to the applied arts stands alongside that of Sophie Taeuber-Arp, Sonia Delaunay-Terk, and Meret Oppenheim, although like much of Loy's visual artwork, most of it fragile and often incorporating found material, none of her lamps is known to survive. Yet they are not entirely lost. Throughout the past century descriptions and images have surfaced in memoirs, photographs, and newspaper clippings. Close-up photographs featured in articles like the one in a 1927 issue of *Arts & Decoration* provide a sense of their effect: her "Red Fish" lampshade conjures an aquarium. A parchment shade painted with a caged parakeet gives the impression of looking at the bird "through a glass."[11]

Loy sold her shop in 1930 with the intention of focusing on her writing and painting. In *Memoir of an Art Gallery* Levy recalls that during this time, "Mina's book, though only partially finished, was already some five hundred pages long and one of the most remarkable manuscripts I have had the opportunity to read."[12] Levy also describes the Paris apartment Loy purchased in 1929 with a loan from his father, a New York real estate entrepreneur, as "by Loy out of the *Marché aux Puces*." Located in the same building as her close friend Djuna Barnes, who was writing *Nightwood* (1937) at the time, Loy lived at 9 rue St. Romain with her youngest daughter, Fabi, until moving to New York City in 1936. Here she generated *The Child and the Parent*, and it is difficult to imagine a setting more likely to give rise to the work's abstract, visionary texture. Levy describes rooms "divided by wirework or wickerwork cages in which birds flew or hopped about. Doors were always glass, the panes covered with translucent material so that there was privacy but also light. Indoor plants were living everywhere. Whatever patching of crumbling walls, or decorative coloring there might be was mostly done with scraps of metallic paper—wrappings from countless bonbons pasted together in floral collages. And colored cellophane everywhere."[13]

The apartment's opaque glass doors and cellophane evoke Loy's lampshades and the antique glass bottles she often used as bases and continued to gather, store, and sell after closing her shop. As if transported into the novels, in both books a row of glass bottles in front of a fanlight unlocks the child's "first concrete impression of phenomena" when she encounters them on the landing of the family doctor's house. As she is carried downstairs, the afternoon sun filters through them "firing the drastic reds and yellows in a double transparency that was so bright it caused a blazing explosion" within her. In this electrified moment the child begins to separate, or decompose, into a self, apart from the whole.

A version of this glass bottle scene also appears in Loy's celebrated long poem "Anglo-Mongrels and the Rose," first published in three parts from 1923 to 1925, and her manuscripts offer a rare glimpse into the way she transported material across genres. The first installment of the poem debuted in the "Exiles' Number" of *The Little Review*, followed by a second *Little Review* segment and a sequence in Robert McAlmon's Paris-based *Contact Collection of Contemporary Writers* (1925). With this initial publication, the poem kept company with the most significant avant-garde modernist writers, although it would not circulate in its entirety until collected in *The Last Lunar Baedeker* (1982). As with the novels in this volume, the poem focuses on a female protagonist, here named Ova, and draws heavily on characters modeled after Loy's parents. The father is named Exodus, and Ada, the mother, has the same name as the bride in *The Child and the Parent*. As the writer Alex Goody suggests, "Exodus embodies patriarchal control over language, identity and economics," and Ada, in part, personifies "degenerate, sentimental, and restrictive Victorian culture."[14] Ova's mongrel hybridity places her outside both forces of oppression and grants her the creative potential *The Child and the Parent* champions and that Linda struggles via a life in art to attain.

In the "Anglo-Mongrels and the Rose" version of the glass bottle scene, the infant Ova "projects" her "entity" onto the bottles, craving what she sees although the objects are out of reach:

> The prismatic sun   show
> of father's physic bottles
> pierced by the light of day
> extinguishes
> as she is carried away
>
> Her entity
> she projects
> into these sudden colours
> for self-identification
> is lost in recurrent annihilation
> with an old desperate unsurprise.[15]

Despite her attraction to the bottles Ova is able to draw the world closer only when she acquires language.[16] Several stanzas later, she overhears the word "iarrhea"—a clipped form of "diarrhea"— spoken by a voice "half inaudible." "It is/ quite green" declares a voice belonging to one of the "armored towers" bending over her baby sister's bassinet. Comically, marvelously, it is the word "iarrhea" that unlocks the "cerebral mush" of Ova's mind, producing poetry. The poem cascades into a series of green-infused images that glitter like glass, and Loy arranges her words to create a bottle shape on the page:

> A
> lucent
> iris
> shifts
> its

irradiate

interstice

glooms and relumes

on an orb of verdigris

By coincidence or careful preservation (it is impossible to know which), handwritten pages reworking these two stanzas are among the few remnants of this signature poem in Loy's papers (fig. 4). Across the front and back of two notebook pages Loy wrote and rewrote variations, changing words and experimenting with line breaks. She circled the twelfth and last version, noting immediately to the right of the poem, "O.K." In pencil she added, "immediately Visualizing a cat's eyes in my mothers Brooch."[17] Intriguingly, in a handwritten addition to *Islands in the Air* Loy carried a condensed, prose version of the poem's "iarrhea" and "lucent iris" passages into chapter 6, as found in the present volume. Unlike "Anglo-Mongrels and the Rose," however, Loy places the moment long after the dazzling bottle scene, thereby detaching the material from the ecstatic encounter. Instead, it is set within a montage of vivid, unsettling images and directly follows a description of one of Linda's earliest artworks, which she assembles from found materials. Given Loy's keen ability to turn castoff liquor bottles into elegant bases for her lamps (and the trash of the Bowery into arresting portraits), this placement eloquently articulates Loy's aesthetic values.

Unlike *Islands in the Air*, *The Child and the Parent* does not incorporate the "iarrhea" and "lucent iris" material from "Anglo-Mongrels and the Rose." The glass bottle encounter, however, is indispensable to both books, and Loy's subtle reworking of the scene as she moves it from *The Child and the Parent* into *Islands in the Air* illustrates the way she shaped each text's unique vision as she rewrote her narrative. *The Child and the Parent* version of the scene opens by outlining the context of the experience, specifically a stay at the house of the family doctor to keep the narrator "out of the way" while her younger sister is born. Dr. Monks, the man carrying her down the stairs, is described as having "one of

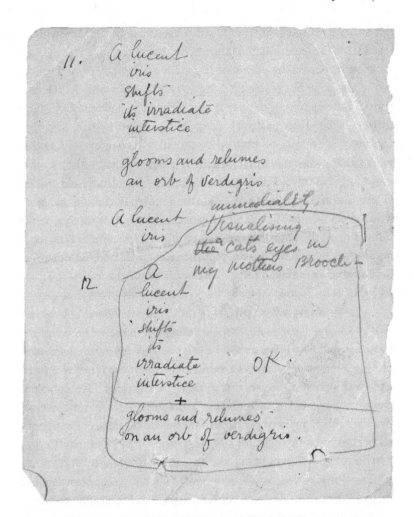

Fig. 4. "Anglo-Mongrels and the Rose," fragment (Mina Loy Papers, Yale Collection of American Literature, Beinecke Rare Book and Manuscript Library, by permission of Roger Conover)

those bulbous purple faces that have practically disappeared with the caricaturists who exploited them." After this context is established, the child's vivid, sense-based encounter with the bottles unfolds. This conventional movement from context to experience effectively guides the passage: only after the stage is set does the action begin. Loy uses this structure throughout *The Child and the Parent,* weaving individual scenes into the experimental fabric of her larger text.

In repurposing the scene for *Islands in the Air,* Loy reused much of the language but rearranged the sequence and withheld all contextual information until after the experience is described. All that matters is the elastic desire to merge with the glass bottles. After describing the experience, Linda then provides the context, telling the reader that it was only upon hearing the story at age twelve that the event fully emerged. Further refining the memory from the point of view of the analytic adult self, Linda then makes the comment about Dr. Monks's face and its relationship to caricature. This resequencing reflects upon the nature of experience and the function of representation. Just as Linda's infant experience can come into full presence only after she understands it as a story, the very existence of the doctor's face is intimately attached to the artistic style of his time.

In both novels, after remarking on Dr. Monks's face Loy moves swiftly on, giving the moment a light touch. At the same time, her repeated attention to faces across the two books is significant. Loy's narrators take notice of the faces around them, often use "face" as a verb, and favor idiomatic phrases that incorporate the word. Also, concepts "surface," borders are "effaced," and London streets are remembered "ineffaceably." Furthermore, one of the essential scenes of both novels occurs when the narrator sees her own face in the mirror for the first time. Before this moment, she says, "I had no identity," and the encounter ultimately leads to a statement of alienation between self and image: "The unreal distance between myself and 'it' disquieted me."

In *The Child and the Parent* this mirror moment occurs in the novel's last chapter and is presented impressionistically, as part of a montage of scenes that reflect on the chapter's title: "Being Alive." In contrast, when Loy moved the event into *Islands in the Air* she anchored it in a narrative context. Here, Linda is seven years old and visiting a family friend's tailor shop in whose windows her father had "rented seats for the Lord Mayor's 'show.' " By setting Linda in a shop window as if she were a mannequin on display Loy intensifies the estrangement Linda experiences upon seeing her own face for the first time. She initially placed this scene at the end of chapter 5 but subsequently added handwritten notes to all three copies of the *Islands in the Air* manuscript, moving it to the end of chapter 7, which is where it appears in the present volume. In this position the scene directly follows a series of grotesque images from circus sideshows and exhibition halls that spiral into a nightmare in which Linda's mother is a whirling mechanical dressmaker's dummy whose face dissolves as Linda reaches toward her for protection. It is in this threatening atmosphere, where non-normative bodies are turned into sideshows and mothers become sharp, faceless instruments of conformity, that Linda comes face-to-face with her own face for the first time.

Throughout *Islands in the Air* Loy continuously uses the figure of the face to explore the tension between societal expectations and individual self-definition. For instance, when Linda recounts that her teenaged ideal of beauty was "the maiden who lost her eyebrows in Burne-Jones's *Love among the Ruins*," she shows her younger self to have fallen for Pre-Raphaelite depictions of femininity popular during her time. Simultaneously, her satiric adult description of the lost eyebrows disempowers the ideal, reveling in its absurdity. By the end of the novel Linda reconfigures her own face by taking up a corncob pipe ornamented with an albino fly, a performance of self that anticipates Dada and rejects traditional femininity. In disrupting expectation of how her face should look, the pipe renders her illegible (and ineligible), ejecting her from the bourgeois symbolic system. Ironically, Linda's adoption of the pipe comes at the same time she performs the role of the Madonna in the art school tableau, narrowly escaping a fiery death during a rehearsal when the lamp she's holding bursts into flame and only the "janitress" remains to help her. In contrast, the pipe liberates Linda, introducing her to her "first anarchist" and the community of bohemian German and Russian art students with whom she spends the remainder of her time in Munich.

Loy's attention to the power that society's images have over the female body, intellect, and psyche plays an equally important role in *The Child and the Parent*. This is particularly vivid in the "Outraged Womb" chapter in which Loy figures the feminine as a socially unacceptable "seismic" and "gory giantess," filled with an "eternal river of blood." Loy contrasts this authentic image of femininity with the socially acceptable appearance of "pale clients" who are "pinked up" and painted to look "as much like a bon-bon as possible." Loy proposes that the painful dissonance between experience and image is the result of women being considered a *"terrain vague"*—a wasteland. Consignment to the wasteland is an "act of violence" that ensures that women remain sexually, psychically, and intellectually unfulfilled, for it guarantees that they will never know who they truly are. Instead, they will model themselves after the latest empty fashion.

Not isolated to these novels, Loy's fascination with the face infuses other writing, as well as her inventions and visual artworks. For instance, her undated late poem "Film-Face" (1996) critiques celebrity culture, featuring an image of the actress Marie Dressler as "the enduring face of, / the ruined body of, / the poor people" floating along with a "garbage-barge," while her *Auto-Facial-Construction* (1919) pamphlet advertises a unique method for revitalizing facial muscles. Sketches of faces peer out from the margins of her drafts, and the "Drawings and Design" folders in her papers include a series of unidentified faces, often drawn and colored on thick cardstock and cut out (fig. 5). While poignant in and of themselves, they also stand as evidence of a lifetime of portraits now largely lost. Much of Loy's public success as an artist was portraiture: salon records for the 1905 *Salon d'Automne,* which would become famous for its fauves, list her as an elected member contributing a portrait and three "Études de Tête bretonne." In 1914 as the sole British representative at the *First Free Futurist International Exhibition* she exhibited three portraits of F. T. Marinetti, one of which she titled "facial synthesis." Later sketches of figures such as Marianne Moore, Sigmund Freud, and Man Ray are treasured survivors inhabiting private collections. Loy's own face was the subject of captivating images by several of the most significant photographers of her time: Man Ray, Berenice Abbott, and Lee Miller.[18]

The cardboard faces in Loy's archival papers also resonate with the faces that so movingly populate her New York multimedia artwork. She

Fig. 5. "Head no. 10," recto (Mina Loy Papers, Yale Collection of American Literature, Beinecke Rare Book and Manuscript Library, by permission of Roger Conover)

called these pieces *refusées*—a word that combines "refugees" with the French *refuser*'s refusal, refuse's waste, refuge's harbor, and also perhaps refers to the Salons des Refusés—and they depict the impoverished residents of yet another terrain vague, New York City's Bowery neighborhood. Exhibited in 1959 at the Bodley Gallery, an Upper East Side venue for surrealist and contemporary art known for showing Max Ernst, Yves Tanguy, and Andy Warhol, most of these works are lost to time. Abbott's photographs, however, document these beatific "lepers of the moon, all magically diseased," as the gallery invitation card calls them, quoting Loy's 1922 poem "Apology of Genius." Except for published reproductions of select images, Abbott's photographs and negatives themselves were lost for several decades. Now recovered, Loy's carefully rendered faces peer out from Abbott's luminous gelatin silver prints.[19]

A valentine that ticks, inscribed with the phrase "My heart beats for you" and including a cheap watch. A device for washing the outside of windows from the inside of a room. A handsome bracelet that doubles as an ink blotter. Mainly dating from the 1940s when she was desperate for income, Loy's inventions span from the whimsical to the practical, but were for the most part never manufactured. Now known only through the sketches, descriptions, and patent proposals preserved in her papers, these ideas were generated during the time Loy is thought to have written *Islands in the Air,* and the three alphabet games she proposed to F.A.O. Schwarz in August 1940 particularly resonate with the novel.

Loy's proposal includes a copy of her introductory letter, a hand-painted script demonstrating how to play the games, and diagrams of two letter sets (fig. 6). In the game she called "The Alphabet That Builds Itself" small magnets are fitted into the sides of letter pieces. Another, similar game called "BUILD YOUR OWN A B C" consists of "pieces with which to form letters, and a board having slightly raised ridges at intervals to hold the letters in line." The accompanying script demonstrates play between an adult and child as the latter learns that "All the letters are made of I and O and pieces of I and O" (fig. 7). In playing with the toy, the child arranges the pieces on the board, a

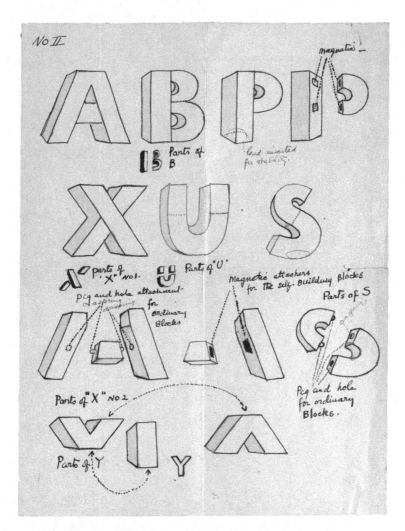

Fig. 6. "The Alphabet That Builds Itself" (Mina Loy Papers, Yale Collection of American Literature, Beinecke Rare Book and Manuscript Library, by permission of Roger Conover)

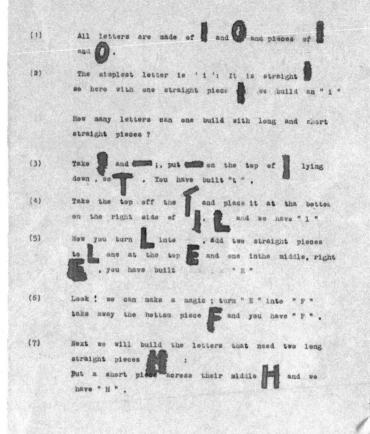

BUILD   YOUR   OWN   A B C

(1)   All letters are made of █ and ● and pieces of █
      and ●.

(2)   The simplest letter is ' i ': It is straight █
      so here with one straight piece █ we build an " i "

      How many letters can one build with long and short
      straight pieces ?

(3)   Take █ and ▬ ;, put ▬ on the top of █ lying
      down , so T . You have built "t " .

(4)   Take the top off the T and place it at tha bottem
      on the right side of █ , L and we have " l "

(5)   Now you turn L into E . Add two straight pieces
      to L one at the top E and one inthe middle, right
      , you have built E " E "

(6)   Look ! we can make a magic ; turn " E " into " F "
      take away the bottem piece F and you have " F " .

(7)   Next we will build the letters that need twe long
      straight pieces H :
      Put a short piece across their middle H and we
      have " H " .

Fig. 7. "BUILD YOUR OWN A B C" [instructions], I. [1] (Mina Loy Papers, Yale Collection of American Literature, Beinecke Rare Book and Manuscript Library, by permission of Roger Conover) process that "grips the child's interest." In a third design, called "An Alphabet Toy" or "Jack in the Box Alphabet," the alphabet blocks open, each containing a small toy that corresponds with its letter. The block "B," Loy explains, would harbor a small bird. The preferred version of the game includes more than one toy for each letter, "held in reserve for changes made by the adult teaching the child" and illustrating language's multiplicity.[20]

"All the letters are made of I and O and pieces of I and O": these games brilliantly foreground the material nature of language so prominent in Loy's writing practice. As early as 1918, four years after her poetry began to appear in print, Ezra Pound pointed to Loy's work to exemplify "logopoeia, or poetry that is akin to nothing but language, which is a dance of the intelligence among words and ideas and modification of ideas and characters," initiating a long tradition of critical attention to her dazzling puns, neologisms, and use of multiple languages.[21] An avid worker of crossword puzzles, she often includes in her drafts word lists created via anagram, a form of wordplay based on multiple combinations of fixed elements. For instance, on the back of the last page of an early typescript draft of "The Bird Alights" chapter, Loy handwrote a list of words that can be created from "immediate," a word that appears in the beginning of the next chapter (fig. 8). On the front side of the draft the type is peacock blue and ends with a concrete poem made by typing the word "Loy" in a triangular form that elegantly repeats her name both in the interior and along all three sides of the periphery (fig. 9).

While the precise role such language games played in Loy's artistic process remains a matter of speculation, it is hardly a coincidence that she developed her alphabet game proposals around the time she rearranged material from *The Child and the Parent* into *Islands in the Air*. Much like an anagram, Loy recombined elements of the earlier draft into the later draft. Furthermore, the novels reserve a special place for coming into written language, which offers entry into the "composite brain of humanity," the "final answer to the whole question." In contrast with her alphabet games, which emphasize the

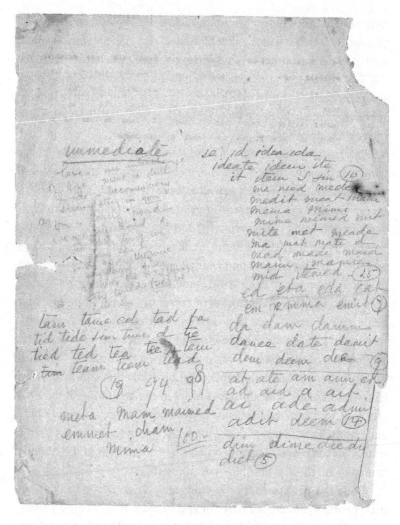

Fig. 8. "The Bird Alights," verso (Mina Loy Papers, Yale Collection of American Literature, Beinecke Rare Book and Manuscript Library, by permission of Roger Conover)

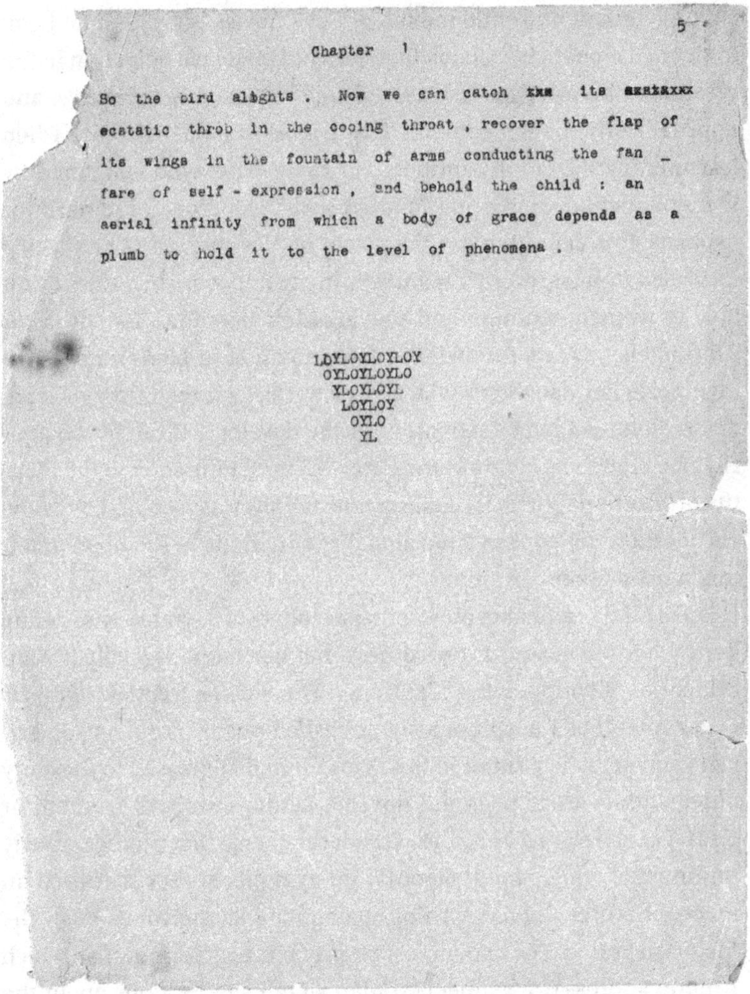

Chapter 1

So the bird alights . Now we can catch ~~the~~ its ~~ecstaxxx~~
ecstatic throb in the cooing throat , recover the flap of
its wings in the fountain of arms conducting the fan _
fare of self - expression , and behold the child : an
aerial infinity from which a body of grace depends as a
plumb to hold it to the level of phenomena .

```
LOYLOYLOYLOY
 OYLOYLOYLO
  YLOYLOYL
   LOYLOY
    OYLO
     YL
```

Fig. 9. "The Bird Alights," recto (Mina Loy Papers, Yale Collection of American
Literature, Beinecke Rare Book and Manuscript Library, by permission of Roger
Conover)

child's freedom, the child in both of Loy's novels is given "a fat book of rhymed alphabets," a book that does not invite participation in the creation of knowledge. Instead, the child is meant to memorize and internalize the book's content. This comes to an acute point when learning that "Z is for Zantippe," Socrates' wife, who is defined by the alphabet book as being "a great scold." Moreover, the narrator explains, this definition has the power of "destiny." As *The Child and the Parent* unfolds, destiny manifests in the impoverished roles available to women, stunting and souring their potential. *Islands in the Air* funnels this fate through the determination of Linda's mother to extinguish her daughter's will, as well as through the misogynist social structures Linda encounters as she develops. If the fat book of rhymed alphabets confines the letter "Z" to "Zantippe" and the identity of "Zantippe" (with its connotation of "wife") to "scold," Loy's novels question the book of life's alphabet of options in the hope that it might open other definitions.

Like Linda's alphabet book, other accounts of Socrates' wife define her by her outspoken shrewishness, but her name is spelled "Xanthippe" or "Xantippe," not "Zantippe." The noted exception to this is Edgar Allan Poe's posthumously published poem "From an Album" (1911), an acrostic written in the 1830s for and addressed to the early nineteenth-century poet and novelist Letitia Elizabeth Landon, or L.E.L., as she signed her work. Popular for verse that was decorously sentimental while simultaneously implying its author harbored an indecent secret, L.E.L.'s writing maintained its appeal through the Victorian period. Poe's poem responds to L.E.L.'s "Warning," in which Landon addresses a younger woman whom she cautions about the fleeting nature of love. Poe takes "Elizabeth" as his acrostic's anchor word, and its "Z" gives rise to "Zantippe," whose "talents," Poe writes sarcastically, "enforced so well" L.E.L.'s avowal to "Love not!"[22] Caught in the same brutal web of misogynist destinies that Loy's novels confront, however, Landon had numerous reasons other than shrewishness to guard against romantic love.

While mapping Poe's acrostic onto Loy's Zantippe charges her unusual spelling with great energy, we cannot know whether she had

Poe's poem in mind. But Loy did publish a poetic homage to Poe in *The Dial* in 1921 and included it in her 1923 collection *Lunar Baedecker*. While she also wrote both published and unpublished tributes to writers and artists such as James Joyce, Gertrude Stein, Constantin Brâncuși, Isadora Duncan, and Joseph Cornell, Poe holds a special place in Loy's constellation as the only figure who was not a contemporary. Even so, because Loy often spelled phonetically, she may have unknowingly selected the unusual spelling of Xantippe. In addition, Xantippe was a popular character in Victorian alphabet books, and although no examples of the unusual spelling have been found, her "Z is for Zantippe" might come from a historical source.[23]

Regardless of whether the spelling is accidental or intentional, Loy's alphabet games and incorporation of the alphabet book into her novels occur in the context of her significant interest in language's inherently recombinant nature. She explores this across her work in many forms, including anagrammatic play with her own name. For instance, her poem "Lion's Jaws" (1920) has the lines "Nima Lyo, alias Anim Yol, alias / Imna Oly / (secret service buffoon to the Woman's Cause)." Loy also used the anagram name Imna Oly as a stage name when she acted in Laurence Vail's 1920 drama *What D'You Want.*[24] In further name play, in the prose work from the thirties "Mi & Lo" (2011), a philosophical dialogue unfolds between "Mi" and "Lo." In another act of self-fashioning Loy changed her birth name from Lowy to Loy in 1904 and regained her legal right to resume it after her divorce from Stephen Haweis in 1917. She found significance in the closeness of her last name with Arthur Cravan's, whose birth name was Fabian Avenarius Lloyd. Loy often signed official documents, including her letter proposing her alphabet games to F.A.O. Schwarz, as "Mina Lloyd." This version of Loy's name contains, among other words, the name Linda.

Applying the strategy of the anagram to her own name, Loy suggests that a self, like a word (like the pieces of "I" and the pieces of "O" that create the alphabet), might be taken apart and put back together in multiple configurations. Although there is freedom in this model of self-making, there is also formidable constraint. Just as the letters of the alphabet are confined to what the pieces of "I" and the pieces of "O" can create, the self, understood in this way, is delimited by the possibilities it is given at birth. Throughout *The Child and the Parent* and *Islands in the Air* Loy brings awareness to these limits, foregrounding the stifling gender expectations into which female children are born. She also draws attention to women's infliction of these restrictions on each other. The ladies in the aviary "nibble" and "gobble" and "trammel" the "fallen woman." The Baroness nefariously plots to compromise Linda in return for profit. Moreover, the figure of the "Voice" painfully reveals the corrosive process of internalization that limits female potential from within.

A combination of the protagonist's mother and cultural expectation, the "Voice" is born in both novels when a domino flies out of the child's hand and breaks a window. Acceptable girls don't break things, exert physical force, or let their bodies lose control. In so doing, the child trespasses the boundaries of gender that define how she should exist in the world. The Voice sweeps through the child and uses the accident as proof that she harbors "evil" inside herself. From that moment forward she is hounded by the Voice, often in the form of a stream of abusive, disciplining dialogue from her mother. By the end of *Islands in the Air* the Voice has been internalized: "the record of the Voice playing on my mind periodically accumulated such confusion it exceeded my capacity."

However, all is not lost. Counterbalancing the Voice's monolithic weight, Loy incorporated a multitude of other voices into her novels. Family, friends, and acquaintances contribute lines of dialogue. Colloquial turns of phrase, often ironically employed, are frequently set off from the surrounding language with scare quotes. Quotations from the Bible, Dante Gabriel Rossetti, Shakespeare, popular music, and cabaret songs such as the German playwright Frank Wedekind's "Ilse," delivered untranslated and unattributed at the end of *Islands in the Air,* enter the narrative and then exit. A sound bite of advertising, "cloth boards, 2/6," satirizes a despised governess's devotion to the Bible. Non-English words, puns, and nontraditional spelling increase vocabulary beyond what is monolingual and correct. Some of these voices support the limitations inflicted by the Voice; others reject, challenge, or operate entirely otherwise. In any case, their inclusion insists on an array of languages, of vehicles of expression, far in excess of the plot points of any individual's life.

The only known recording of Loy's voice is an interview Paul Blackburn and Robert Vas Dias conducted with her in Aspen in August 1965, the year before her death. At the age of eighty-two she retains her British accent and sharp wit, interspersing stories from her life with readings of poems from the 1958 *Lunar Baedeker & Time-Tables,* her second published book of poetry and the last volume released during her lifetime. Nearly halfway through the interview she reads from "Love Songs," which is a version of the long poem "Songs to Joannes" that scandalized readers with its fragmentary form and erotic content when its first four sections appeared in the inaugural issue of *Others* magazine in 1915. Loy interrupts her reading to comment throughout, "That's clever!" and "But that's why they said I was so frightfully immoral," and "Wasn't I funny?" Between two of the poem's most daring passages she takes a longer pause to speak of her "home life" as a child where "this woman was shrieking and driving us cracked with her bad temper." She then describes leaving home to study at an art school in Munich under Angelo Jank. There she lived "in a house with a baroness" who "was always trying to get me into trouble, so she wouldn't have to account for the money my people sent."[25] There is great pleasure in listening to Loy recount plot points from *The Child and the Parent* and *Islands in the Air* in the midst of her most provocative poem. Loy's voice, fragile yet strong over the hiss of the tape recorder, carries a message to the Lindas of the past, present, and future. Do not allow yourself to be defined by the strictures of your time.

Appendix

FRAGMENTS

The Child and the Parent

These inexpressive lives are ugly lives and I who have been to so great extent privileged to share that ugliness with the disinherited of the earth, thanks to my miraculous education; I who have been tangled in the fringes of many insanities, been ashamed and slandered, have loved and starved and above all been so ridiculous, when I look back on that ugliness with the intention of describing it, in spite of my certitude that it is out of such dross I can extract an indispensable radium of truth, my mind on the road to evocation dawdles, as if memory feared to be crushed itself in reacting to that tedious process of redrawing light from darkness; it dillies and dallies, preferring to make pretty pictures of ladies in bird-cages or preliminary excuses for women by embroidering more or less graciously on the tabued subject of her frequent frigidity as if wishing to pretend to more seemly recollections than those to which it is entitled.

That individuality, like a bottled viable explosive, is conditioned by each man having as label a face which he alone of all his fellows can never see.

Islands in the Air

London is an atmospheric envelopment, a misty isolation of the individual for which a gregarious luxury is the only appeasement.

At home, the nursery-man's trees outside the windows stood as if shrouded for upright burial. In a strange diminished light, inside, the morning-room, the same uneven row of books showed through the glass doors of a narrow book-case locked since I found a Ouida there. An invalid chair in the corner, left over from Father's convalescence, had like himself still more broken down. Ida, presiding over the hodgepodge of the breakfast table, eyed me with mysterious retention measured to line the Voice; for the time being it was quiet here, the Voice prolonging holidays was absent for my return. At last like a talking island, my sister greeted me:

"I have given Mamma my solemn word of honor not to let you set foot outside the house." She was snug with regency.

On those dim first mornings Father, before going to business, would pace before us, dropping on his "beat," watchwords from his restricted ideation to be our safeguard through the dangerous day. Among his protective hints was some reference to girls who became "bad women." He had, exceptionally, touched on a subject to which I could intellectually respond.

"But I'm afraid," I proffered eagerly, "our present outrageous social system makes the poor wretched prostitute inevitable: a sort of moral sewer."

It was not because he understood a word of it that that spontaneous utterance finished me with him, rather his horror that the unexpected sequence of verbal sounds should take the place of the "Lor! Pappa, how shocking!" he must have invoked. It did not disturb him that Ida made no comment. A searching analysis might have revealed his subconscious assuring him he need have no apprehension of his unuttering daughter accosting a man on the street.*

The Voice, returning, tore through the house under its jailer's eyes; raising Father's temporary self-assertion as watchman. He fell to trembling again. Ida, untouched by what "went on," would later make it seem that the nervous system can be modified by environment without communicating its experience to the mind.

As sometimes neglected illness will put an end to itself, at intervals the sheer desperation of my being alive abated, clearing the way for spells of apparently rootless courage; when these occurred I became indiscriminately militant on behalf of my sisters who seemed quite contented as they often were. Exhaustive argument had resulted in their being transferred from the muddling school they attended to one I considered ideal. Co-educational, with cultured teachers, attended mostly by the offspring of famous artists, it recommended itself to me as likely to combat my parents' obsession of the peril of

---

* Today there are still thousands of daughters of American immigrants trapped in such parental obsession. Recently, in a low shop on Third Avenue, I heard a suspicious mother ask her daughter, fidgeting to slip off with her Beau:

"You're going to de movies? What time will yer be back?"
"Tomorrow morning," I answered pat, bubbling with sympathy for the young girl whose otherwise quite lovely flesh seemed to have expanded under the exclusive pressure of the poultry concept of life. The mother at once relapsed in a laugh of reassurance. She had heard of, but never met, a living confirmer of the glorious liberty of American adolescence. The girl's anxiety lessened also in the hope I had averted the danger of her man (who had been looking bored) shelving her for some daughter of modern parents. Such girls, in America, have a court of appeal; they can write to Doris Blake and, showing their Ma the answer in the News, *perhaps* convince her as to where she "gets off." Age, in my day infallible, has become suspect.

confronting the sexes, providing topics of conversation other than my original sin, curing my sisters' aesthetic of our "interior" decoration.

Ida strutting serenely into the "Chaucer" school with no let-up of her intensive musical studies soon became "Captain" of the school. The silly smugness dropped from the flattish handsome outspread of rosepetals and cream on her proud face. An impersonal peacock with the enamel insignia of "Chaucer" assigned to the head pupil hanging from a chain round her neck against the daffodil green of the school uniform.

Certain that in Ida my father's vision would materialize, I could see her passing from the suburbs of the incognoscenti whose self-respect is suspicion of one's fellows into that illuminated core of a metropolis, the safety-zone of accomplishment to justify the family's existence while between us the blood-tie coagulated. To my younger sister I felt "related." Born when already our queer urges toward occupation had convinced my mother we were socially hopeless, my mother swore that Marthe would be brought up "my way." Locking the nursery door against my "coming near her" to save, she said, this brown-eyed baby for whom with proud delight I had trimmed a bonnet with ostrich-tips, from my "moral contamination." As I hung around that key-hole in the outer hell of bewildered childhood, a draconian "inferiority" gnawed at my vitals.

Cloistered with the Voice, which substituted speech for an absolute lack of knowledge, I longed to hear words of significance. Ida brought her female professor home to tea. Although she surprisingly, so much I felt atrophied by my ignorance, decided I was an intellectual snob, we formed a thoroughgoing friendship. She invited me to a meeting of the positivists; they spoke of Auguste Comte, of whom as of all theorists I knew nothing. Here, again, surprisingly, a professor of philosophy gaped over his tea: "You are *young* to have made so profound a study of the philosophies." My idea of the philosophical, common to the illiterate, that of remaining calm under an annoyance, was put to a severe test when I found it unavoidable to be seen home by this professor in his cab. I had had, on arriving, to implore him not to get out of the [*fragment breaks off here*].

Editor's Notes

ABBREVIATIONS

JLGR   Julien Levy Gallery Records, Julien Levy Papers. Philadelphia Museum of Art, Library and Archives

LLB 82   Mina Loy, *The Last Lunar Baedeker*, ed. Roger L. Conover (Highlands, N.C.: Jargon Society, 1982)

LLB 96   Mina Loy, *The Lost Lunar Baedeker*, ed. Roger L. Conover (New York: Farrar, Straus and Giroux, 1996)

NDPCR   New Directions Publishing Corporation Records, circa 1932–1997, Houghton Library, Harvard University

YCAL MSS 6   Mina Loy Papers, Yale Collection of American Literature, Beinecke Rare Book and Manuscript Library, Yale University

YCAL MSS 778   Carolyn Burke Collection on Mina Loy and Lee Miller, Yale Collection of American Literature, Beinecke Rare Book and Manuscript Library, Yale University

INTRODUCTION

1. The first chapter of *Islands in the Air* was published in Antonella Francini, "Mina Loy's *Islands in the Air* (Chapter 1)," *Italian Poetry Review* 1 (2006): 236–244. In addition, Roger Conover published three short fragments in the "Ready Mades" section in Mina Loy, *LLB* 82, 314–316. The phrase "fugitive prose" is from Conover.

2. For biographical information see Carolyn Burke, *Becoming Modern: The Life of Mina Loy* (Berkeley: University of California Press, 1996); Roger Conover, "Time-Table," *LLB* 82, lxiii–lxxix; Jennifer R. Gross, "Truant of Heaven: The Artist

Mina Loy," in *Mina Loy: Strangeness Is Inevitable,* ed. Jennifer R. Gross (Princeton: Princeton University Press, 2023), 2–103; Marisa Januzzi, "A Bibliography of Works By and About Mina Loy," in *Mina Loy: Woman and Poet,* ed. Maeera Shreiber and Keith Tuma (Orono, Maine: National Poetry Foundation, 1998), 507–539.

3. See Sandeep Parmar, *Reading Mina Loy's Autobiographies: Myth of the Modern Woman* (London: Bloomsbury Academic, 2013), 174–175.

4. Mina Loy to James Laughlin, June 1952, MS Am 2077, box 162: 1035, NDPCR; James Laughlin to Elizabeth Sutherland, 26 September 1961, MS Am 2077, box 425: 2611, NDPCR.

5. *The Child and the Parent* is based on the manuscripts housed as "The Child and the Parent," box 1, folders 10–20, YCAL MSS 6, and drafts of chapters 2 and 3 housed with the "Islands in the Air" manuscript in YCAL MSS 6, box 4, folders 59–60. *Islands in the Air* is based on the manuscripts housed as "Islands in the Air," YCAL MSS 6, box 4, folders 58–69.

AFTERWORD

1. Mina Loy, "Notes," YCAL MSS 6, box 1, folder 10.

2. Sara Ahmed, *Living a Feminist Life* (Durham, N.C.: Duke University Press, 2017), 17.

3. Mina Loy to Julien Levy, ca. 1930, YCAL MSS 778, box 1, folder "Loy, Mina to Joella Bayer and assorted others, circa 1934–1949, 1960"; Mina Loy to Julien Levy, January 5, 1934 (see also May 5, 1934; July 30, 1934), box 31, folder 1, JLGR; Mina Loy to James Laughlin, n.d., MS Am 2077, box 162: 1035, NDPCR; Joella Bayer to James Laughlin, March 15, 1960, MS Am 2077, box 425: 2611, NDPCR.

4. Joella Bayer, "Notes," YCAL MSS 6, box 1, folder 10.

5. Sandeep Parmar, *Reading Mina Loy's Autobiographies: Myth of the Modern Woman* (London: Bloomsbury Academic, 2013), 95–96. Parmar also provides dates (1925–1930) for the composition of "Goy Israels" (*Reading Mina Loy's Autobiographies,* 173).

6. The appendix material and the typescript fragments incorporated into *The Child and the Parent* are found in Mina Loy, "Islands in the Air," YCAL MSS 6, box 4, folders 70–71.

7. Mina Loy to Julien Levy, November 28, 1932, box 30, folder 12, JLGR. In this letter Loy writes that she thinks she rewrote the "first bit" of her Book "2,000 times."

8. Amy Feinstein, "Goy Interrupted: Mina Loy's Unfinished Novel and Mongrel Jewish Fiction," *MFS Modern Fiction Studies* 51, no. 2 (Summer 2005): 339.

9. Parmar, *Reading Mina Loy's Autobiographies,* 132.

10. On Loy's spiritual beliefs, see Lara Vetter, *Modernist Writings and Religio-Scientific Discourse: H.D., Loy, and Toomer* (New York: Palgrave Macmillan, 2010), and Tim Armstrong, "Loy and Cornell: Christian Science and the Destruction of the World" in *The Salt Companion to Mina Loy,* ed. Rachel Potter and Suzanne

Hobson (Cambridge: Salt Publishing, 2010), 204–220. Mina Loy, "Islands in the Air," YCAL MSS 6, box 4, folder 64.

11. See Eric B. White, *Reading Machines in the Modernist Transatlantic* (Edinburgh: Edinburgh University Press, 2022), 99–106; Carolyn Burke, *Becoming Modern: The Life of Mina Loy* (Berkeley: University of California Press, 1996), 365–370; Susan Rosenbaum, "Mina Loy's Lamp Shop," in *Mina Loy: Navigating the Avant-Garde*, ed. Suzanne W. Churchill et al., University of Georgia, 2020, https://mina-loy.com/chapters/surreal-scene/5-paris-era-exhibitions/.

12. Julien Levy, *Memoir of an Art Gallery* (Boston: MFA Publications, 2003), 119.

13. Levy, *Memoir of an Art Gallery*, 120.

14. Alex Goody, "Empire, Motherhood and the Poetics of the Self in Mina Loy's *Anglo-Mongrels and the Rose*," *Life Writing* 6, no. 1 (2009): 65–66. Although the mother and father figures are unnamed in *Islands in the Air*, on one copy of chapter 7 Loy changes the phrase "my father" to "the master." She carries this change into the first few pages of chapter 8, then abandons it.

15. Loy, "Anglo-Mongrels and the Rose," LLB 82, 137–142. All passages from "Anglo-Mongrels and the Rose" are from this edition.

16. See Virginia M. Kouidis, *Mina Loy: American Modernist Poet* (Baton Rouge: Louisiana State University Press, 1980), 88–89.

17. Mina Loy, "Anglo-Mongrels and the Rose, fragment," YCAL MSS 6, box 5, folder 75.

18. Mina Loy, "Film-Face," LLB 96, 125; *Salon d'Automne*, 1905, miscellaneous art exhibition catalogue collection, 1813–1953, Archives of American Art, Smithsonian Institution, https://www.aaa.si.edu/collections/items/detail/salon-d-automne-8797. For Loy's association with photography, see Linda A. Kinnahan, *Mina Loy, Twentieth-Century Photography, and Contemporary Women Poets* (New York: Routledge, 2017), 29.

19. Burke, *Becoming Modern*, 434; Berenice Abbott, Mina Loy, and Amy E. Elkins, "From the Gutter to the Gallery: Berenice Abbott Photographs Mina Loy's Assemblages," *PMLA* 134, no. 5 (2019): 1094–1103.

20. Mina Loy to F.A.O. Schwarz, 6 August, 1940, YCAL MSS 6, box 7, folder 184.

21. Ezra Pound, "Marianne Moore and Mina Loy," in Pound, *Selected Prose 1909–1965* (New York: New Directions, 1973), 424.

22. Edgar Allan Poe, "From an Album," in *The Complete Poems of Edgar Allan Poe*, ed. James H. Whitty (Boston: Houghton Mifflin, 1911), 141.

23. See Burke, *Becoming Modern*, 445n26.

24. Susan Gilmore, "Imna, Ova, Mongrel, Spy: Anagram and Imposture in the Work of Mina Loy," in *Mina Loy: Woman and Poet*, ed. Maeera Shreiber and Keith Tuma (Orono, Maine: National Poetry Foundation, 1998), 512.

25. This interview is transcribed in Mina Loy, "Interview with Paul Blackburn and Robert Vas Dias, Introduction by Carolyn Burke," in *Mina Loy: Woman and Poet*, 222–223. The sound recording is available online at "Mina Loy," PennSound, University of Pennsylvania, https://writing.upenn.edu/pennsound/x/Loy.php.

Acknowledgments

This book is dedicated to Mina Loy scholars and editors for continuously deepening the past, present, and future of her work. The arrival of these novels into print is particularly indebted to Sandeep Parmar, whose scholarship renders the value of Loy's autobiographical prose undeniable. Without the editorial work and estate stewardship of Roger Conover there would be, at best, an impoverished version of Loy, and I am deeply grateful to him for his enormous generosity. Thank you to the Beinecke Rare Book and Manuscript Library at Yale University for granting me an H.D. Fellowship in English or American Literature for the study of Loy's papers, which seeded this book, and for the assistance of the reading room staff. In preserving Loy's papers and making them accessible, the Beinecke has made this project possible. My boundless appreciation to curator Nancy Kuhl for her unsurpassable knowledge and radiant thinking. Thank you to Jennifer Banks, my editor at Yale University Press, for her belief in this project; to Abigail Storch and Eva Skewes for their resourcefulness; to Susan Laity for her keen eye; and to everyone at Yale University Press for giving this book a body and a home. Thank you to Susquehanna University for research support. To Dan Beachy-Quick, Stephanie Larson, and Brian Cassidy, thank you for sharing information about Xantippe and the technologies of reproduction. Thank you to Eleni Sikelianos for "Anglo-Mongrels and the Rose," and to Cole Swensen and Susan

McCabe for their encouragement. To Richard Deming, Poupeh Missaghi, Donna Stonecipher, G. C. Waldrep, and Elizabeth Zuba: thank you for your insights, friendship, and conversation. To Mary and Dave Kelsey, thank you for your belief in me. Alan Gilbert, thank you for your peerless editorial eye, brilliance, and unfaltering support. All that is good you amplify.